Hasty Retreat

Dhal lifted his hands in a gesture of peace, but his movement only frightened the child even more. Then three males ran toward Dhal, all naked but armed with throwing spears usually reserved for fish. Behind them came others, nets forgotten, singing ended.

Dhal panicked. Lifting his hand, he quickly found the ring's invisible crack and willed the stone's colors back to gold and himself back to his own world.

Bodies and strange voices were closing around him, but he kept his eyes on the stone, not daring to look away even for a second. Gradually, the lakeside voices began to fade. The last thing he heard was a softly whispered word that sounded like: "Stay."

WHERE THE NI-LACH

M.J. BENNETT

A Del Rey Book

BALLANTINE BOOKS • NEW YORK

A Del Rey Book
Published by Ballantine Books

Library of Congress Catalog Card Number: 82-90937

ISBN 0-345-30876-X

Manufactured in the United States of America

First Edition: July 1983

Cover art by Carl Lundgren

Chapter 1 🖎

> *Where the Ni-lach,*
> *the Green Ones,*
> *they of the Draak Watch?*
> *Are they dead*
> *or only hiding?*
> *Only the mountains know*
> *and they are silent.*

THE DAY HAD BEEN QUIET, THE STILLNESS OF THE DEEP BROKEN only by bird and insect noises. Dhal had been out gathering since early light, and his sack overflowed with the wild herb lilsir.

Resting against the trunk of a mighty aban tree, he glanced up through the heavy foliage to the patches of mint-green sky above. Ra-shun, the larger of the twin suns, was falling to the west. Ra-gar, her sister, was still high overhead. Though the day had been mild, Dhalvad sensed the change in the air and was glad he had worn his overvest. The cold passage would soon be upon them.

Ver-draak was a green world, a land of growing things, where shifting shadows of viridian, emerald, and lime melded one into the other until sky, land, and water became locked together in an unending circle of green. The twin suns lighted Ver-draak twenty-two out of thirty hours, allowing the living green of tree, bush, and blade to feed and grow with astonishing speed. Only when the axis tilted away from the suns during the cold passage did the green world slow its growth, hemisphere by hemisphere, turn and turn about.

Deciding it was time to start home, Dhalvad stood and reached for his gathering sack. Suddenly, before he could swing the sack to his shoulder, he heard a hiss off to his right, followed by the crackle of branches. Too long a resident of the Deep not to recognize the warning cry of a draak and be fully aware of the risks in confronting one of the cold-blooded, scaly carnivores, he dropped his sack and jumped for the branch just above his head.

He was climbing to the next higher branch when a small animal burst out from behind a genna bush just a few strides downtrail. It was an olvaar, one of the small fur children who inhabited the Deep. And right behind him ran a baby draak, its long neck outstretched, its mouth open and reaching. The young draak was closing on the olvaar.

Dhalvad quickly lowered himself until he sat astride the branch, legs locked around it, then leaned over to peer down through the leaves. Holding tight to his perch, he loosed a whistle greeting and lowered his right arm, inviting the olvaar to join him on his perch.

The fur child looked up as he dashed beneath the branch, then he was gone, putting on a burst of speed that took him out of sight around the aban tree.

Pulling himself up, Dhalvad watched as the baby draak followed the olvaar, hissing its excitement. It took but a moment to realize that the olvaar was leading the baby draak in a circle. To Dhalvad that meant that the olvaar had recognized his whistle greeting and was coming back for assistance. He lay down the length of the branch and waited.

A minute or two later a whistled plea floated upward. "Needing help. Where are you?"

"Large aban tree. Come up," Dhal responded. Though most of the olvaar within the Deep spoke some form of trader, only a very few of the wilders had ever taken the time to learn the olvaar's whistle speech. Dhalvad was one of those few. Olvaar whistle speech came to him easily, as he had known the fur children for a long time.

The olvaar had resided in the Deep longer than any others, save the draak. Intelligent yet shy, the fur children were few in number and rarely seen by any but the wilders, men such as Dhalvad, who had learned to trust the child-size creatures and to share in their forest wisdom. Because they desired privacy and preferred deep forest homes, the olvaar often moved from a territory when man moved in, delving deeper into the forest and jungle wilderness.

The olvaar normally walked upright, waddling slightly because of their small round bodies, but in full flight they ran on all fours. Dhalvad grinned as the olvaar appeared below. No stranger this, but a friend of long standing. "Here, Gi!"

The crackle of bushes uptrail announced the return of the baby draak. Gi backed several paces and made a running leap for Dhalvad's outstretched hand. Though just under a half-meter tall, Gi had no problem with the height of the jump. As his small furred hands latched onto Dhalvad's arm, Dhalvad started to pull him up. A moment later Gi and Dhalvad sat together on the limb and watched as the draak broke out of cover and ran downtrail, hissing in anger at the meal that had disappeared. Gi made a thrumming noise in his throat: It was the olvaar laugh.

Leaning over, Dhalvad brought himself down to Gi's eye level. Gi's eyes, black irises in pools of gold, were large and wide-set, the only parts of his body not covered with the short, rust-colored fur of the adult olvaars; even his ears and nose were lost in fur, his mouth visible only when he spoke. His well-rounded waist was a testimony to his skill at foraging.

Tilting his furred head forward, Gi greeted Dhalvad in man speech. "Avto, friend Dhal."

Dhalvad shook his head. "Another minute and there would have been no more avtos for you, my friend. When are you going to learn not to tease baby draak?"

Big golden eyes regarded Dhalvad calmly, all innocence. "Was not teasing, Dhal, was running from."

"Then you had best improve your running, Gi, because one of these days you are going to tease the wrong draak and you'll find your fun has become a matter of survival."

Gi-arobi reached over and laid his small furred hand on Dhal's, patting it in a show of comfort. "Dhal has warmth for Gi," the olvaar said softly. "Thanking Dhal, but not to worry. Gi promises he will be careful."

"Does that mean you'll stop teasing baby draak?"

Gi thrummed his amusement. "Gi not say that, friend Dhal. Only say would be careful."

"You are incorrigible." Dhal swung his leg over the branch. He paused a moment just to make sure all was safe below, then lowered himself down and dropped to the ground.

"Incorrigible," Gi repeated perfectly. "New word. Good or bad?"

Looking up, Dhal grinned. "On you it's good. I would have you no other way." Lifting his arms, Dhal signaled Gi to jump. The olvaar launched himself into the air, trusting Dhal to catch him.

Gently Dhal set Gi on his feet, then turned to retrieve his gathering sack, hoping that the baby draak had not trampled it in passing. Lilsir was a tender herb that needed much care in picking and drying. Assured that his work for the day had not been ruined, he turned to find Gi-arobi watching his every move.

Thinking that the olvaar was hinting for a treat, Dhal reached into his belt pouch and withdrew a soft gumball made of boiled drenberries and mint leaves, a favorite with the olvaar.

Gi surprised him by ignoring the offering.

"Not hungry?"

"Not," Gi replied.

Shrugging, Dhal pulled the leaf wrapping off and popped the gumball into his mouth. Bending over, he reached for his sack, but before he could get it off the ground, Gi patted his leg to get his attention.

Dhal looked down. "Something wrong, Gi?"

"Dhal knows there are stranger men in the Deep?"

"Stranger men? How many?"

"Lar-aval says four hand counts." An olvaar's hand count was four.

"From which direction do they enter the Deep?"

Gi pointed one of his stubby fingers south.

"Annaroth. That would make them Sarissa. I wonder where they're going."

"Not going anywhere," Gi answered. "They circle now. Lost."

"Did Lar-aval say where he saw these strangers last?"

Gi-arobi nodded. "This morning they near Great Bend where they try to ford river. Water too deep." There was a slight lisp to Gi's speech, as if his small black tongue had trouble forming around some of the man words. Dhal listened carefully as Gi continued.

"Some afraid of black water. Talk together, then go west. Lar-aval says stranger men follow river."

"And by now they are in the lower fen. Did they have a guide?"

"Lar-aval says not."

"Stupid! No stranger should ever enter the Deep unguided!" Stupid wasn't the right word; suicidal would be more accurate, he thought.

"Do you go to find stranger men, friend Dhal?"

"They could be no more than an hour away and I doubt there are any closer than I, Gi. Someone must help them."

"What if danger?" Gi asked, tilting his furry face upward.

"In the fen there's always danger, Gi."

"Gi does not speak of mudboles or gensvolf," the olvaar responded. "Stranger men could be danger."

"But if they're lost and in need of help, surely they would offer me no harm if I came to aid them." Gi regarded Dhal silently. Something in his silence told Dhal that there was more. "Gi, is there something about these men that makes you think them a danger?"

Gi nodded, a quick downward bob of the head. "Lar-aval says they follow Haradan—as gensvolf hunting."

"Haradan's back?"

"Yes."

"You're sure?"

"Gi has not seen, but Lar-aval says is true. Gi comes to find Dhal to tell him."

"How long have you been looking for me? When did Lar-aval see Haradan?"

"Morning. Dhal going home now?"

Dhal thought a moment. If there were strangers in the Deep and they were following Haradan, then it seemed wisest to talk to Haradan before launching any rescue parties. The cabin was only a half-hour walk away. "Yes, Gi, I'm going home. Coming along?"

Gi whistled an affirmative. Shouldering his gathering sack, Dhal turned and followed Gi's small form downtrail. Running five steps to every one of Dhal's, the olvaar stayed in the lead, his fat furry legs pumping tirelessly. Dhal smiled to himself as he thought back on the first time he had seen those round, rust-colored legs, sticking out of the yellow and orange coils of an echar vine.

The echar was a strong, carnivorous creeper with long sticky tendrils; usually its victims were insects, snakes, and rodents but occasionally it caught a small animal such as a young olvaar.

When he freed Gi-arobi, Dhalvad won himself a friend who would be both companion and teacher as the years passed.

As Dhal walked along, his thoughts turned to Haradan, five weeks gone, two overdue. Haradan sar Nath was a wilder by profession, a gatherer of herbs and spices. He was a large man with broad shoulders, long arms, and big hands. His hair was black and unruly, his eyes dark brown. He seldom laughed aloud yet did not lack humor. His was a silent laughter that touched the eyes and spread his lips wide in a slow grin.

For twenty-four of his twenty-six years Dhal had walked the forest trails with Haradan, learning how to spot the danger of mudboles and bogs; memorizing the look, taste, and texture of the plants they gathered; learning how to defend himself against attack by draak and gensvolf; absorbing all the information that would allow him to survive alone in the Deep.

Though Dhal couldn't remember anything before Haradan's cabin or the Deep, he knew that Haradan was not his father. When he was old enough to understand, Haradan had explained how he had come into his care. The story began with a burning cabin on the edge of the Deep and ended with the discovery of a lone survivor, a small child found hiding under a clump of bushes.

Dhal was elated by Gi's announcement of Haradan's return to the Deep. He wondered how well the trading had gone, and what gift Haradan had brought back for him this time. He was in desperate need of a new pair of pants; the ones he wore had been mended so many times that the patches were beginning to wear through. He also needed a new pair of boots. But what he really wanted was a knife; his had a broken point, and though it served for cutting grass and vine it was most inconvenient for gutting fish or peeling fruit.

Dhal worried about Haradan's being followed. The Sarissa were said to be an unfriendly, arrogant people who looked down on anyone not of the Escarpment. To them, the field workers of Blazee and the swamp merchants of the Deep were little better than slaves from the other side of the Enzaar Sea. Tolerated because their goods were needed or useful, the field workers and swamp merchants were allowed into the rock city of Annaroth, but inside the main city they were barred from certain places, such as the regent's quadrant or the people's warrens.

Dhal had never visited the Escarpment. As a child, he had been left with Dreena and Xarlan on their farm on the southern edge of the swamp while Haradan saw to trading with the Sarissa. For the last twelve years, Dhal had been left on his own, to continue the work of gathering the herbs that provided their only income. Haradan had repeatedly promised to take

him trading, but each time he had found an excuse to go alone.
Why? Was Haradan trying to protect him from something, or
was he just afraid of losing his foster son?

Dhalvad loved the Deep. But recently he had begun to feel
that something lay beyond it, something that called to him. A
restlessness had pushed him to rove farther and farther away
from the cabin each day. He tried to relieve this strange uneasiness by exploring new sections of the Deep, but even that did
not satisfy. He felt as if he searched for something without
knowing its name.

When he had tried to explain these feelings to Haradan one
night at the supper table, Haradan had grinned and told him
that he was finally growing up. Dhal had asked him what he
meant.

"That you need what every man needs sooner or later—a
woman."

Dhal remembered the heat that had warmed his cheeks and
the strange look that had swept across Haradan's face, a haunted
look that completely wiped away his smile.

"Is something wrong, Haradan?"

"Wrong? No—nothing."

Dhal pressed him. "There *is* something wrong. What is it?"

"Women," Haradan growled. "You'll not be finding any
women in the Deep. And those on the fringes have been spoken
for long ago. If it's a woman you want or need, the nearest
place to find one is Annaroth."

"So I go to Annaroth," Dhal responded.

Haradan had looked up from his plate. "You are handsome
enough, and have had your manners taught you, but you are
not Sarissa nor ever will be! There are some who would couple
with a wilder, but few if any who would marry one. You are
landless, have no money, no servants, and no future!"

Haradan started to say something else, but the words caught
in his throat and he pushed away from the table, heading for
the front door. When he reached the porch he stopped and for
long moments just stood there, looking out into the deep green
twilight.

"Haradan, what is it? What's wrong?" Haradan's strange behavior had frightened Dhal.

Dhal never received an answer to his question. Swearing softly under his breath, Haradan left the porch and climbed down out of sight, disappearing into the bushes below their tree home.

Two days later he had left for Annaroth.

Chapter 2

THE CABIN WAS BUILT TWENTY METERS ABOVE THE GROUND, ON the lowest branches of an aban tree. Dhal lifted Gi to the first of the spiked branches that provided a natural ladder upward. It took but moments to climb to the porch. Swinging his gathering sack from his shoulder, Dhal reached for the door latch. Gi-arobi stood before the door, waiting patiently.

The main room was dark—the two small windows to the south, one on either side of the door, were so overshadowed with vine that little light managed to penetrate the interwoven wood grills.

The cabin comprised two rooms covered over with a wood-thatched roof overlaid with sod. There was a small stone-and-clay fireplace at the north end of the main room, a long eating table in the center, and by the west wall there stood a series of three wooden water basins used for the washing and preparing of the wild herbs they gathered. There were woven fiber rugs on the floor and two handmade chairs by the fireplace, and overhead hung a series of drying racks.

Off the main room, Haradan had built a bedroom which he and Dhal shared. Once or twice Haradan had spoken of building another room to the east, but he had never quite found the time to begin.

Dhal leaned his sack against the table leg, and reached for the dish of matches that always sat in the center of the table. Next to the dish there was an old oil lamp. Striking a match, he turned the wick up. "Gi, do you think Lar-aval made a mistake? Perhaps it was someone else he saw in the Deep, not Haradan."

As light pushed back the darkness, Dhal picked up the sack of lilsir and carried it to the largest side basin. "I'll put this to soak, then I'll start us some supper. If Haradan's on the trail, he'll be hungry when he gets here. How about you, Gi? Hungry?"

When there came no answer to his question, he turned, "Gi?" The olvaar was standing five or six paces from the table, his back to Dhal, his eyes on the far end of the room near the fireplace where shadows were still deep.

"Gi, what's wrong?" With the light from the lamp shining in his eyes, Dhal couldn't pierce the shadows.

Dhal started forward, but he had taken no more than a few steps when he heard something move in the shadows. He stopped, the light behind him. "Who's there?" he demanded, his hand moving to his knife.

Darker shadow within shadow; a sudden movement to the left of the fireplace caught his eyes. He saw the silhouette of a man slowly rise from the chair that was Haradan's. Though he couldn't see the man's face, size alone told him who it was.

Breathing a sigh of relief, Dhal released his knife and moved toward his foster father. "Haradan, you startled us. Why didn't you answer? Lar-aval said he saw you in the Deep. Gi came to find me. How long have you been waiting?"

Haradan's fist caught Dhal on the point of the chin. The explosion of pain in Dhal's face was followed by the shock of his body slamming against the floor. For a moment or two his brain went numb. It was Gi-arobi's shrill whistled warning that stirred him to his senses.

Dhal felt hands on his tunic front, pulling him up. A hand

slapped across his face. His eyes flew open. Haradan's face was only a hand's length away. Stunned by the attack, Dhal tried to speak, but with his tongue and mouth numb and slick with blood, the words came out mumbled.

Scowling, Haradan shook Dhal. "What did I tell you before I left?" he roared. He shook Dhal again, hardly giving him time to think. "Damn it! What did I tell you?"

Grabbing Haradan's wrists, Dhal tried to regain his feet, but Haradan's right fist lashed out again, knocking the young man backward into the table.

A shock of pain caught Dhal in the lower back, then he was on the floor bracing himself on his hands and knees. He shook his head, trying to clear the fuzziness that clouded his eyes. He saw Haradan's boots in front of him. A hand caught in his hair, jerking his head back and up. Haradan's strength was too much for Dhal. Flopping him over onto his back as easily as he would turn and skin a nida, Haradan knelt over Dhal, his eyes hard and angry.

The last Dhal remembered was hearing Gi's whistled challenge, then a wave of darkness descended.

Dhal woke to the touch of something cool and wet resting on his forehead. When he opened his eyes he found himself lying on his bed. He could hear Haradan moving around out in the main room. What had prompted the older man to attack? Dhal wondered. What wrong had he done? When he turned his head to the lighted doorway joining the two rooms, the dull ache that had been with him upon waking rumbled to life.

Sure that Haradan's violence would have frightened the olvaar away, Dhal was surprised to find Gi still there. A sharp intake of breath alerted Gi-arobi to Dhal's waking. Gi pushed his furry face down near Dhal's and spoke softly in trader. "Dhal not move. Hurt. Blood on face."

He gently patted Dhal's chest.

Dhal started to answer but stopped when he heard Haradan's footsteps approaching. Gi read the apprehension in Dhal's eyes; leaning close, he blocked his friend's view of the doorway. "Haradan not angry now. Not to be afraid."

As Haradan entered the room, Gi moved back against the wall, but one small furred hand stayed on Dhal's shoulder. Dhal watched as Haradan set a pan of water on the floor and pulled up a chair. Sitting, Haradan leaned over the table between their two beds and brought the candle to the edge of the table so he could better see the damage done.

Their eyes met, and Dhal wondered if Gi had misread Haradan's temper, for the scowl on his face was anything but comforting. Haradan glanced over at Gi-arobi, then without a word he squeezed out the cloth he had left soaking in the pan of water.

Dhal closed his eyes, willing the pain to go away, while Haradan washed the blood from his face. Then, letting his mind turn inward, he made a quick survey of the broken blood vessels in and around his nose and mouth. He found all of them in the process of clotting. Once assured that no bones had been broken and that all bruises were minor, he turned his attention to the small amount of blood seepage. The repair work was minimal. Before Haradan had rinsed his cloth a second time, Dhal was finished with his self-healing.

After inspecting his work, Haradan's eyes locked onto Dhal's. "I told you to stay in the Deep, did I not?" he growled softly. "And you promised me that you would. But you couldn't keep that promise. No, you had to go wandering."

"Only to Drimdor, Haradan. With Xarlan," Dhal said quickly. "He asked me if I would help him with a load of bread wheat. Surely it wasn't wrong to help Xarlan."

"Wrong to help him, no! But I can't say the same for the boy you healed! You know what I've told you, that you were to keep your healing hands off people!"

"But he was bleeding to death, Haradan! He would have died!"

"Better him than you!"

"But I was in no danger," Dhal protested.

"Not then, you young fool—now! Your healing of birds and animals is one thing, but when you start healing men how long before someone starts asking questions? I made record time from Annaroth the minute I heard the rumor about a miracle healer in Drimdor. I knew it was you. And it won't be long before others know!"

"But what wrong is there in saving a life, Haradan? What wrong in healing men?"

Haradan shook his head. "It's time for the truth. I knew it would come." His scowl was gone. Reaching out, he pushed the hair back from Dhal's forehead.

It had been a long time since Haradan had raised his hand to discipline; by the way Haradan now touched him, Dhal knew he was sorry for his actions.

Haradan turned Dhal's face to the lamp light. "How long has it been since you've washed your hair? Or eaten the brannel I left for you?"

Hair? Brannel? Dhal was at a loss. Had Haradan been drinking?

Haradan's voice softened. "Answer me, Dhal. How long since you've eaten any brannel?"

"You know I don't like it."

"How long?"

Dhal thought back. "Two weeks, no longer. But I feel all right without it, Haradan. Perhaps I've outgrown my need for it. But what has my eating brannel have to do with—with what happened in the other room, with my healing the boy?"

"Everything," Haradan answered. "It's all tied together. By leaving the Deep, by healing that boy, you made a terrible mistake, one that may just cost you your life! I tried to warn you, but then, who can keep a draak in its shell forever?"

Dhal shook his head. "Haradan, I don't understand a thing you're saying. Hair, brannel, draak shells . . . What are you talking about?"

Haradan drew a deep breath. "There's something you must be told, Dhal, but I don't know how to start. You are—" Haradan seemed to choke on his own words. Cursing softly, he dropped his head. "God help me, I can't tell you!"

Dhal laid his hand on Haradan's arm. "Tell me."

Haradan took Dhal's hand, holding it in a crushing grip. His eyes searched the younger man's face, then he nodded, somewhere finding the strength he needed to continue.

"Dhalvad, before I tell you what I must, I want you to know that I think of you as a son, a true son. That between us nothing is changed or ever will be. I was angry a little while ago because I was deathly afraid for you. When I came home and found you gone I feared that they had come before me, that I would never see you again. And then you came in, so carefree and happy. I struck out at you when it was only you I wanted to protect. I know this isn't making any sense, but please believe me when I say that I do love you, that no matter what the future holds, I mean to share it with you."

Haradan was not a demonstrative man, never one to fondle or caress. For him to openly avow his love was little less than astonishing. Startled, Dhal lay still, hardly daring to breath, wondering who "they" were and what danger Haradan foresaw for him.

"You asked me what hair, brannel, and draak shells have in common. The answer is nothing, unless *you* put yourself in the place of a baby draak before it breaks through its eggshell. There's safety in concealment, Dhal, for the baby draak and for you. The draak hides inside its shell, you hide behind the dye with which you wash your hair and the brannel that I've forced you to eat all these years."

Dhal frowned. "I wash my hair with dye?"

Haradan nodded. "You always were a trusting child. All these years and you never once questioned me. Without the special soap I make every cold passage, your hair would be green, Dhal, not brown."

"Green?"

"Yes. And without the brannel you have eaten all these years, your eyes would be crystal gray." Haradan hurried on. "Dhal, you are Ni-lach, one of the Green Ones, those who were hunted out of existence by men who feared what they couldn't control."

Dhal frowned, sure that Haradan had been drinking.

"You don't believe me," Haradan said softly. "I can see it in your eyes." He stood. "You don't believe me, do you?" he demanded. Looking down at Dhal, his fists clenched as if he would like to use them once more, Haradan growled a curse, then turned and went to the small table between their beds. He rummaged in the top drawer for a moment.

What is he after? Dhal wondered. Haradan withdrew something from the drawer. Dhal felt a twinge of uneasiness as Haradan returned to his side.

"I can't blame you for not believing," he said, "but this should be proof enough. Look into this and tell me what you see! It's called a Dron mirror, named after its maker. It's not as clear as those used by the Sarissa, but it will serve. Look into its surface and tell me what you see!"

Dhal had never seen any kind of mirror. The only reflection of himself he had ever seen was in a still pool of water. He was astonished that Haradan even possessed such a thing, for Dron mirrors, though of a lower quality than Sarissa-made, still must have cost a great deal of money.

As he peered into the smooth, clean surface, all kinds of thoughts flickered through Dhal's mind, including the possibility that Haradan was telling the truth.

To look into a mirror and see oneself for the very first time— it was an experience that would live with him for many years to come. To see himself as others saw him, to visually trace the outlines of nose and jaw, to see the lips soften and smile with delight. Feature by feature, Dhal studied the image before him: the straight nose, narrow nostrils, hollow cheeks, lips that couldn't stop smiling, eyebrows that arched up and out, the straight forehead—and the eyes. To look into eyes that until that moment had only looked outward, to know the thoughts behind those eyes without guessing, that truly was a miracle.

Haradan pushed Dhal's hair back from his forehead. "Look at the roots of your hair, Dhal. What color?"

Dhal felt his delight flicker and die as he saw the difference in color. For a moment or two he had almost forgotten the reason for the mirror. His hair was dyed! The roots were lighter in color than the rest of his hair—but green? Dhal peered closer, straining to see. Haradan moved his hand back slightly, so his arm would not block the light. A sudden chill touched Dhal.

But Haradan was not finished. "Your eyes, Dhalvad, look

at your eyes. Not at the very center where all eyes are dark but around the outside of the colored orb. What color there?"

Dhal did not want to look but he could not stop himself. At first his eyes looked no different than they had only moments ago, brown orb in a sea of white, but then he noticed that the outer edges of the brown were faded, almost colorless, and between brown and white flickered a crystal gray.

"Without the brannel your eyes become a light gray with flecks of crystal glimmering through. You have the eyes of the Ni-lach, Dhalvad, exotic and striking, but death to you if anyone saw."

Dhal closed his eyes, stunned by the truth. He was Ni-lach! He remembered stories, legends of the unmen who killed without cause, who ate the flesh of true men to strengthen their own evil powers. Ugly were the Ni-lach, destroyers of crops, stealers of children, hiders in the dark, killers demon spawned. There were no words gruesome enough to describe such beings! Dhal felt sickness well up inside.

"Dhalvad!" Haradan's fingers tightened in Dhal's hair. "Dhalvad, open your eyes. Look at me! I know what you're thinking but it isn't true! The legends are false! Damn it, listen to me!"

Pulling on his hair, Haradan forced Dhal's head around to face him. Dhal had no strength to resist, but he kept his eyes closed, fearing what he might see in Haradan's face.

Haradan spoke quickly, his voice harsh. "Dhalvad, you are Ni-lach, but don't condemn yourself as some monster until you've heard me out! I must go back in time for you to understand, to tell it all as it should be told. It concerns your parents and how I came to bring you home. The truth this time, not the half truth you have always heard."

Though he didn't want to listen, Dhal had no choice.

"For me it all began when I was little older than you are at this moment. My master was Adan sar Ospa, one of the merchants on the Sadil docks. I had come from the home of an uncle who had raised me since my mother's marriage to a landowner in the Blazee District." Haradan paused to collect his thoughts. "I was twenty-four when I went to work for Saan

Adan. It was my job to keep track of the carts going in and out of the dock loading zone. It was the beginning of my fourth year on the docks when the Sarissa declared war on the Ni-lach. One day I was guarding the docks, the next day I was fighting Ni-lach."

When Dhalvad heard Haradan stand and move away from his bed, he opened his eyes. Though shocked by the knowledge that he was one of the dreaded Green Ones, he heard the pain in Haradan's voice and couldn't turn away from it.

When Haradan turned around and saw that Dhal's eyes were open, he continued his story.

"When I was younger, all I knew about the Ni-lach was what I had heard from others. Because the Ni-lach liked to live near water, many claimed that they originated in the sea, like some kind of fish men. Others claimed that they were aliens from some far-distant galaxy, marooned on Ver-draak in much the same way as true men."

Haradan returned to the chair beside Dhal's bed. "Our historians haven't been kind to the Ni-lach and perhaps there's just cause for some of the things they said about them, but I know for a fact that many of the legends told were just that— legends—based on lies meant to discredit the Ni. Your people were different, Dhal. They were tuned to nature and they understood plants and animals in a way that we never understood them. And some were gifted with special talents, such as prophesy and healing."

"That is why you didn't want me to heal anyone," Dhal said, a glimmer of understanding beginning to dawn.

Haradan nodded. "No one knew you to be Ni-lach and I had hoped to keep it that way, but now that the draak is out of its shell there'll be no going back."

"Haradan, what started the war?"

Haradan took a deep breath and released it slowly. "Fear, greed, envy. The Sarissa envied the Ni-lach their long life span, which is twice what it is for man, and they feared the Ni's special talents, yet at the same time they wanted to share in those talents. Besides healers there were some among the Green Ones who could tame draak; others were capable of sending messages over great distances in mere seconds. The Sarissa never did find out how that was accomplished. It was a fortunate man who managed to hire one of the Ni-lach, for the Green Ones stayed much to themselves, fishing, growing their own foods and creating the most beautiful hand-carved jewelry out of shell, wood, and gemstones. Your people were known for their use of a magnificent green stone in their artistry. They never gave it a name and no one ever learned where the stones came from. It was one of the Ni-lach's most carefully guarded secrets.

"The war between the Ni and the Sarissa was fairly one-sided, with the Sarissa doing most of the killing. I'm not sure what even actually sparked the war. Some claimed that a famous Ni-lach healer went berserk and killed three of the regent's family. Others claimed that it was a larger conspiracy, aimed at the eradication of all Sarissa.

"If that sounds ridiculous, remember that Annaroth is a rich seaport, that all goods traveling north into the Enzaar Sea must pass through the Straits of Annarothal, so whoever controls the city of Annaroth also controls the straits and all passage taxes. Some said that the Ni-lach had been hired by Letsians to destroy the Sarissa government and open the straits to free passage, but no one ever proved that. But since the war, Letsia pays higher shipping taxes, and it wouldn't surprise me to learn that the Sarissa used that last rumor as an excuse to raise shipping rates."

Haradan paused, then continued, urged on Dhal's silence. "There never were many Ni-lach in Annaroth, but along the coast and in the river delta north of the Deep you could see their homes everywhere. When the war started, many of them were caught unknowing of their crimes. Most were killed outright.

"My own part in the war began when one of the captains of the Annaroth Guard came to the docks to ask Saan Adan for men to help gather up a large contingent of Ni-lach hiding on the south side of the Gador River at the edge of the Deep. Four hours later I found myself standing in a double line of men, awaiting orders from a man I had never seen before, a man who told us that no prisoners were to be taken alive."

Haradan shook his head. "It was a strange experience, Dhal, one I never want to repeat. One moment I was a simple dock-worker armed with nothing but the strength of my arm and voice, the next moment I was part of a fighting machine, armed with a sword ready to kill on command."

Haradan was staring at the wall just above Gi-arobi's head, his eyes unfocused, remembering. "Some will tell you that it's easy to kill. They lie. That day I killed and I won't ever forget it. The captain was right. There were Ni-lach by the river. It didn't take much guesswork to see why they had chosen that place to camp. With the river at their back, they had a good escape route. From the number of partially built rafts we found later, it was apparent that they had been preparing to leave by floating downriver to the sea. Another one or two days and they might have made it."

Haradan's words came faster now, as if he would get them all out at once. "There must have been close to a hundred of them hiding in the brush and thickets next to the water, some of them children. When the order came to rush them, they literally exploded from the underbrush. It was like seeing a flock of wild birds startled into the air."

Shaking his head, Haradan's voice softened. "Something ran at me. I didn't even see it, I just reacted. I killed a little girl—she couldn't have been more than eight. I felt others brush by me but all I could do was stand and stare at the child I had butchered. It didn't matter that her hair was green or her skin lighter than my own. All I could see were her small hands lying upward in the grass, her gray eyes looking up, unseeing. I don't remember what happened after that. The next thing I knew I was standing with a group of men, all strangers. They were pointing to a clump of bushes just ahead.

"Suddenly two adult Ni burst into sight, a man and woman. Behind them ran a youth. Each of the adults carried a child. When the male realized that they couldn't outrun the men who followed, he set the child down and pushed it away. Then, seizing a branch, he turned and ran at us. Out of the corner of my eye I saw the youth pick the child up and run on beside his mother. The Ni male fought like a demon, but a branch is little protection against swords and it was only moments before they had cut him down."

Haradan drew a shaky breath, his eyes lowered. "I watched and did nothing. By that time I was totally numb inside. I walked without knowing where I was going. After a while the numbness gave way to shame and anger. The Sarissa were doing wrong. There was no excuse good enough to make war on children, no matter the color of their hair or eyes! I turned around and started back, meaning to go home, but then I came upon two Ni children who had escaped. One was the youth I had seen before—and you, Dhal, were the other, no more than a babe. I stayed with the two of you the rest of the day. When night came I took you back to the river. My plans to return to the Sadil docks were put aside. I couldn't leave you to fend for yourselves, not with the Sarissa army still hunting for stragglers. After dark I swam the river with the two of you in tow.

"Once assured that I meant you no harm, your brother was of enormous help. He kept an eye on you all the time I was gathering wood and vine for our shelter and, as the days passed, he helped teach me what roots, plants, and berries were edible. Though I was older than him by twenty years, it was he who was the teacher, for the river and the forest had been his domain, not mine."

"What was my brother's name?" Dhal asked softly.

"He called himself Bhaldavin."

"You haven't said what happened to him."

Haradan hesitated. "I don't know. One night he was here, the next morning he was gone. I looked for him but I never found him. Nor did I hear of any Ni-lach being caught or killed in the days following his disappearance. So far as I know he still lives, unless he fell prey to gensvolf or draak, and I think that highly unlikely. He was fast on his feet and he knew the ways of the forest. I thought about him a lot at first, wondering why he left, wondering if I had done or said something that had upset him or driven him away." Haradan shook his head.

"His going has remained a mystery to me, one that I will probably never solve."

Haradan looked around the room. "Bhaldavin helped me build a walled-in platform in this tree. I enlarged that platform year after year until it is what you see now. It's a good home. It was then and it is now. I hate the thought of leaving it, but leave it we must. When you were small it was easy to hide you, but as you grew and some of the other wilders found us and came visiting I was forced to disguise you as best I could. I didn't do it because I hated your people, Dhal, or because I wanted you to be different than you were. I did it because I wanted to protect you from the fear I still see in anyone's face when the Ni-lach are mentioned."

Chapter 3

*D*HAL LAY STILL, ALL OF HIS SENSES LOCKED INTO HARADAN'S words. A hundred questions came to mind but before he could voice even one, Haradan turned in his chair and reached for the top drawer once more. "One more thing," he said, pulling out a small wooden box the size of his fist.

Dhal had seen the box many times and had more than once asked Haradan what was inside. Always the answer had been the same: "A secret that will one day be yours, when you are old enough." Dhal had despaired of ever learning the contents of that box.

Haradan reached into the lacings of his tunic and withdrew the light chain he always wore around his neck. On the chain there were two keys. One was to the special herb chest out in the main room, the other fit the small wooden box.

Dhal watched as Haradan slipped the key into place. He heard the click of the lock. Curiosity got the better of him and he leaned forward—and gasped as Haradan revealed what had been hidden for so long. In the middle of the box was a heavy gold ring. It was a piece of master craftsmanship. The intricately woven filigree formed a birdwing setting around a magnificent green stone the size of a thumbnail.

Dhal reached out without thinking, but Haradan pulled the box away. "The ring belonged to your father. Bhaldavin retrieved it from his body on our way back to the river. The morning he left I found the ring tied about your neck on a leather thong. I've kept it safe for you all these years, waiting for the right moment. That moment is now."

Haradan took the ring from the box and placed it in Dhal's hand. "It's yours now. Guard it well. Not only is it a gift from your brother, but it would bring you a goodly sum should you ever decide to sell it. It's a beautiful example of Ni-lach artistry, something that is no longer seen anywhere in the lands of the Enzaar Sea." Sensing Dhal's need to think things over, Haradan left him and went into the other room to prepare supper.

As Dhal listened to Haradan move about, he gazed at the ring and thought over all he had been told. A movement at his shoulder reminded him of Gi-arobi. He turned and looked at the olvaar, for a moment fearing what he might see in his eyes. Would Gi look upon him as one of the dreaded Ni-lach?

Gi leaned over and patted his chest. "Dhal feel better?"

"Yes, Gi, I feel fine. Gi, does it bother you that I am Ni-lach?"

A thrumming noise erupted from Gi's throat. "Gi knew."

Surprised, Dhal sat up, almost throwing Gi off balance. "You knew I was Ni-lach?"

"Gi knows. Lar-aval knows. Funny Dhal not know."

Dhal shook his head. "If you knew, why didn't you tell me?"

"Gi-arobi is olvaar. Dhal is Ni-lach. Why say what is? Can see ring, please?"

Bemused by such logic, Dhal held the ring so Gi could look it over. A moment later the olvaar whistled excitedly.

"Slow down," Dhal said, unable to follow the speed of the olvaar's whistle clicks.

"Fire ring, Dhal! See!"

"Fire ring?" The expression was unfamiliar. Holding the

ring close to his eyes, he turned it from side to side, not sure what he was looking for. Then he saw it, a wink of light, golden orange.

"Dhal see?" Gi pressed, leaning over Dhal's arm.

"I saw something, but now it's gone." He moved the ring back and forth slowly, trying to find the light once more. "There! There it is! I see it. It's like fire. It's almost as if there's a crack in the stone."

Dhal rubbed his finger across the surface of the stone, searching for the flaw that had to be there. But the stone was smooth and unbroken. Holding the ring firmly, he peered again into the center of the stone. A moment later he felt a shiver of excitement. "Look, Gi, there it is!"

When Gi-arobi's furry head pushed close, Dhal's view was blocked, but somehow he managed to stifle the urge to pull the ring away. "Do you see it, Gi?"

"See fire, Dhal."

"Look deeper, past the gold."

Gi was silent for a moment or two, then his head jerked back, as if he had been startled by something.

"Did you see it, Gi?"

Gi-arobi nodded, his golden eyes fastened on Dhal's. "Fire draak inside stone, Dhal. Makes Gi cold and warm together. Gi think ring spirit be very strong."

Fire draak? Dhal knew of blue draak and green, but what was a fire draak? Gi spoke of a ring spirit. Were the words "fire draak" Gi's way of expressing a spiritual essence, or did he mean something else? There were times when Gi's translation from olvaar to trader left one guessing.

Dhal examined the filigree that surrounded the stone. There seemed to be a pattern to it, yet the moment his eyes caught the pattern it would waver and disappear. But the setting, though beautiful, couldn't hold his attention for long, and he turned once more to the stone. Holding the ring so the candlelight fell full on the stone, Dhal moved it back and forth ever so slightly. "There!"

Minutes passed as he watched the shifting currents of golden light. Just beneath the light appeared a myriad of shadow forms that would not hold still long enough for him to name them. He felt both delighted and frustrated.

Ring spirits, Dhal thought silently, be still. Let me see you, let me know the secrets of your tiny world. Gi has named you and I would know the meaning behind his words.

Dhal was not sure how long he watched the interplay of light and shadow, but suddenly he noticed a subtle change in the colors. The golds and oranges faded, to be replaced by cooler colors such as blues and greens. The next moment Dhal was looking through a window into another world. He saw tree branches moving in the wind and the break of green sky above them. The head and shoulders of a man appeared in the scene. He was moving away. Beyond him rose a line of mountains, blue green in the distance. Dhal almost felt as if he could reach into the stone and touch the man he was watching.

Suddenly, the man stopped and turned to look behind him. With bated breath, Dhal watched the man retrace his steps, as if looking for some hidden menace in the bushes and trees surrounding him.

Though the man was half in shadows, Dhal saw his face clearly. He had high cheekbones, a longish nose, slightly winged eyebrows, and eyes that appeared dark one moment, light the next, as if the shadows that crossed his path were reflected back in his eyes. He had a different look about him. In that instant Dhal knew he was seeing one of his own people; his green hair was so dark that Dhal had taken it for black.

The Ni lifted his eyes, frowning. Dhal saw him shrug, as if suddenly chilled. In the next instant Dhal felt his own world tilt with a sickening lurch as the eyes of the Ni met his. He felt himself probed with such piercing intelligence that he actually flinched and, in doing so, lost sight of the invisible crack in the stone.

Drawing a shaky breath, Dhal became aware of the heavy beating of his heart, the tightness of muscles in arms, back, and neck. Forcing himself to relax, he took several deep breaths, all the while wondering who he had seen in the ring. A spirit perhaps?

"Dhal?"

He looked away from the ring and found Gi-arobi sitting quietly beside him, his golden eyes sober. Dhal shook his head, trying to clear his mind of the strange vision he had seen inside the ring stone.

"Dhal quiet long time," Gi whistled softly. "What see in fire stone?"

"I'm not sure, Gi. I thought I saw a Ni. He had the strangest eyes. Even now I can feel them, pulling me back into the stone. I want to look again, but suddenly I'm afraid. I don't know why. Gi, what do you know about these fire rings? What are they? Where do they come from? What I see inside the stone— is it real or only my imagination?"

The questions came too fast. Gi whistled for Dhal to stop.

"Sorry," Dhal said.

Gi patted his arm in a show of understanding. "Gi not know how to answer Dhal. Fire rings belong to Ni-lach. They make. Legends say fire draak dwells in green stones. Guides Ni-lach. True? Not true? Only Ni-lach know. Gi look again?"

Dhal held the ring down to Gi's eye level and watched as the olvaar moved the ring back and forth, searching for the light within the stone. A moment later Gi found the invisible crack. Dhal waited.

"Well?" he asked after a minute, unable to be patient any longer. "What do you see?"

Reluctantly Gi withdrew his gaze from the stone. "No see Ni with strange eyes, Dhal. See only sun colors. Make Gi feel warm inside."

Dhal looked from Gi to the ring, wondering if he had dreamed it all.

Footsteps approached the doorway. Haradan poked his head into the room. "Ready to eat?"

"Yes." Dhal decided he would try the ring again later. Slipping it onto his middle finger, right hand, he stood, picked up Gi-arobi, and followed Haradan into the other room.

Supper consisted of stew, hard bread, and a cup of strong rayil tea. Gi-arobi sat crosslegged on top of the table and drank the liquid portion of the stew out of a tiny spoonlike dipper that Dhal had made for him. When the liquid was gone, he ate the pieces of vegetables with his fingers. Gi was often a guest at their table, and Dhal and Haradan had accustomed themselves to his unusual table manners.

Meals were always a silent affair. When they finished eating, Haradan and Dhal usually carried their second cups of rayil out to the porch where they would sit and talk awhile. But this night Dhal knew it would be different.

From the glances Haradan sent his way, Dhal knew he wanted to talk. Dhal also had something he wanted to say, but finding the right words was another matter. Haradan had taken a great risk in harboring him all of these years. Not only had he saved Dhal's life, but he had loved and protected him as if they were blood kin.

Haradan set his spoon down on the table and looked directly at Dhal. "Am I forgiven?" he asked softly.

"There is nothing to forgive, Haradan."

"You understand why I acted as I did?"

"Yes."

"Is there anything you want to ask me about your people— or anything else?"

"Yes, there's one question. What made you decide to keep me?"

"I suppose it was guilt at first, then a sense of responsibility." Haradan paused, his dark eyes clinging to Dhal in a plea for understanding. "But somewhere along the way I came to love you, and that is something no man can fight. In truth, I didn't put up much of a struggle. I needed you as much as you needed me."

Haradan started to say something else but was interrupted by a whistle click from Gi-arobi. The olvaar's head was turned toward the door leading out onto the porch. The sound of shuffling footsteps brought Haradan and Dhal to their feet.

"Stranger men, Dhal," Gi piped up.

"What's he saying?" Haradan snapped.

"Stranger men in the Deep," Dhal explained quickly. "Laraval said he had seen men following your trail. With all that happened when I got home, I forgot!"

"Damn, I thought I'd lost them!" Haradan started for the

door, then stopped and whirled around, his eyes narrowed in determination. "Get out of here, Dhal! Out the back window and down the vine."

"But Haradan, what—"

"Move!" he hissed, shoving Dhal around the end of the table and toward their sleeping quarters. "It's you they'll want!"

Dhal turned to obey, trusting Haradan to know what was best, but he did not like the thought of leaving Haradan to face the strangers alone. Before he reached the bedroom, the front door banged open and armed men began pouring into the room. Out of the corner of his eye, Dhal saw Gi jump down from the table and scurry behind one of the chairs in the unlighted portion of the room.

Caught in the middle of the floor, Haradan had no choice but to face the intruders squarely. Resting his hand on the hilt of his knife, he challenged them. "Hold where you are!" he bellowed. "What do you men do in my home?"

The indignation in Haradan's voice caught the men by surprise. They stopped where they were, some already into the main room, others in the doorway and on the porch.

Though he had never seen the men before, Dhal recognized them as Sarissa; their tall brown boots and hip-length tunics were emblazoned with the seal of Annaroth. The thick leather chest harness each man wore served as protection against a cutting stroke by knife or sword blade.

"Who are you?" Haradan demanded. "And by what right do you enter my home without permission?"

For a moment there was silence. Then one of the men, bolder than the others, stepped forward. His courage reclaimed, the round-faced man spoke directly to Haradan. "I am Captain Mlar of the Third Sarissa Guard. I'm here under orders of Regent Lasca, who has issued orders for your arrest."

"What are the charges?" Haradan demanded.

"You will be informed of the charges when you are returned to Annaroth," the captain replied stiffly.

As several more men moved into the room, Dhal saw Haradan sign with his left hand, hidden behind his back. The waggle of his fingers told Dhal to get out.

Though he wanted to stay, to stand with Haradan, some inner sense warned him to obey. He took a half step toward the bedroom doorway, then another. No one seemed to notice.

Dhal was almost to the doorway when Captain Mlar snapped, "Stand where you are!"

"Run, Dhal!" Haradan yelled, then drew his knife and lunged toward the captain.

Dhal hesitated only a second, then, turning, bolted through the doorway into the bedroom. He crossed the room in five running steps, jumped onto Haradan's bed, flicked up the two knobs that held the wooden grill in place, and was halfway through the window when a hand caught at the leg of his pants. He tried to kick free but in a moment other hands were grabbing him and he was roughly torn from his perch and pulled to the floor. Dhal fought to break free until four men sat atop him.

"Did you get him?" Captain Mlar shouted from the other room.

"Yes, sir!"

"Bring him back in here!"

Dhal was dragged to his feet and shoved back through the doorway into the main room. There he saw Haradan standing between two men, a knife at his throat. From the way his foster father was breathing, and the blood on his lips, Dhal could see he had put up a good fight before being subdued.

Dhal was brought to stand before the captain, where guards pinned his arms behind his back. "And where did you think you were going?" the captain asked.

When Dhal failed to respond, the captain slapped him across the mouth. His eyes watered from the blow but he did not make a sound.

The captain turned and walked over to Haradan. "You made a mistake by reacting as you did. So did your son. He *is* your son, isn't he?"

Haradan shook his head. "No," he said, avoiding Dhal's eyes. "Only a friend. He came visiting when he heard I had returned from Annaroth."

Captain Mlar smiled unpleasantly. "I think you are a liar, Haradan sar Nath. We followed you out of Annaroth and know you've been home only a few short hours. With all of your neighbors so far away, I doubt anyone knows of your return."

Haradan stood silent.

"You intend to be difficult. Well, no matter, there are others who can tell me what I want to know." Turning to his men he nodded. "Bring him in."

Captain Mlar's men moved aside and through their ranks shambled a small, stooped man. One look and Dhal knew who is was, though he had seen him only twice in his lifetime: Gragdar the Silent, an old trapper who sold the meat and hides of deepland animals to anyone with money enough to buy. Gragdar was said to be drogo, a man who controlled spirits of the dead. Many believed that Gragdar's ill wish could bring disease or death. Haradan had taught Dhal that such claims were nonsense, that men such as Gragdar used superstition to their own benefit, gaining power over others through fear.

Bearded, dirty, unkempt, Gragdar moved into the room, his dark eyes glittering. An overpowering smell of decay wafted toward Dhal as the old man stopped several paces away.

"Do you know the man before you, Gragdar?" Captain Mlar asked, carefully maintaining his distance from the old man.

Gragdar nodded. "He is called Dhalvad sar Haradan."

The captain turned to Haradan. "Do you still deny him, sar Nath?"

Haradan shrugged, "Does it matter? You came to arrest me. Arrest me and have done with it."

"Oh, but we did not come to arrest you alone. Your son is also wanted."

"But he has done nothing wrong! He wasn't even with me in Annaroth. If I broke one of your laws, I should be punished, not him!"

"Silence! It wasn't something you did in Annaroth, as you well know, but something your son did in Drimdor."

Haradan shook his head. "What are you talking about?"

Dhal could not help but admire the way Haradan was playing his part. As the captain continued speaking, Dhal realized with a sense of helplessness that Haradan had been right. Healing the child had been a mistake.

"Some days ago a certain rumor reached the regent's ear, a rumor stating that a healer had appeared in Drimdor, a healer with the most extraordinary powers. One of the regent's men was sent to investigate. When he returned, he brought this man with him." Turning to the old man, the captain said, "Tell sar Nath what you saw in Drimdor, trapper."

Gragdar's gaze fastened on Dhal. "I saw him working magic. His hands were red with the child's blood!" Gragdar's upper lip raised in a grimace of loathing; his voice changed to a whine. "He healed, then stole what was not his to take. Ni-lach filth! Stealer of souls, he is! Not fit to live!"

Suddenly Gragdar lunged forward, something shiny glinting in his hand. But the captain had been waiting for just such a move. Slamming his fist down across Gragdar's arm, Captain Mlar caught the trapper about the shoulders and whirled him around, then let go and kicked the old man in the buttocks, sending him sprawling onto the floor under the table.

Captain Mlar signaled to two of his men. "Watch him!"

After straightening his harness, the captain turned and looked at Dhal. "Well," he said softly, "are you what he says you are, Dhalvad sar Haradan?"

Dhal glanced at Haradan. The shake of his head was barely perceptible, but it was enough. "I'm a wilder, Captain. Just because I'm versed in herbs and medicines and know how to staunch the flow of blood doesn't mean that I'm Ni-lach."

Haradan spoke up. "Gragdar is an old man, Captain. His wits are addled after all the years he's spent in the Deep. He doesn't know what he's talking about half the time. Ask others! They'll tell you what kind of a man he is!"

"But he is not our only witness, sar Nath. There were several others who saw your son work his 'miracle healing,' and it wasn't simply a matter of staunching a wound. The child's arm was severed. Severed! No physician, no matter how clever, could repair such a wound. A good physician might have saved the child's life by cauterizing the stump of the arm, but no man—no *man*—could have saved both boy and arm!"

Captain Mlar looked down at Gragdar, who sat where he had fallen, one of the guards standing over him. "That old man may be insane, sar Nath, but I think not. For one thing, he was the only man in Drimdor who would lead us into the Deep to find your home. That he succeeded in doing so tells me that his mind is not entirely gone. He's dirty, he stinks, and he has a foul mouth, but his attack on your son speaks for itself. He believes what he told us is the truth! And that truth must be tested."

There was silence in the room following the captain's statement. All eyes were turned to Dhal, as if he were some swamp monster caught in a net. Dhal noticed that the two men holding his arms had both managed to sidle a half step away, as if they might become contaminated by his very nearness.

Dhal looked to Haradan, and saw no fear there, no hate, only frustration and a sign that Dhal should admit nothing.

But Dhal was not the only one watching. Captain Mlar turned and walked over to stand before Haradan. Though the two men were equal in height, Haradan's broader shoulders gave him the appearance of greater size. "I saw your frown, sar Nath. You warn your son to silence, yes? No matter. There are ways of getting him to admit his bloodlines. We thought it might come to this. As you know, a man's word cannot be trusted, but his actions seldom lie. The regent decided upon a little test. When the test is over I shall make a judgment as to whether or not your son is Ni-lach."

"And then?" Haradan asked.

The captain raised an eyebrow and turned to look at Dhal. "If he passes the test, he goes with us to Annaroth. If he fails, he is welcome to stay here for the rest of his life."

Haradan frowned. "What is this test?"

"This!" The captain swung around, his movement controlled. Dhal saw the captain's knife sink deep into Haradan's stomach. Haradan screamed only once, then he was fighting for breath. The two men who held him laid him down on the floor. With icy calm, the captain withdrew the knife and stepped back.

Dhal struggled between the two men who held his arms. "Let me go!"

The captain nodded. "Release him."

The two men obeyed so quickly that Dhal fell to his hands and knees in his haste to reach Haradan. The captain stepped back as he pushed past his legs.

Haradan lay on his side, knees up, clutching his stomach. His eyes were open. Dhal touched him. "Haradan. Haradan."

"No!" his foster father hissed. "Leave me alone!"

Dhal thought it was only pain talking and ignored his protests. Only later would he remember Haradan's refusal of help and the soft words of Captain Mlar: "Heal him at your own peril, Green One."

Reaching out, Dhal touched Haradan's forehead, numbing the pain center in the brain. Several seconds later Haradan's body relaxed. Quickly Dhal pulled Haradan's tunic up and out of the way. After he pushed Haradan's hands aside, he untied the leather thongs at the top of his pants and pulled them down to expose the wound. It was deep and welling blood. Laying both hands over the bleeding hole, Dhal closed his mind to all save the healing power that allowed him to enter a broken body and mend.

Awareness came, the *seeing* of the damaged tissue, the layers of fat and muscle, the torn blood vessels. He began to work, picturing everything in his mind, not as it was but as it should be. Slowing the blood flow was essential. That accomplished, he envisioned the torn blood vessels as whole, then went on to repair the severed muscle and the slit in the coils of intestine. Slowly, carefully, he mended the wound, his hands glowing with a green aura created by the outpouring of energy.

At last he reached the outer layers of skin where Haradan's blood had spilled freely those first few moments. Directed by his will, the layers of tissue pulled together and held, interlocking cell with cell. A minute later Dhal sank back on his heels, his task completed. Where the knife had entered, the skin was now smooth, though still slick with blood. He could hear the murmur of voices above and behind him, but they were no more than whispers in his mind. As he looked down at his hands, red with Haradan's blood, a wave of darkness threatened.

He shook his head, trying to stay awake. Healing used vast

amounts of energy from within. Dhal felt himself slipping away and knew it was useless to resist. Both mind and body demanded rest. The last he remembered was hearing the old man's voice.

"Kill him, Captain. Kill him while you have the chance, else all will be changed for mankind on Ver-draak."

Chapter 4

DHAL WOKE TO A SWAYING MOTION. FOR LONG MOMENTS HE LAY still, trying to fit the movement into some remembered pattern. Then he heard a swishing noise, and the sounds made by man or animal as they walked through tall grass.

He opened his eyes, full awareness returning. He was being carried in some kind of litter. Ahead of him he could see the head and shoulders of a man, one of the Sarissa Guard who had invaded Haradan's cabin. When he tried to sit up he discovered that he was securely lashed to a makeshift stretcher formed of two stout branches and several blankets.

He lay still, remembering: Gi-arobi and the baby draak; Haradan's confession; the ring; Captain Mlar and the testing. He remembered it all, though at that moment it seemed more dream than reality.

The green of open sky above was deepening. Ra-gar was nearing the western horizon. Soon it would be night. How long have I been unconscious? he wondered. Certainly no longer than a few hours.

He heard voices coming from behind him and thought of Haradan. Was he there or had they left him behind? The thought that he might be alone among enemies filled him with panic. "Haradan! Haradan!"

The men carrying the litter came to an abrupt halt. "He's awake, Captain," one of the men announced. There was a slight bump as Dhal was lowered to the ground.

"What's wrong?" Captain Mlar snapped, coming up from behind.

"The Green One is awake."

"So?"

"I thought—we thought you would like to speak with him, sir," the man stammered.

"Later. Pick him up again and let's get moving. Gragdar says there's a camping spot about fifteen minutes ahead, a clearing. I want to get there before its completely dark."

As the two men bent to pick him up, Dhal called out once more. He had to know if Haradan was there. "Haradan, can you hear me?"

"Here, Dhal!" came a quick reply from somewhere behind him.

Haradan's response was followed by the sound of flesh striking flesh. "Silence! You will not speak to him!"

The moment of relief he had felt at the sound of Haradan's voice instantly turned to anger. The Sarissa were known for their brutality. That they should strike Haradan for so simple a crime as answering his call was a signal to him that he and Haradan had become something less than slaves.

Twenty minutes later Captain Mlar called for a halt. Gragdar had located the promised campsite. While some of the men began clearing away brush, others gathered dry wood for a fire. Left in the center of the clearing under the watchful eyes of four guards, Haradan and Dhal took the opportunity to talk, their whispered voices drowned out by the sounds of the other men moving around.

"How are you feeling, Dhal?"

Dhal was lying at such an angle that he was just able to see Haradan's face in the early-evening light. Sitting with his head bent slightly forward and down, the movement of Haradan's lips was hidden in shadow. "I'm fine," Dhal replied softly. "You?"

"I'm alive, thanks to you. For years I've watched you heal your animal friends and I knew you had the power, but not until I looked down at the place where the captain drove his knife in did I really begin to understand the value of your gift. I realize now that such power is wasted in the Deep, that I should've taken you to Letsia or some other place where you might have had a chance to live in peace and use your gift where it would be appreciated. But then, I never had the money for passage, and the only overland route goes through the Mountains of the Lost and it has been years since anyone has even attempted that route."

"You did the best you could, Haradan. I love the Deep. It was a good home. I'm sorry I brought all of this trouble to you. If I had obeyed you, no one would have known about my being Ni-lach."

"Don't blame yourself, Dhal. It would've happened eventually. Hsst! Someone comes this way."

Captain Mlar approached with four of his men. While three stood guard, Dhal was released from the litter and allowed to stand and walk a few times around the fire, then he was taken back to sit beside Haradan. After a few more minutes of freedom, Dhal's arms were drawn behind his back and tied. Ropes also bound his ankles.

During the brief time his hands were free, he noticed that something was missing. "The ring you gave me is gone, Haradan," he whispered.

"I took it," Haradan answered quietly. "Before they tied you onto the litter, they let me wash the blood from your hands. I took the ring before anyone else could."

"You have it with you?"

"No, I think your little friend might have it now. I saw him hiding under one of the chairs near where you lay. I slipped the ring under the chair when everyone was busy getting you ready to travel. But if he didn't take it, it'll be safely hidden under that chair."

Silently Dhal agreed; yet he was sorry to have been so quickly parted from the strange and beautiful fire ring. He looked around the camp and saw the men beginning to settle down to sleep. "The open sky tells me we've left the Deep. Where do they take us?"

"Annaroth."

"What will they do to us?"

There was no response. Haradan was sitting very still.

"Haradan?"

"You ask a question I can't answer, Dhal. Captain Mlar has named me a traitor. He claims that by sheltering you all these years I have acted against Regent Lasca and his government. The last I knew, anyone judged a traitor by Sarissa law was publicly executed." Haradan paused, his eyes sliding away. "As for you, much will depend upon the regent and how he looks upon one of your race. The time of war is long past, but the superstitious fear of Ni-lach magic that started it all still exists."

Haradan shook his head. "Your gift of healing may be natural to you, but to most men it appears as no less than magic. Good magic, I'll grant, but still magic, and to the Sarissa magic means evil. Of course it's entirely possible that the regent wants you for other purposes. Long before the war some of your people aided the Sarissa with their special talents. Perhaps Regent Lasca would have you healing those people his own physicians are unable to help, but—"

"You don't think so," Dhal finished for him.

Their eyes met. This was no time for comforting lies. "No, Dhal." Haradan said softly, "I fear yours will not be so kind a fate."

The night was short, as were most nights on Ver-draak, five hours out of thirty during the summer months, ten during the cold passage. As the first light of day touched the sky, Haradan and Dhal were roused from sleep and given a drink of water. A little while later one of the captain's men came over and offered them each a piece of cheese and a hard roll that had been warmed by the morning fire.

When Dhal asked to be released so he might feed himself, the man shook his head and held a roll to Dhal's mouth. The thought of feeding from Sarissa hands brought a flush of heat to Dhal's face, but before he could refuse the offering, he saw Haradan.

Swallowing his pride and his anger, Dhal took a bite of the bread, carefully avoiding the man's eyes. The bread was tough and took some chewing, but it helped to fill the empty place in his stomach.

Soon the captain ordered the men to prepare to leave. Thoughts of escape were in both their minds as Haradan and Dhal were freed from the ropes about their legs and helped to stand. But Captain Mlar was not about to give them any chance of escape. After ropes were tied about their chests and arms, another rope was fastened about their necks linking them together in such a way that should one misstep, he would pull the other off balance.

They reached the outskirts of Drimdor early in the afternoon. News of their arrival had preceded them. Drimdor, not a large village, had no more than sixty inhabitants. Because it was the middle of the day, a time when most of the people would usually be out working in the fields, it was a surprise to find so many villagers on the main street.

As the Sarissa and their prisoners passed down between the one-story wood buildings that lined both sides of the main road, Dhal became aware of the silence among the people. Several of the men he recognized, but most he did not, as his trips to Drimdor had been few. Remembering his last trip to the village with Xarlan, Dhal wished that he had never left his greenland home.

Dhal caught Haradan nodding to a man and woman standing just within a doorway to a small inn. The woman's hair was white gold, denoting not age but Letsian bloodlines. The man was tall and broad shouldered. His light-brown hair was rumpled, as if he had just been roused from sleep, but the sharp, steady look he gave Captain Mlar as the Sarissa Guard passed told Dhal that the man was alert and fully aware of what was going on before him.

Dhal believed that Captain Mlar had planned on resting in Drimdor for a few hours before moving on but that something in the attitude of the swamp farmers had made him change his mind. For a moment or two Dhal thought the farmers were there just out of curiosity, to see the Ni-lach captive taken from the Deep, but the eyes that followed their progress down the dirt road were more on the captain and his men than on his prisoners. Dhal wondered what had stirred the Drimdorians from their work.

The captain's men unconsciously closed ranks. Haradan and Dhal looked at each other. Haradan's knowing smile told Dhal that he was well aware of the strange undercurrent of unrest passing through the people of Drimdor and that he saw good in that unrest.

One of the captain's men passed by with hurried steps. "Sir," he said, stopping at the captain's side, "the old man is gone. He must have dropped out just as we entered the town."

Captain Mlar nodded. "Never mind, we don't need him any longer."

"Sir, are we stopping here?"

"No, Amsa, we'll go on. We have a good eight hours of daylight left. We can camp early and the men can rest then."

"Sir, have you noticed the looks we're getting? Something's wrong here. They didn't act this way before."

"Perhaps that's because they didn't know our reason for coming before," the captain answered without turning, "and now they do."

"You think they resent our taking of the Ni-lach?"

"These are ignorant people, Amsa, primitive. Don't even try to understand them. Our goal at this moment is to get the prisoners to Annaroth. When that is accomplished, I may just return to Drimdor with more men and teach these people a lesson in hospitality." The captain watched both sides of the street as they neared the center of the village. "Amsa, tell the men to keep their eyes open and their hands to their swords."

"Yes, sir."

No one tried to stop them as they passed through the center of Drimdor. Their pace increased slightly. A smile broke the sternness of Haradan's features. Dhal tried to share that amusement but found himself unable to do so. So the Drimdorians had frightened the Sarissa into passing right through their village. How did that help the prisoners?

Chapter 5

SIX HOURS AFTER LEAVING DRIMDOR, THE CAPTAIN CALLED A halt and a temporary camp was set up. Once again Dhal and Haradan were fed, given water, and allowed a few minutes of freedom from the ropes about their arms and chests. From conversations among the captain's men, they learned that they were to reach the Sadil docks by late afternoon the following day. Several guards commented on the people of Drimdor, but a stern look from Captain Mlar silenced them.

With the coming of full darkness, Captain Mlar posted three guards and ordered that the watch be changed every two hours. When it came time to sleep, Haradan and Dhal were separated, allowing them no chance to talk or plan escape.

One of the men slapped at Dhal's legs. "Turn around here," he growled. Dhal obeyed, knowing the uselessness of fighting. The guard brought his rope out and began wrapping it around Dhal's ankles. Jerking the rope tight, he knotted the cord until satisfied that Dhal couldn't wiggle free.

Haradan and Dhal exchanged glances across the fire. Haradan's nod was a sign not to give up hope.

Suddenly the men around the campfire were silent. Dhal looked up and saw three strangers walk out of the darkness into the firelight. He recognized one of the men instantly—he was the tall, broad-shouldered man who had been standing in the doorway of the inn.

Startled by the unexpected arrival of the Drimdorians, Captain Mlar and his men scrambled to their feet. But before any weapons could be drawn, the tall Drimdorian stepped forward holding out his hands palms up, signaling that he was unarmed and presenting no danger.

"Peace, Captain Mlar, we have only come to talk."

"Who are you?" the captain demanded. "How did you get past my men?"

The Drimdorian looked at his two friends, then back to the captain. "We saw no men, sir. We must have missed each other in the darkness."

"What is your name?"

"I am Thalt," the tall man responded. "My friends and I come from Drimdor. We are here to ask a favor."

"Favor be damned!" the captain snapped irritably. "You and your friends will find that . . ." Mlar's voice dwindled away. There was movement in the shadows just beyond the firelight.

"You would be wise to order your men to put down their weapons, Captain Mlar," Thalt said. "We far outnumber you, and unlike myself, those in the darkness *are* armed."

As the Sarissa peered into the darkness surrounding them, the captain faced Thalt. "What do you want?"

"We want a friend returned to us," Thalt answered quickly. "Haradan sar Nath is a good man. For years he has traded with us, and never once during that time has he taken advantage of our poverty. He has provided us with herbs and medicines at a quarter of the cost quoted by Sarissa merchants in Annaroth! Though he never lived among us, we think of him as friend, and so we can't allow him to be taken away against his will. The laws of Annaroth are hard on a man who can't prove pure

Sarissa bloodlines. We fear there would be no justice for Haradan in your courts."

"You are wrong, Thalt," the captain argued, "about our courts and about the man you call friend! He is a traitor, to us and to you! For years he has harbored one of the Green Ones!"

"No," Thalt snapped back. "Not harbored! That word is wrong. Haradan took pity on a child, a foundling who had no family. You cannot condemn a man for having a heart!"

Captain Mlar shook his head. "You don't understand the danger the Ni represents! There's no telling what powers lay dormant in the Green One. We're just lucky that we discovered him before he had time to do great harm to your people!"

Thalt looked at Dhal for a moment. "I don't follow your reasoning, Captain. Not once has Dhalvad done any wrong in Drimdor. On the contrary, he saved a child's life."

Dhal heard the mutter of voices. The captain and his men stirred uneasily.

Unconsciously Dhal strained against the ropes that held him. He did not like the thought of being caught in the middle of a battle between the Drimdorians and the Sarissa Guard when he could not move to protect himself. He saw Haradan get to his knees.

"Give us Haradan sar Nath, Captain," Thalt said, "or else we will be forced to take him from you."

The captain hesitated just a moment too long. Haradan was on his feet and moving. In five strides he had passed two of the captain's men. Before they could recover and attempt to block his passage, he had passed Captain Mlar. Six more strides and he was standing before Thalt. Arms bound tight to his sides, Haradan turned to look at the captain, a wide grin on his face.

Thalt barely held back his own smile as he addressed the captain. "You were wise in your choice, sir. I'm glad that this didn't come to bloodshed, for we are a gentle folk and do not take kindly to warfare."

The captain was on the defensive. Angered by the turn of events and the sudden loss of one of his prisoners, he glared at the swamp farmers. "You don't fool me, Thalt! You"—the captain looked out into the darkness—"all of you would like nothing more than to spill Sarissa blood! Only you dare not! When the regent hears what you've done here, he'll send an entire regiment to Drimdor and what you call home shall be home for you no longer! Drimdor will be—"

"Enough of your threats, Captain," Thalt snapped. "If you want your three guards back alive I would suggest you save your insults and threats for later." Thalt reached out and took Haradan by the arm. "Come, friend, it's time to go."

The grin on Haradan's face quickly changed to a scowl. "Thalt, what about my son?"

Thalt looked past the captain. His eyes found Dhal. "He isn't your son, Haradan," he said quietly. "He is Ni-lach. Gragdar said it was proven."

"But you know what will happen to him if they take him to Annaroth," Haradan cried. "You know what they'll do to him! He's done nothing to deserve death, nothing! Please, I beg you, let him come with us!"

Thalt shook his head. "We can't. Already we've done enough to lose us our homes. Should we take the Ni we would be hunted down just as they were. We have our families to protect, Haradan. Don't ask more of us than we can give."

"If you won't take him, at least free him from his ropes and give him a chance to run. At least do that!"

Captain Mlar broke in. "If you do that, Thalt, it will be as you said: Each and every one of you will be hunted down and killed! You have the man you came for. Take him and leave!"

"No!" Haradan cried, but hands caught at him from both sides.

Dhal watched as Thalt and another man wrestled Haradan backward into the darkness. He wanted to call out, to tell Haradan that it was all right, that he wanted him to go with Thalt and the others, but the words wouldn't come. He was afraid to be left alone with the Sarissa.

As Thalt disappeared into the night, Captain Mlar drew his sword and swung about to face his men. "Arm yourselves and keep watch on him," he said, nodding in Dhal's direction.

"Amsa, you, Bran, and Gydon with me. Each of you bring a torch!"

As the captain and his men left camp to search for the missing watch, a single voice floated back to camp: "Look for me, Dhal. Look for me!" Dhal felt a small glimmer of hope.

The Sarissa started out early the next morning. From the way the captain kept turning to check their back trail, Dhal guessed that he was worried about the Drimdorians changing their minds. Should Haradan somehow persuade Thalt and his friends to return and demand Dhal's release, the captain would have no choice but to fight, and judging from the sounds coming out of the darkness the night before, it was apparent that the Drimdorians had outnumbered the guard.

They reached the Sadil docks by late afternoon. Safe now from the Drimdorians, they slackened their pace. For thirteen hours they had maintained a steady march. By their high color and heavy breathing, Dhal could tell that the captain and his men were not used to hurrying. But Dhal, used to such exercise, was still breathing easily and the discomfort of the guardsmen delighted him.

The trail they followed wound through dense underbrush and scrub trees that showed signs of being hacked off in periodic clearings. It was not easy to keep trails open on Ver-draak, where everything green grew visibly by the day. Dhal heard the sea before he saw it, and felt excitement stir within. When they broke out onto the grassy beach, he was so awed by the openness before him that he just stopped and stared. Several of the Sarissa bumped into him and cursed, not understanding why he had stopped.

"Move!" one of them growled, pushing him forward.

Walking in a near trance, he allowed himself to be shoved along, fascinated by the sea. Though he had wakened with a heavy heart that morning and walked many hours with despair, it was impossible to hold those feelings a moment longer. It didn't matter that he was alone among enemies or that he was probably walking to his death. All thoughts of personal danger ceased as he beheld the great body of water called the Enzaar

Sea, beauty of the Dradarian continent. Its blue-green color captured the eyes, its movement beckoned. The breath-like rise and fall of the waves sent chills down Dhal's back. It was beautiful and alive and unlike anything he had ever seen before.

As they approached the first run of docks, only fifteen or twenty paces from the water's edge, Dhal moved away from his captors, no longer aware of anything but the need to reach the sea.

"Watch him! Don't let him into the water!" someone shouted.

Suddenly hands grabbed him, pulling him back. Dhal fought back, kicking and biting. But the battle was short and ended with him lying on the beach, his face in the sand. He was dragged, dazed, away from the water and up a slight rise to the docks. There he was left with four guards while the captain ordered two of his men to go down to one of the small inns along the dock to buy wine for their midday meal.

While the rest of his men dove into their packs for food, Captain Mlar stood over Dhal. "I know what the legends say about your people, Green One. Did you think to escape into the sea?"

Dhal looked up but didn't answer. Never having gone farther out of the Deep than Drimdor, all he knew of the sea was what Haradan had told him. Words such as *deep*, *tides*, *waves*, and *dangerous*; words that seemed so inadequate now that he had seen for himself. So often he had begged Haradan to let him go with him to Annaroth, but always there had been some excuse. He began to wonder if it had had something to do with Annaroth's proximity to the sea. Dhal searched his mind for facts about the Green Ones, but all he had ever heard was that the Ni-lach often chose homes near water and that they were excellent fishermen.

The captain hadn't finished. "They say your kind turn into fish men when you enter the water. Is it true?"

Fish men? Was the captain serious? Dhal had always loved the water and could not remember a time when he did not swim, but to change into a fish man? That was one he had never heard!

"I was young when the Ni-lach were hunted out of Sarissa

territory," the captain continued. "So I never saw very many myself. Most of us thought such as you gone from our land forever. Are there more of you in the Deep, Green One?"

Dhalvad did not respond.

Captain Mlar frowned at Dhal's silence, then shrugged. "Keep your secrets, Green One. There are others who can make you talk, but I don't think you'll like their methods."

While the captain and his men shared their midday meal, Dhal turned toward the sea once more. Sitting quietly, he watched the shifting of the waves as they glided closer and closer to the beach.

As one of the small sailing boats left the dock and headed out to open waters, Dhal looked to the horizon, wondering where the boat was going. Though he strained his eyes, he couldn't see any land beyond. Once, long ago, Haradan had drawn a map of the Enzaar Sea for Dhal to study, so he knew that on the other side of the water there was a country known as Amla-Bagor, a sparsely settled land where draak were said to roam in great numbers.

Haradan had often spoken to Dhal about the countries and people of the Enzaar Sea. From the way in which he spoke, Dhal concluded that his foster father was more traveled than he claimed.

Dhal was aware of the voices around him, but they had ceased to have meaning. His inability to see beyond the horizon had left him feeling very much alone. He sat quietly and tried to think things out.

First of all, the world was much larger than he had ever dreamed. Second, he had much to learn, about himself and about his people—if he would be allowed time enough to learn. Despite Haradan's promise to come after him, Dhal held out little hope that his foster father would be able to help. He feared that once inside the city, he would be lost to Haradan forever.

Annaroth was a fortress carved out of solid stone, with narrow stairwells and climbing streets. The main city, with its shops and trade centers, lay in the cliffside overlooking the main docks; inside, deep in the heart of the rock, lay the warrens, the homes of the Sarissa. Haradan had explained that the Sarissa homes—made snug and comfortable with rugs, wall drapes, and pillowed furniture—were kept warm by fire-heated air pushed through vertical and horizontal vents by a system of fans operated by slave labor.

Dhal wondered what it must be like to live day after day doing nothing but tending fires, to be surrounded by a mountain of rock and never see the light of day. Did such a fate await him? Better to die, he thought, than to live enclosed in rock.

"Up!" One of the guards brought Dhal to his feet with a jerk on his arm.

As he walked along the docks absorbing all the sights and smells around him, Dhal was barely aware of the looks he was getting from the dock workers they passed.

When they approached the first flight of stairs leading up into the main city, the captain's men fell into pairs, enabling them to pass between the narrow, waist-high walls that formed either side of the stairway. Twisting, turning, but ever rising, the steps wound deeper and deeper into the rock until the walls were well over Dhal's head. Whenever they came to a landing or another flight of steps leading in another direction, there were painted letters on the wall. Unable to read or write, except for those symbols Haradan and he used to mark their herbs and spices, Dhal had no way of knowing where those other stair-ways led.

From almost any observation point Annaroth looked more like a great jumble of rock than a city. Except for the docks, any passing ship would see the Sarissa capital as nothing but high jagged cliffs with natural rock caves.

At last the stairways ended. Captain Mlar took the lead. Passing through a series of tunnels that led ever inward, with only hints of light coming from man-made fissures overhead, Dhal was taken deep into the City of Rock. Forced to walk single file now, to allow for the passage of someone coming from the other direction, they moved like a gigantic snake along a mud trail.

The echo of shuffling boots coupled with the semidark of tunnel streets and the knowledge that he might never again walk forest paths made Dhal shiver uncontrollably. The guard directly behind him, guiding him by a hand on his shoulder, must have felt that involuntary shudder, for his hand moved to Dhal's neck and clamped tight, as if he feared Dhal might try to bolt.

Minutes passed and it seemed as if the tunnelways would have no end, then suddenly there was a splotch of light ahead. Moments later they entered an open area that overlooked the main harbor. It was a gigantic horizontal arc cut out of solid rock.

Dhal had seen market days in Drimdor, and it took but one glance to realize that this long shelf of rock was a marketplace. Underneath the overhang there were selling stalls. For those who had not come early enough to claim one of the enclosed stalls, there was an open area in the center of the arc where a man could lay out his goods on rugs or woven grass mats.

Haradan had described it many times, so Dhal was not completely unfamiliar with the scene. But one thing Haradan had not prepared him for was the sight of slaves being paraded before customers, the marks of whip and chain all too evident on their naked bodies.

Dhal looked away. There were no slaves in the Deep, not any in Drimdor. He felt sick with the thought of any one man or woman owning another.

Opening off the trading arc were many narrow tunnels, all of them lighted with strange glowing ovals of luminescence that sat in niches along the walls every fifty paces or so. The light within the glass globes came from a form of sea rock that had to be renewed once every forty days. Haradan had spoken about such lights but had never had money enough to purchase one.

Having chosen one of the narrow tunnels, Captain Mlar dismissed all but six of his men. Placed in the center of the remaining guards, Dhal silently cursed his captors as they reentered the tunnelways. He soon became disoriented. Not only did the tunnels twist and turn back upon themselves, but there were endless stairways, several actually passing each other, one up, one down.

A sense of helplessness slowly ate into Dhal's mind. With-

out a guide, escape from such a maze would be impossible.
How could Haradan, who had never been beyond the trading
arc, ever manage to find him in this maze of rock?

At that moment Dhal likened the Sarissa to a pack of gensvolf that made their homes in caves and underground dens. As
the gensvolf were dangerous, so too were the Sarissa, dangerous and forever his enemies.

Chapter 6

*D*HALVAD'S JOURNEY ENDED IN A CELL OF STONE. THRUST IN-
side and unbound, he sat in the dark on a scattering of
damp straw and tried to restore the circulation in his hands and
fingers. It was a painful task.

Some time later he explored the confines of his cell. It was
five paces square; the only exit was the stone slab door. By
standing on his toes he could touch the ceiling. The floor was
level but rough, as if unfinished. Embedded in the wall were
several rings, one at shoulder level, another down toward the
floor. Dhal wondered at their use.

There was no way to judge time in darkness. Hunger pains
came and went several times before the door to Dhal's cell
opened and he received his first visitors. He stood up as the
door swung outward into the tunnel. Squinting into the glare
of light beyond the open portal, he saw several figures. Then
someone stepped into the cell bearing a glowing ball of light.
As Dhal shielded his eyes with his hand, he heard the scuffling
of boots on stone, then felt the point of a blade touch his chest.

"Stand quietly, Green One."

Dhal didn't recognize the voice, and his eyes had not suf-
ficiently adjusted to the light for him to tell if it was one of
Captain Mlar's men. He lowered his hand and turned his head
to the side, trying to focus on the man directly in front of him.

A strange smell aroused his curiosity. It was not a bad odor,
only different, as if the man had bathed in some herb concoc-
tion. Then Dhal remembered Haradan telling him about the
Sarissa upper class and their penchant for wearing expensive
perfumes.

His visitor wore a floor-length tunic and an embroidered
overvest. Wooden clogs kept his feet from the cool stone floors.
Like most Sarissa, he had dark curly hair and dark eyes; unlike
the clean-shaven guards standing around him, the man wore a
short neatly-trimmed beard. His lips were full, his cheeks hollow.

For long moments no one said anything, then this man
spoke. "Feed him and give him water and in two hours bring
him to the regent's hall, third level."

"Yes, sir," one of the guards responded quickly. "Saan
Drambe, is he to be secured in any special manner?"

"A neck collar and manacles should be sufficient, I think.
He is not overlarge, and from Captain Mlar's report, he's been
quite docile."

A flush of anger warmed Dhal's face. He would not hear
himself discussed as if he were no more than a nida kit caught
in a trap. Docile! He took a half step forward. He would show
them docile!

The sharp prick of a sword point brought him quickly to
his senses. He was not yet ready to die. He moved back, away
from the touch of the blade.

A moment later Dhal realized that the Sarissa had been
testing him. Saan Drambe's low chuckle rumbled forth. "Captain Mlar did call you tame, Green One," he said, speaking
directly to Dhal this time. "But he was wrong, wasn't he?
When the odds aren't in one's favor, one is wise to postpone
action until the odds change. Right?"

Dhal remained silent.

The man shook his head. "It's been a long time since any of your race have been 'guests' in Annaroth. I'm old enough to remember your people and their end and to know that they were an intelligent race who had delved into mysteries that we are now only beginning to uncover. Tell me, are you full Ni or only half-blood?"

What point in claiming himself either, Dhal thought, since it would mean no change in his status as prisoner?

One of the guards poked at him with his sword. "Answer!"

Saan Drambe reached out and touched the guard's arm. "No, not that way. There are other ways to get the information we want. There's no need to fight us, Green One. Your best interests lie in cooperating. Believe me."

Following Saan Drambe's departure, Dhal was fed. Any thoughts of refusing the food were quickly overcome by hunger. Unused to having an audience while he ate, he took the wooden platter and turned to the wall, presenting his back to the three guards who stood watching over him.

When he finished eating, he was ordered at the point of a sword to lie stomach down on the floor. Cursing silently while his hands were fastened behind his back in a pair of manacles, he fought to keep his temper, knowing full well that any violence on his part would only bring him violence returned and in double measure.

Wait, he thought silently. Wait and pray for the right moment. Escape from such a prison of rock would take time, patience, and a good deal of luck.

Two hours after Saan Drambe had left his cell, Dhal was escorted through another section of the warrens and up three long flights of stairs to the level reserved for Regent Lasca and his immediate family. In the regent's quadrant the tunnelways were wider and better lighted.

Suddenly Dhal felt a sharp jerk on the chain that was attached to the metal collar at his throat. "Hold!" the guard beside him ordered.

Angered by being treated like some half-tame gensvolf, Dhal deliberately stumbled into the guardsman and stepped on his foot. His weight threw the man off balance; that man, in turn, fell into another of the guardsmen, who was thrown against the wall.

The next few seconds was a confusion of pushing and shouting. Caught in the middle of the skuffle, Dhal ducked a fist aimed at his face and lunged into his attacker's legs, knocking him over. The guardsman cried out as his elbow smashed against the wall. Confusion turned into chaos.

Rolling out from under the tangle of legs, Dhal was sitting up when a nearby door opened and Saan Drambe appeared with two other men. "What's going on here?" he shouted.

Dhal was hauled to his feet and pushed up against the tunnel wall. As Saan Drambe listened to the stammer of excuses being offered, he watched Dhalvad, who returned his look with what he hoped was his most innocent expression.

Interrupting one guard's description of an escape attempt, Saan Drambe approached the prisoner. "Did you try to escape, Green One?" he asked calmly.

"No," Dhal replied, keeping his own voice steady.

"He's lying! He was—"

"Silence!" Saan Drambe roared at the guard. Softening his voice, he added, "I would hear what the prisoner has to say."

The guardsman started to object but then thought better of it. "Yes, Saan, your pardon."

Saan Drambe turned back to Dhalvad. "If you were not trying to escape, then tell me what happened here."

Dhalvad indicated the man to his right. "He pulled on the chain at my neck. I fell and one of the others attacked me. He was clumsy and fell over me. The only thing I was trying to escape was being trampled."

One of the guardsmen cursed. Saan Drambe turned on the man. "You have something you wish to say, guardsman?"

The man started to speak, then hesitated, glancing at his comrades. Finally he shook his head. "No, Saan, nothing."

"I see. Well, I'll look into this matter at a later time. The regent's waiting now and there's no more time for delays. Two of you will stay with the prisoner, the other two will remain on duty out here.

"Come, Dhalvad sar Haradan," Saan Drambe said, taking

the lead on his collar. "It's time for you to be presented to our regent, Dramnal sar Lasca."

The two men who had entered the tunnelway behind Saan Drambe, and who had remained silent throughout the exchange of accusations, moved back a step, clearing the doorway. From their long tunics and fancy overvests, Dhal assumed them to be more of the Sarissa upper class—either that or officials of the government of Regent Lasca.

Saan Drambe paused before the open doorway and gave last-minute orders to the two guards stationed in the tunnelway. "Let no one enter except by order of Regent Lasca or myself. Is that clear?"

"Yes, Saan," two voices agreed.

Following Saan Drambe through the doorway, with the two guards stepping close on his heels, Dhalvad felt apprehensive. Regent Lasca was reputed to be a man of great vitality, a leader who demanded complete obedience from his followers and whose greed was matched only by his lust for more power. It was no secret that the regent's ambitions included gaining control over every port on the Enzaar Sea. Already he had made pacts with the Bagorians of Port Cestar and the Ruling Council of Port Bhalvar. It was Letsia's turn next and, according to Haradan, if the Letsians were not careful they would find themselves annexed and under the authority of the Sarissa regent before the year was out.

They passed through a series of five small rooms, and Dhalvad felt himself to be entering a strange new world. Never had he envisioned such lavishly furnished rooms. There were cushioned platforms for sitting, hanging globe lights in rainbow colors, wall tapestries, rugs, and intricately carved wooden tables on which rested all sorts of delightful-looking objects. Haradan had once spoken of the Sarissa penchant for games; Dhalvad wondered if the inlaid patterns on each table were gaming boards rather than mere designs.

Saan Drambe slowed his pace as they entered a narrow corridor that was dark and long. One of the guards at Dhalvad's back placed a hand on his shoulder. As they neared the end of the corridor, Saan Drambe glanced behind him. "If you value

your life, Green One, keep a civil tongue and answer only
those questions that are asked."

When Dhalvad failed to respond, Saan Drambe stopped and
turned, confronting him. "Did you understand me?" he asked
softly. The warning note in his voice was all the more mean-
ingful for its lack of volume.

"I understand," Dhal answered, but in truth he did not. Why
should Saan Drambe caution him at all? If by chance Dhal
were to anger the regent and be punished, it would not be Saan
Drambe's back that would feel the whip.

The man gave him one last warning look then, tugging
gently on the neck chain, he stepped out of the corridor into a
well-lighted chamber the size of a great hall, with a ceiling six
times the height of a man.

Startled by the dimensions of the hall, Dhalvad moved behind Saan Drambe as one in a dream, lost to the brilliant glitter
of crystal that hung below the globe lights on the ceiling. Here
all was light, as if the suns had somehow found a wedge through
the tons of rock that formed the roof to the warrens. In the
center of the hall there was a large pool and a fountain that
rained water continuously. Around the poolside there were
beautifully carved statues of men and women, some in erotic
poses. The floor of the hall was laid with small colored stones
that swirled in patterns of blue and white. Never before had
Dhal seen such fine stonework.

They passed among a scattering of banquet tables. Then
Dhal saw a gathering of people at the other end of the room.
In a raised chair, overlooking the heads of the crowd, sat a
man of huge proportions: Regent Dramnal sar Lasca.

As Saan Drambe approached the official seat of State, the
thirty or so men who were attending the regent moved to clear
an open pathway. Stopping five or six paces from the first step
of the platform, Saan Drambe bowed from the waist, as did
the two guards. When Dhalvad failed to follow their example,
one of the guards hit the back of his legs and pushed him down
to his knees, holding him there by a hand on his shoulder.

Out of the corner of his eye, Saan Drambe saw what happened. Standing to his full height, he glanced in warning at

Dhal, then turned to face the regent. "Please excuse the Ni, Reverence. He was found in the Deep and, I fear, is ignorant of our customs."

For several moments the regent sat quietly gazing down at Saan Drambe. Then he looked at Dhalvad and stepped down from the platform. He was dressed in a long-sleeved, floor-length tunic, a furred overvest, and a pair of soft leather slippers. Tunic and slippers were black, the vest gray. The colors of rock, Dhalvad thought.

Though the regent wore no jewelry about neck or arms, his fingers were weighted down with golden rings. As he stopped a pace or two away, Dhal became aware of a spicy odor emanating from him. The heavy scent far overpowered the perfume worn by Saan Drambe.

"Let him stand," Regent Lasca said.

Dhal was quickly pulled to his feet, his arms held by the two guards.

"He certainly hasn't the look of the Ni-lach," the regent said, moving a step closer. "Yet Captain Mlar has told us that he displayed unusual powers of healing."

All eyes were on Dhalvad as the regent reached out and took a firm grip on his hair. Moving as one, the guards stepped forward to restrain Dhal's legs. Regent Lasca pulled on Dhal's hair, forcing his head up and back. The regent's eyes were as black as the tunic he wore. Feature by feature, he studied Dhal's face, then hair.

"It's dyed, Reverence," Saan Drambe offered.

"Yes, I can see it. What about his eyes?"

"Look close, Reverence, and I think you'll see what you look for."

"I didn't think it possible to change eye color, Saan Drambe. How is it done?"

"Probably some plant or drug, sir. The Ni-lach are well versed in such things. If we restrict his diet, the eye color should revert to normal in a few weeks. Of course, there is the possibility he is only half-blood. If so his eye color might be natural. You will note, however, that he doesn't need a shave. In fact, I doubt he ever has. Another Ni-lach characteristic."

It was true. Dhal had never shaved. Haradan had always told him that beards came with maturity. He had assumed that at a later age he would have to shave, as Haradan did. The truth came somewhat as a shock. What other things was he to learn about himself?

When finished with his examination, the regent released Dhal's head and moved back to stand beside Saan Drambe. "Strip him."

Rather than free Dhal's wrists from the manacles, the guards chose to cut his clothes away. Suppressing the urge to fight back, Dhalvad stood quietly, eyes down, waiting for it all to be over. His fear of being killed outright had left him. They wanted something from him. He was sure of it. So as long as he didn't give them what they wanted, he would be safe. He hoped.

Slowly the regent walked a circle around him. "No sign of scales," he noted.

"Scales?" someone echoed. "I didn't know they were scaled."

"Some, not all."

Twice Dhalvad felt the regent's hand on his body. Anger quickly drowned all shame. "Note the color of his skin where it's been protected by clothes," the regent continued. "Was any Sarissa ever so pale, even as a babe?"

"Some of the Letsians are fair," someone commented.

"Yes, but not like this."

The regent returned to stand beside Saan Drambe. "Have his healing powers been tested other than by Captain Mlar?"

"No, sir," Saan Drambe responded, "not to my knowledge."

The regent turned to Dhalvad. "I believe you have been told the charges against you. Answer the charges truthfully and you have my word that you will be granted mercy." He paused, then asked, "Are you Ni-lach; one of the Healers?"

Dhalvad swallowed his anger. "I am a wilder. No more, no less."

"A wilder. A wilder who has the power to heal? Tell me, how do you come by such power if you are not Ni-lach? Or do you disclaim Captain Mlar's witnessed account of your healing ability?"

Dhalvad was silent. There was no way to answer the question without condemning himself.

"Saan Drambe, a knife please," the regent said softly.

Saan Drambe hesitated, then drew a knife from beneath his overvest, proffering it to the regent hilt first.

A moment later the knife was laid next to Dhalvad's throat. "I am curious as to the nature of your power, Green One," the regent said. "Should this knife slip and cut your jugular vein, could you stop the bleeding before you died? Shall we try it?"

Dhalvad felt the knife blade press against his throat and pulled back as far as he was able. The knife followed, but before the test could be completed Saan Drambe interceded.

"Reverence, please, should he die we would lose—" He paused and began again. "We would lose the chance to find out if there are more of his kind in the Deep."

A murmur of surprise passed among the onlookers, and it was evident to Dhal that Saan Drambe had overstepped himself.

Regent Lasca withdrew the knife and turned to Saan Drambe. He smiled, a strange, knowing smile that failed to reach the eyes. "I know what you're afraid of losing, Saan Drambe, and it has nothing to do with the threat of more Ni-lach in the Deep."

The look on Saan Drambe's face was enough to tell everyone there that the regent had touched upon a truth. But what truth? Dhalvad wondered.

Regent Lasca motioned to a man standing to the right of the raised platform. "Bring the tray." The tall, brown-haired man approached. He was dressed much as the others except for an additional leather harness that crisscrossed his chest and held three knives in sheaths. The man was one of the elite bodyguard who served the regent.

Dhalvad looked down at the tray and caught his breath. The glitter and shine of metal and gemstones was awesome. Rings, necklaces, bracelets—it was a great concentration of wealth. Regent Lasca picked out one of the smaller items and held it up for Dhalvad's inspection. "Do you know what this is, what it represents?"

Dhal's eyes widened in disbelief. His ring! Where had they—

no. No, it wasn't his ring. The green color of the stone was darker and the setting was different. Dhalvad raised his eyes and found the regent watching him closely.

"Your eyes betray you, Green One. You know what it is, don't you? The work is unmistakable. The Ni-lach had a way with such trinkets. It is our belief that this collection is but a small sampling of the Ni-lach treasure the legends call the Tamorlee." The regent paused. "If you are Ni-lach, then you know about this Tamorlee and its whereabouts. Such knowledge could conceivably buy you your freedom. Do we deal?"

Treasure? Was this then the real reason he was there, Dhal wondered, to lead the Sarissa to some kind of fabled treasure? How to answer? Even if he wanted to bargain for his freedom, he knew nothing about the Tamorlee. Should he admit to being Ni-lach and fail to give them the information they wanted, they would never believe him.

They left him no choice. "I am a wilder, Regent Lasca. I know nothing of the Ni-lach or the treasure you speak of. A mistake has been made. I have done you and yours no harm. I asked to be freed."

For long moments all was silence, then the regent shook his head. "No, I think not, Green One. We had hoped you would cooperate, but I can see that such is not the case. We'll have the information we want, one way or the other." He turned to a heavyset man standing next to Saan Drambe. "Saan Omna, you and Saan Dulth shall be responsible for our guest. You will devise tests that will help us learn the truth concerning both this man's bloodlines and his knowledge of the Tamorlee. There must be various ways to test his power of healing without killing him. As Saan Drambe pointed out, *if* he is Ni, we have much to learn from him."

"And if he is not?" Saan Dulth asked.

Ignoring Saan Dulth's question, the regent turned away. "Keep me informed as to your progress. I shall expect full reports daily."

As the two guards led Dhalvad away, he locked glances with Saan Drambe. Was it frustration he saw in the man's face, or pity?

Chapter 7

*S*AAN DULTH AND SAAN OMNA LOST NO TIME IN BEGINNING THE work assigned them. Chained to his cell wall at wrist and ankle, Dhalvad endured hours of questioning. He quickly learned that silence did nothing but infuriate his captors, so rather than let himself be cut to pieces by the lash Saan Omna wielded so expertly, he answered as many questions as possible.

But Dhalvad did not always have the answers the two men wanted. As the hours dragged on, the lash fell more and more often. Fearing that self-healing would be a confession of his power, he simply blanked out the pain as best he could.

Time passed. Exhausted by their efforts to try to make him speak of things about which he had no knowledge, such as the use of Ni-lach artifacts or the whereabouts of the fabled Tamorlee, Saan Dulth and Saan Omna abandoned their task to take council with some of the other ministers on the regent's staff.

Before they left the cell they ordered the guards to see that Dhalvad's hair was washed daily. "Soon you will have no shields to hide behind, Green One," Saan Omna said, looking down at him.

Saan Dulth moved toward the cell door. "Personally, I don't see that his hair color matters much. We all know he's Ni-lach. The regent seemed more interested in learning about the Tamorlee. I suggest that is where we concentrate our efforts in the future."

"You may be right," Saan Omna agreed. "Still, the regent did say he wanted positive proof of his bloodlines, and proof is what I intend to give him."

As the two men turned to leave the cell, one of the guards asked, "Saans, is he to be fed?"

The two councilmen shared a glance. Saan Omna answered. "No. Give him water but no food. Hunger can be a very effective tool in obtaining cooperation, even from such as that one."

"Get him up."

Dhalvad opened his eyes and saw that he had company again. Hands pulled him to a sitting position and removed the chains from his wrists and ankles. Dumbly, he lifted his head and looked up at Saan Omna and Saan Dulth. That slight movement caused him to lose his balance, so that he fell against the guard who had freed his hands.

"Get him to his feet," Saan Omna ordered.

Dhalvad bit back a cry as rough hands closed on the bruised and tender flesh of his arms. He felt himself being pulled to his feet, but his legs had no strength to stand.

"He can't walk," one of the guards said.

"Then carry him!" Saan Omna snapped.

"He's too weak," Saan Dulth protested, "What if he should drown?"

"He will *not* drown! The Ni are supposed to be fish men, remember!"

"That may be, but I don't think this is necessary. We've been at this for three weeks now. His bloodlines are plainly evident. Look at his eyes and his hair! And if that isn't enough, his surviving the tests we've given him is proof that the creature has a life force greater than most, that he's used his healing powers to survive. Though he hasn't confessed, we've proved he's Ni. Someone else will have to get him to talk about the Tamorlee. We've tried everything we can think of."

"All you say is true, but since we both know what the regent will do to him once he has the information he wants, I can see no harm in one last test. I'm curious about the stories of the Ni being able to turn themselves into another form when in water. If such is possible, I would like to see it."

"He's been uncooperative up to this point, Saan Omna. What makes you think he'll cooperate now?"

Saan Omna motioned to the two guards. "We won't know until we try. Bring him along. Carry him if you must."

Catching his arms over their shoulders, the guards took Dhalvad's weight. He managed to pick up his feet for five or six steps, then his legs gave way and he was dragged out through the doorway.

"Are you coming, Saan Dulth?" Saan Omna asked.

For a moment the other man did not respond, then he fell in behind the guards. "I hope you know what you're doing. If anything happens to the Ni before the regent gets the information he wants, we will be—"

"You worry overmuch. Just this one last test and then we'll give the regent our final report. A few hours will make no difference."

Though lost in a maze of dimly lighted tunnels, Dhalvad knew they were descending into the bowels of the rock city because the air in the tunnelways became cooler and damp against his naked body. Fighting to retain consciousness, he breathed deeply. He understood only that this last test had something to do with water.

Finally they reached the end of a long tunnelway that sloped gently downward. Dhalvad watched as Saan Omna removed five metal slide bolts from the door that blocked their passage. When the door swung inward, he could hear the sound of water slapping against rock.

Saan Omna turned. "Bring him."

The guards carried him down the ramp and stopped. "Over

there." Saan Omna pointed. "That pool should do. Saan Dulth, light four of those torches and bring them. They'll give us all the light we need."

A few moments later Dhal stood at the brink of a salt-water pool, one of a series of catchbasins created by high-tide over-flows into the honeycombed caverns at the base of the city.

Saan Omna took one of the lighted torches from Saan Dulth, then turned to the guards. "Put this collar aound his neck so we don't lose him, then put him in."

As the two men pulled him up and pushed him toward the edge of the pool, Dhal felt all fear leave him. All that was happening could have been part of a dream. For weeks they had kept him chained like some savage draak. Every third or fourth day they had fed him scraps of bread, just enough to keep him alive. Using knives, ropes, and firebrands, they had tortured him. Too long had fear shadowed Dhal's every breath. He looked at Saan Omna, numb and resigned to whatever the councilman had planned. Dhalvad hardly cared what came next—even death seemed to have lost its meaning.

A hand in the middle of his back pushed him forward, then he was falling. He gasped at the shock of cold water as it closed over him. Water swirled into his mouth as he went under.

But the will to live is strong and is born in every life form. Though his mind said to let go, to breathe in and end the struggle, his body fought on. Striking for the surface, his arms and legs moved of their own free will. When he reached air, he spat up water, clearing nose and throat.

Though he was unable to sustain his weight on land, Dhalvad had just strength enough to keep himself afloat. But the weightlessness he experienced only enhanced the dreamlike state that muddled his thinking. Slowly he kicked toward the edge of the pool.

"Don't let him out!" Saan Omna cried. "Use your torches! Keep him swimming!"

Dhal heard the order but didn't comprehend its meaning until he reached the edge of the pool and had a ball of flame thrust at his face. Instinctively he slipped beneath the water, pulling his arms up over his head to propel himself down and away from the danger.

A few seconds later he resurfaced trying for another side of the pool. But one of the guards was there ahead of him, walking the edge of the pool and presenting his torch each time Dhal tried for a hold. He retreated to the center of the pool and tried to rest his arms and legs by floating.

The shock of cold water had worn off, but he knew that if he didn't keep moving he would become too numb to keep afloat.

Suddenly he felt a tug on his collar. He was being pulled to the side of the pool. Thinking Saan Omna was finished, Dhal turned over and grabbed the rope, allowing himself to be drawn in. But when he reached the edge of the pool, he saw Saan Omna bring his torch down close to the water.

"Has he changed?" Saan Dulth wanted to know.

Saan Omna stepped on Dhal's fingers and pushed the torch at his head. "No, not yet," he growled. "Back into the water, fish man! Do whatever it is you supposed to do and we'll let you rest."

Dhal tried to rest in the water, but Saan Omna would not allow it. By using the collar and rope and a long pole, he forced Dhal to swim.

Dhal fought back by splashing water on the torches. Though he did manage to put one out, it did no good, for the wet torch was used as a club whenever he neared the side of the pool. Exhaustion crept upon Dhalvad like a gensvolf stalking prey. His movements became slower. He had all he could do just to keep his head above water.

"I think the legends are false, Saan Omna," Saan Dulth called across the pool. "Let's end this foolishness."

"Just a little longer. I want to be sure."

"No! No more for me! You're only playing with him! You've no interest in the old legends or anything else! All you want is some helpless creature to torture. Let him out before he drowns!"

Saan Omna's laugh echoed around the chamber. "I hear you, Saan Dulth, and know you for the weak man you are. *Go* if you have no stomach for this. I'll meet you later and we can discuss what we will tell the regent."

As Saan Dulth left the cavern, Saan Omna turned back to the pool, ordering the guards to hold their positions. Poking at Dhal with his long pole, Saan Omna tried to make him move.

Dhal grabbed the pole and somehow managed to hang on. Cursing, Saan Omna laid his torch on the rock floor and began pulling Dhal in toward the edge of the pool. There followed a brief wrestling match, which Dhal lost. Slipping beneath the water to avoid being struck in the head with the pole, he suddenly realized that he had lost all feeling in his legs. Still holding his breath, he felt himself slowly rising, but he knew that when he reached the surface he would not be able to keep himself from slipping back under.

His head broke the surface. Pushing down with his hands, he forced himself up high enough to allow him a chance to breathe. A great splash sent water swirling into his mouth.

He became aware of raised voices, then he heard another splash and someone was floundering in the water. He opened his eyes and saw shadowed forms moving around the poolside. A tug on his collar turned him over onto his face and, with the last of his strength, he reached for the rope. Then he was being pulled through the water. Holding his breath, he fought to turn over, but his legs wouldn't obey the simplest of commands.

He began to release the air in his lungs, knowing he was dead, then his hand bumped against something and he felt fingers catch at the metal collar around his neck. His head was drawn up and out of the water.

Gasping for air, Dhal tried to pull himself out of the pool, but his strength was gone. He clung desperately to the rock, and he coughed up more water.

"Dhal. Dhal?"

A shudder ran through his frame as the familiar voice sounded in his ear. "Gi?" he whispered, hardly daring to believe.

"Here, Gi," another voice said. "Let me have him. Let go the rope." Strong hands fastened around Dhal's wrists and he was pulled up out of the water. Though he had his eyes open, he could not see anything but shadows.

But he could hear. "Haradan."

When Dhal woke, the first face he saw belonged to Saan Drambe. The shock of seeing him rather than Haradan brought a flood of despair. He was still a prisoner of the Sarissa. He fought back tears. Blinking rapidly, he looked past Saan Drambe to the wall behind him. The wall was rough-cut stone, the shadows caused by the unfinished surface creating strange patterns.

He tried to move and found it impossible. He was swathed in heavy blankets. "Where am I?" His voice sounded strange to his ears. He tried again. "Where am I?"

Saan Drambe leaned over and spoke in a low voice. "You're in a secret chamber beneath the Kniat Temple. You're safe here."

"Safe?"

"Yes. Only I know of this place, I and my son, Efan. We were lucky to get you out when we did. A few more minutes and you would have been beyond help."

"It was you who came to the pool?"

"Yes."

"I thought—I dreamed it was Haradan and Gi. I thought they had come for me."

Saan Drambe's lips softened into a smile. "They did." Moving to the side, he motioned to the other side of the room. "Look."

Dhalvad turned his head and saw a blanketed form asleep on the floor not more than three paces away. That mop of unruly, dark hair was unmistakable. "Haradan." The tears he had fought now came with relief.

"He hasn't left your side since we brought you here three days ago," Saan Drambe said softly. "He fell asleep just a little while ago, as did your little furred friend. They've been very worried about you. We all have. It's been quite a struggle to get you to take any food or water. How are you feeling now?"

"I don't know. Numb. It's hard to think. How did they get here, Haradan and Gi?"

"I brought them. When you were given over to Saan Omna, I knew what would happen. He always enjoyed hurting others." Saan Drambe shrugged. "Fearing you might be permanently harmed, I sought ways to free you. When logic and bribery failed, it left nothing but direct action. I knew about your foster father and decided that if anyone would be willing to help me help you, it would be he. It took me a week to get in touch with him, then we made some plans. Since it was impossible to take you out of your cell—too many guards coming and going—we had to make other arrangements. When I learned from Saan Dulth that Saan Omna had one last test he wanted to make, at the lower pools, Haradan and I decided it would be a good place to attempt a rescue. Saan Omna was foolish not to bring more guards with him."

"What happened?"

Dhal saw a grim smile touch Saan Drambe's lips. "The son of Omna is dead. He and his two guards were found floating in the pools yesterday morning. According to the rumor being circulated, you are responsible for their deaths. Some say that after you killed them you turned yourself into a fish man and swam out to the sea through one of the submerged channels in the rock. Those who disbelieve the legends of fish men are now busy searching the lower tunnels to ensure you won't kill again."

"What happened to Saan Dulth?"

"We saw him pass and waited until he was out of sight."

Dhalvad looked at Saan Drambe, one question filling his mind. "Why?"

"Why did we let Saan Dulth go, or why did I help you?"

"The last."

"I will be truthful, Dhalvad. I want something from you, though finding you in the condition we did, I begin to doubt your ability to give me what I desire. But time enough for talk later. Rest now, you are safe here."

Chapter 8

*A*S THE DAYS PASSED. MUCH OF HIS TIME WAS SPENT EITHER eating or sleeping. Dhalvad was so weak those first few days that Haradan had to hold him up while he spooned a meat and grain stew into his mouth. Coming and going at irregular intervals, Cerl sar Drambe supplied them with food, water, and information. Several times he sat down with them and spoke about escape from the warrens; Dhal knew that it was his weakness that was holding everything up.

One week from the day Haradan had pulled him from the underground pool, Dhalvad stood for the first time and, with Haradan's support, walked around the confines of the rock-walled room. Gi walked in front of him, watching his every step and giving encouragement with soft whistle clicks. When Dhal returned to his pallet, Gi came and sat beside him, leaning carefully against his leg.

"Tired?" Haradan asked, taking a seat across from Dhal.

"Yes, but it feels good to move. How much longer do you think before I'll be strong enough to leave here?"

"I know how you're feeling, Dhal. You aren't the only one who will be glad to leave this place. And I swear, once I get out of Annaroth, I'll never again enter another Sarissa city, even to trade." Haradan looked down at the olvaar. "I think Gi feels much the same."

Gi-arobi whistled an affirmative, his golden eyes going from Dhal to Haradan. Several days before, while Gi lay sleeping, Haradan had told Dhal that he had returned to the cabin to find Gi waiting. Later, when Haradan left to discuss Dhal's release with Saan Drambe, the olvaar had not allowed himself to be left behind.

Surprised by Gi's determination to find him, Dhal had begun to reassess the bond that was between them. No pet this, but rather a friend, a thinking, loving being who cared enough to sacrifice his home and comfort for a chance to help. Dhal rubbed the back of Gi's neck and watched as the olvaar's eyes closed in pleasure.

He looked over at Haradan. "You didn't answer my question. How long do you think we'll have to wait here?"

"You should be strong enough in another day or so. Then it will depend upon Saan Drambe."

"Do you trust him, Haradan?"

"Yes, as long as we have something he wants."

"Meaning me?"

Haradan nodded. "He wants you to heal his son. He said he would bring me safely to Annaroth and get me into the warrens to help you escape if you would heal his son, Efan."

"What's wrong with his son?"

"Crippled in a fall, according to Saan Drambe."

"How long ago did this happen?"

"Two years this spring."

"Haradan, what if I can't help the boy?"

"You healed me."

"Your wound was new. I've never tried to heal a hurt that was old. What if I fail? Would Saan Drambe go back on his bargain and turn us over to the Sarissa guard?"

Haradan's silence set a chill on Dhal's heart.

* * *

Waking to the sound of voices, Dhal found Gi-arobi sitting within the circle of his arm, staring at a point just above Dhal's shoulder.

". . . so you have told me time and time again, but what I don't understand is if he can heal others, why couldn't he heal himself?"

"Saan Drambe," Haradan said in a low voice, "you saw the condition he was in when we brought him here. He was starved. It requires strength to heal, strength which must come from food. If you ask him to heal your son now, you risk having him deplete the little energy he has managed to store these past few days. He's up and walking, but it may be days before he's strong enough to attempt that which you would ask of him."

Dhal lay quietly, listening, but some change in his breathing or a slight movement of his body caught Gi's attention. His golden eyes dropped to Dhal's. Before the olvaar could whistle a greeting, Dhal pursed his lips, cautioning him to silence.

"How many days before he's strong enough to move?"

"Why?" Haradan asked.

"The regent has ordered that the entire warrens be searched, every room, every tunnel. A diligent search of the temple would, I fear, uncover this room."

"Damn! What do we do then?"

"It should take the guards at least two days to reach this level. We'll just have to move you tonight, to my rooms."

"Won't they be searched?"

"They already have been, so you should be safe there, at least for a little while."

"What about your family? Won't they object to your harboring a fugitive Ni?"

"My wife is dead. My son and I share our rooms with only one servant. No one will object to your presence. I'll go now and return with suitable clothing for the two of you to wear. The supper hour is long past and soon the tunnelways will be relatively empty. We'll move you then. Agreed?"

"Agreed."

* * *

The black-hooded robes changed them from obvious in-truders to temple priests. When they were ready to leave, Har-adan lifted the hem of his robe and Gi slipped under.

"Dhalvad," Saan Drambe said, "you'll walk beside me and pretend to be ill. Whatever happens, keep your hood up and your eyes down. If anyone should recognize you, we would all forfeit our lives. Haradan, you follow close behind and hunch over a little. I can't think of one priest in all the warrens with your height."

They passed single file through a small tunnel, then reached the open rooms of the temple. Saan Drambe paused to make sure no one saw them emerge from what appeared to be solid wall. He stepped out quickly, then motioned them to follow. Moments later they left the temple and continued down another larger tunnelway to the first stairway leading up. With his arm around Dhalvad's waist, Saan Drambe gave him support while climbing the steps. "We're in luck so far. I hope it continues to hold."

From that point on it seemed like a steady climb. Saan Drambe stopped when they reached the fifth level above the temple. "Are you all right, Dhalvad?"

"Yes."

"Liar, you tremble with every step. But we can't stop now."

"I could carry him," Haradan offered.

"You may have to. We have three more levels to go."

"I can make it," Dhal protested. "Just let me rest a minute."

"All right, but only a minute. If someone finds us loitering here, it would mean questions. Do you want to sit down on the steps?"

Dhal shook his head, though he doubted either man could see him in the semidark at the foot of the steps. "Afraid to sit," he told them. "Won't be able to get back up."

The seconds passed. Gradually the trembling in his legs stopped. Looking up the thirty-odd steps ahead of them, Dhal felt a great fatigue slip over him. He would never make it.

When he signaled that he was ready to go, Saan Drambe moved in and supported him once more. He was aware of reaching the top of the stairs and looking down a long dark corridor, then everything began to take on a dreamlike quality. His legs ceased to be a part of his body and the lights in the tunnel blurred into small suns.

Suddenly there were shadow forms standing in front of him. He felt Saan Drambe's arm tighten around him.

One of the shadow forms spoke. "Name yourselves, and give reason why you pass this way."

"I am Cerl sar Drambe, Captain. I know it's late for anyone to be about, but I was in the temple praying when one of the initiates fell ill. Priest Glacon and I are taking him up to the infirmary."

"What's wrong with him?"

"We don't know, but the sooner we get him to the infirmary the better."

The guard stepped forward. "I'm not supposed to let anyone pass this level without proper identification, Saan. What is the initiate's name?" As he asked his question, he reached for the hood of Dhal's robe.

But before the guard's fingers could close on the material, Dhal's legs finally gave out, and Saan Drambe caught him before he fell to the floor. "Damn! He's fainted again! Captain, please let us pass. Regent Lasca would be greatly displeased to hear that you hindered us in aiding his nephew."

"It is Janor sar Lasca?"

"Yes."

"Saan, I'm sorry. I didn't realize. Please, let us help you with him."

"No. No, it's all right. Your duty is here. We can see to him. Now, may we pass?"

"Yes, surely."

Dhal felt himself being lifted, the hood of his robe being pulled down about his face by a hand he couldn't see. Saan Drambe started forward, only to be halted once more. "Saan," the guard said. "We believe the Ni-lach prisoner is loose on the lower levels. I think it wise if you all stayed out of the temple area until we've found him. Pray elsewhere for the next few days."

"A wise suggestion, Captain," Saan Drambe said. "Be assured it is advice we will follow."

Once out of the captain's sight, Haradan moved up alongside Saan Drambe. "Here, let me carry him." Dhal felt himself being passed from one pair of arms to another. "Dhalvad? Are you all right?"

Dhal formed the word yes but couldn't get it past his lips.

"He isn't faking," Haradan said. "He has fainted."

"He could not have timed it any better had he planned it," Saan Drambe commented. "Come, we have two more levels to go. Pray that we don't meet any more posted guards."

Gradually the darkness that had closed over Dhal's eyes ate into his thoughts. As he slipped into unconsciousness, he could hear Haradan's hearbeat strong against his ear. It was a hollow, thumping noise that brought warmth and the feeling of security.

Chapter 9

DHALVAD STOOD IN FRONT OF A FLOOR-LENGTH MIRROR GAZING at the strange apparition that was his image. Was he truly that thin, green-haired, pale-skinned being that looked back at him with large, crystal eyes?

Looking deep into those twin orbs, he searched for that part of him which had not changed. Are you there, Dhalvad? No need to be afraid, he thought. Though outward appearances have changed, we are the same . . . or do I only wish it were so?

He ran fingers through his freshly combed hair. There was no mistaking the color now—it was as green as the needles of the rilror pine.

They had been five days in Saan Drambe's apartments, which were located on the upper level of the main warrens. Escape wasn't going to be an easy matter. Saan Omna's death had caused a stir in Annaroth and had served as a reminder to the Sarissa that the Green Ones *were* dangerous, no matter how few their number. The war that had left Dhal an orphan had been revived.

And who is to blame? he thought. You, Dhalvad sar Haradan, all because you saved a child's life.

His thoughts were interrupted by the sound of voices. Turning from the mirror, he crossed the stone floor and paused in the narrow archway that opened onto the next room. There Haradan and Gi-arobi sat on a raised cushioned platform opposite Efan sar Cerl, Saan Drambe's son. Between Haradan and Efan sat a playing board. Judging from the number of pieces still on the board, Dhal guessed that the game had just begun.

Efan was a tall boy of fifteen years. Like his father, he wore his dark hair drawn back in a club at the nape of his neck, a sign among Sarissa males that he had left his childhood and become a man. Efan was a handsome youth with lively brown eyes and very expressive hands. He was fascinating to watch as he emphasized each thought with motion, as if his body was trying to compensate for the crippled limbs that forced him to sit while others ran.

Though Dhal had had several chances to talk to Efan alone, not once had they spoken of the boy's injured body or Saan Drambe's hopes that Dhal might be able to help him. Was it possible that Efan knew nothing about his father's plans? Knowing Saan Drambe's doubts about his ability to heal, Dhal could see the wisdom of keeping silent until he had more proof. Why raise the boy's hopes only to destroy them later?

Dhal let his eyes wander from Efan to Gi. He smiled to see the olvaar so intent upon the gaming board. Such things were not a part of the olvaar's world, yet he seemed to be following the game with some understanding. Would he ever be content to return to his home in the Deep after all this? Teasing baby draak would hold little appeal after matching wits with the Sarissa.

Sensing Dhal's eyes upon him, Gi-arobi lifted his head and piped a whistle greeting. Haradan turned to see Dhal standing in the doorway. "About time you woke up," he said, smiling.

"Come and join us. Efan has won the last two games and I'm beginning to think I need some help."

Dhal witnessed the small flicker of amusement that touched Efan's face. According to his father's boasting, dacor was one game Efan had thoroughly mastered.

Efan watched Dhal cross the room, his eyes flicking from the top of Dhal's head down to his legs. Did the boy envy him his freedom, Dhal wondered, or was he only satisfying his own curiosity about the Green One his father had brought into their home? As their eyes met, Dhal decided that it was a little bit of both.

Haradan moved over so Dhal could sit by his side. Gi greeted Dhal with several pats on the arm, then settled himself in Dhal's lap.

"How are you feeling?" Haradan asked.

"Fine, though it seems as if I can't get enough sleep."

"So we noticed. This makes three naps today."

"Are you hungry, Dhalvad?" Efan asked politely.

Dhal smiled and nodded. "Always."

"We ate just a short time ago." Efan brought around a tray from a nearby table. "We saved some for you." On the tray were slices of cheese, rolls, a bowl of jellied fruit, and bite-sized squares of cooked fish. "If you want something to drink, there's a pot of rayil tea in the kitchen. It's probably cool by now but can be easily warmed." Efan started to reach for his crutches.

Standing, Dhal set the tray down. "Please, continue with your game. I know where the kitchen is."

As Dhal headed for the kitchen, Gi-arobi padded across the floor after him. "Thirsty?" Dhal whistled.

"No. Gi has something for Dhal. Give in secret."

"Sounds interesting. But tea first."

In the kitchen, Dhal sat down on the warm stone floor in front of the hearth. It would be a few minutes before the rayil was hot enough for his taste—time to find out what Gi wanted. He nudged Gi's well-rounded stomach with a finger. "How about that secret?"

Ducking his furred head, Gi dug his fingers into the fur

around his neck and lifted out a piece of vine. Pulling the vine up and over his head, he stepped closer.

Dhal recognized the object dangling from the vine the moment he saw it. "My ring!" Hidden deep in the plush of Gi's fur, vine and ring had remained safe and invisible. Gi cut the vine with his teeth, then carefully placed the ring in Dhalvad's hand.

"You've had it all this time?" Dhal asked, slipping the ring onto the middle finger of his right hand.

"Haradan worried for Dhal. Forget ring. Gi keep. Dhal happy?"

"Yes, happy! I never thought to see it again. I only held it for a few short hours, yet somehow it seemed that I had owned it all my life." Gently, he touched the olvaar on top of the head. "How can I thank you, Gi?"

"Gi look fire ring sometimes?"

"Any time you wish, friend. Any time."

Dhal poured himself a cup of hot rayil, then returned with Gi to the other room where Haradan and Efan continued their game.

While Haradan was contemplating his next move, Efan caught Dhal's eye. "May I ask you a question?"

"Certainly."

"When you left the room a few minutes ago you were making strange sounds, whistling sounds like the olvaar makes. Do you understand his noises?"

"As a second language. Gi is an excellent teacher."

Efan looked at the olvaar. "I never thought of them as having an actual language. Does he understand us—I mean, right now?"

"Yes, or at least most of it."

Efan shook his head. "Fascinating. Do you think—could you—" he hesitated, embarrassed.

"Could I what?"

Eyes wide in hope, Efan looked at the olvaar. "Could you teach me the olvaar language?"

Dhal looked down at Gi and winked. "Could we, Gi?"

"Yes," Gi whistled.

"Your first lesson, Efan. Gi said yes."

"I hate to interrupt," Haradan said, "but could we get back to the game now? I made my move over a minute ago."

"Sorry," Efan apologized. He took a half minute to scan the pieces, then made his next move.

Haradan frowned. "Damn! I was sure you had no way out of that!"

Efan looked up and grinned, pleased to be causing Haradan so much trouble. "While he thinks about his next move," he said, "perhaps we could talk."

"About?"

"About you and why my father brought you here."

Dhal saw Haradan's eyes lift and knew he was listening. "Do *you* know why?" he asked calmly.

"I think so. It was rumored that the Ni captured in the Deep was able to heal. I belive Saan Dram—my father—brought you here hoping that rumor to be true." After a moment Efan asked softly. "Is it?"

Dhal decided that he had underestimated young Efan. Realizing that it would serve no purpose to lie to the boy he answered truthfully. "I'm a wilder by profession, Efan, as is Haradan. We've been dealing with healing herbs for a long time. At some point in my growing up I discovered that I had a certain talent for repairing broken things, not inanimate objects like chairs or pots, but real living things. Cuts, broken bones, hurts within the body that weren't always visible from the outside. All I had to do was picture the wounds 'right' and they changed. I can't explain how it works. Call it a talent or just a gift, whatever its name, it works. Or at least most of the time."

"Has it ever *not* worked for you?" Efan asked.

"Yes. Once I found a baby nida that had been mauled badly by a gensvolf. The wounds were too extensive and it took too long to try to undo the damage. The kit died in my lap."

Efan was silent for a few moments, his eyes straying to the game board. Dhal knew the question he wanted to ask. Why didn't he speak? "Efan, would you like me to try to heal your legs?"

Efan looked up. "Do you think you could?"

"I don't know. I can try. Your injuries are old and I've never attempted anything like that before."

Moistness filled Efan's eyes. "It would be wonderful to walk again, to stand alone."

Haradan and Dhal shared a glance. "Are you up to it, Dhal?" Haradan asked.

"I won't know until I try." He looked at Efan. "Shall I try?"

Efan hesitated, then shook his head. "No," he said softly.

"No?" Haradan echoed. "If Dhalvad is willing to try, why not?"

"My father. I can't risk putting him in danger. I know he wants me to walk again. I know that's why he brought you here. But should you perform the miracle he hopes for here in Annaroth, everyone would know where you are hiding and who was responsible for your escape."

"Efan," Haradan said. "Hasn't your father thought this all through? Perhaps he has plans of which you aren't aware."

The boy frowned. "He's spoken of taking a trip upcoast to Port Bhalvar."

"Were you to accompany him?"

"I don't know."

"This trip—did he say if it was for business or pleasure?"

"I assume business. Father deals in imports from Letsia and works through a buyer in Port Bhalvar."

"Does he have his own boat?"

"Yes, sir. We have a small sailboat down at the fourth run of docks, but it isn't large enough for cargo. When my father sails upcoast on business he usually rents one of the larger trade ships available."

Haradan had one more question. "Efan, does your father ever sail directly to Port Sulta?"

"No, not anymore. Port Sulta has been closed to all Sarissa vessels for nine months now. Though we aren't exactly at war with the Letsians, the relationship between our two nations is anything but friendly. The Letsians believe that we intend to subjugate all the nations on the Enzaar Sea, if not by actual combat, then by trade embargoes and ship piracy. It's no secret that during the last few years the Letsian fleet has diminished as our own fleet has grown."

"Pirating can be very profitable. How does your father feel about it?" Haradan asked, watching for Efan's reaction.

"He doesn't approve," Efan replied calmly. "It's his belief that trade is only profitable when it is free of restrictions. But then, my father is only one voice against many and he hasn't the power to change things."

Efan paused, looking hard at Haradan. "Do you hope to take ship to some Letsian port?"

"It's a thought," Haradan responded. "Tell me, what do you know of the old port on the Gadrocci Inlet? Might it provide refuge for Dhalvad and myself?"

"Possibly, if you can reach it. It's on the other side of the Mountains of the Lost and lies just within the fringe of Letsian territory. Not many ships sail there anymore. If you could find passage, it might be enough out of the way so you wouldn't be followed or molested there."

Dhal left Efan and Haradan discussing alternative destinations, and returned to the kitchen for another cup of tea. Gi-arobi followed. When they were alone, the olvaar asked to see the ring.

"Already?" Dhal asked.

"Dhal say any time. Any time is now, yes?"

Smiling at the olvaar's logic, Dhal sat down and let Gi look into the stone. For long moments Gi was silent, then he thrummed deep in his throat. "See fire draak, Dhal."

Freeing his hand from Gi's grasp, Dhal lifted the ring to his eyes, adjusting it until he found the invisible golden crack that had once before taken him into another world. He felt a shiver of excitement. Who was the Ni he had seen in the ring? Where was his world? Was it real? Because the ring was Ni-lach, he thought, anything was possible.

Eyes locked onto the moving shadows, Dhal waited, willing the gold to disappear. The shift from warm colors to cool was so subtle at first that he almost missed the change. Then suddenly all was blue and green. As he watched, the colors flowed together like shadowy mist over a lake then, as quickly, they parted and he found himself looking at a quiet dell where the shadows of evening were tinged with blue.

He felt a breath of cool night air touch his face and was startled. Where was he? Where were Gi and Saan Drambe's kitchen? Around him he saw nothing but dark bushes and trees. A sudden fear trickled down his spine. Where was he—dreaming? Yes, surely that was the answer. He was sitting by the kitchen hearth, dreaming. All he had to do was wake up.

A flicker of light and the sound of voices drew his eyes to the right. He couldn't feel his legs move, yet he seemed to be gliding toward the light. The sky above was dark green: Night was closing fast.

The light of the small campfire revealed two men. Both wore cowled tunics and hide breeches that covered all but faces and hands. The younger man turned his head to the side. He looked familiar. The old man bent to stir the fire. Wisps of white hair showed out from under his hood.

Dhalvad became aware of the sound of water bubbling over and around rock. Water, open ground—obviously a well-traveled trail, he thought, and a good place to stop the night.

The old man turned to reach for a nearby sack—and saw Dhal. For long seconds he just stared, then he said something to the younger man beside him.

Slowly the young man stood up, facing Dhal. He spoke, but the words were strange to Dhal's ears. When Dhal failed to respond, the older man spoke, this time in trader. "Welcome to our fire, stranger." The accent was strange but Dhal understood.

Stunned by the knowledge that both men actually did see him, he felt his heartbeat quicken. Hardly realizing what he was doing, he nodded.

The young one beckoned. "Do you come in peace? Step out of the shadows and join us."

Dhal approached, feeling again that gliding sensation, as if he walked without touching the ground. He stopped ten or twelve paces from the younger man. Recognition came. It was the same man—no, Ni! It was the same Ni he had seen the first time he had looked into the ring.

"Your name should be silence, stranger," the old Ni said. "We didn't hear you approach."

"Are you alone?" the young one asked, looking beyond Dhal to the dark under the trees.

Dhal said yes, but no sound came forth. Startled, he tried again. Still no sound. How was it that he could hear and see and be seen, yet not be heard?

The old one rose. "Is there something wrong? Are you ill?"

Suddenly the young Ni's eyes went round in fright. "It's him, Lafa! The one I told you about! Only his eyes are different this time. He's one of us!"

"You're sure he's the same one?" the old one asked.

"Yes, I swear! And he came out of nowhere just like he did before. Look how he's dressed. That is no tunic for travel! What does he want? Why does he follow me?" The young Ni's hand slid to his knife sheath.

"Be easy, Fantar," the old one said. Gently he placed his hand on Fantar's arm. "There is no need for weapons. He doesn't look to be armed."

The old Ni turned back to Dhal and introduced himself. "My name is Lafa. This is my friend, Fantar. We're on our way to the Gathering of Val-hrodhur to gift the Tamorlee. Fantar says that he's seen you before. Do you also travel to the mountains?"

Dhal had never heard of Val-hrodhur, but the word Tamorlee sent a chill down his back. Regent Lasca had spoken of the Tamorlee and had offered Dhal his freedom for knowledge of its location. Was it possible that the Tamorlee was not a reality of his own world, but rather a part of the mysterious Ni-lach ring world? Or was all of this just his own imagination? The last seemed most probable—all Dhal had to do was find some way to wake himself up.

"Your silence does little to reasssure us, stranger," the old one continued, keeping his voice soft. "Would you not give us your name?"

Once more Dhal tried to speak. His lips moved but there was no sound.

Lafa started to say something, only to be interrupted by

Fantar. "No more," he said, shaking his head. "He doesn't understand you. Let's go. I want no more of his silence!" The young Ni pulled on Lafa's arm. "Come!"

After a moment's hesitation, Lafa nodded and together the two Ni retrieved their packs from beside the fire and disappeared into the darkness. Dhal wanted to call them back, to ask them what they knew of the Tamorlee, but, still voiceless, he couldn't.

He was standing alone in the darkness wondering what he should do next, when he heard his name being called. "Dhalvad!" Haradan's voice. Something struck his face, then he saw a swirl of colors and felt hands on his shoulders, shaking him.

"Wake up, Dhal! Wake up!"

He opened his eyes to find Haradan squatting in front of him, his face only a hand span away. Their eyes locked. "Dhal, are you all right?"

He managed a nod. "Yes, I think so."

"What happened? You've been out here for over an hour. When you didn't come back I grew worried. Then when I found you on the floor and I couldn't wake you up, I thought—"

"I'm sorry, Haradan," Dhal said. "I didn't mean to worry anyone. It was the ring. It has some kind of a mesmerizing effect. I saw something in the stone, a campsite and two Ni. It was like a dream."

"Are you talking about the ring I gave you, the one that belonged to your father?"

"Yes. Gi returned it to me." Dhal turned to find the olvaar silently watching him. "Gi, did you see the Ni by the campfire? Did you hear them speak?"

"No see, Dhal," Gi whistled. "Gi watch Dhal close eyes. Sleep. Then Dhal talk but not to Gi. Gi wait for Dhal to return."

"What's he saying?" Haradan demanded.

"Gi looked into the ring too, but he didn't see what I saw."

"Perhaps you were only dreaming?" Haradan offered.

"That's what I kept thinking, but everything seemed so real, the air, the sound of the water.... And, Haradan, they spoke of the Tamorlee, the place Regent Lasca asked about. They said that that was where they were going, to gift the Tamorlee, whatever that means."

"What else did they say?" Everyone turned at the sound of Saan Drambe's voice. Standing beside his son in the open archway, he studied Dhal with intense interest.

Haradan stood and gave Dhal a hand up. He nodded a greeting at Saan Drambe, then turned back to Dhal. "Did they say anything else?"

"No. The one called Fantar was afraid, I think. I tried to talk to them but couldn't make myself heard."

Haradan shook his head. "It sounds like some kind of a trance to me—or a dream."

"No," Saan Drambe interrupted, "not necessarily. It's been reported that the Ni-lach were capable of controlling a variety of mysterious powers. If they did make the ring you wear, it's very possible that it is useful as well as decorative. They are not to be underestimated. May I see the ring?"

Dhal looked at Saan Drambe's outstretched hand and was instantly wary and loath to part with the fire ring.

"You seem to know a great deal about the Ni-lach, Saan Drambe," Haradan observed. "How is that?"

Alert to the sudden tone of distrust, Saan Drambe dropped his hand. "I'm a student of the Ni-lach, Haradan. I, unlike many of my friends, have never looked upon the Ni as a curse, but rather as a mystery to be solved. What were their origins? Where did their powers come from? Were they learned or natural? What form of government did they have? Why did they never create any cities? In the years following the annihilation of the Green Ones, I became obsessed with learning all about them. After studying all the written reports available, I quickly came to the realization that although the Ni-lach had always lived among us, we knew almost nothing about them. What we did know was mostly conjecture; still, where there is talk there is usually substance. It's taken me ten long years to begin to pull some of the information together and though I'm still woefully ignorant about many facets of Ni-lach life, I have closely studied their artistry and believe that many of

the Ni artifacts the regent has collected are functional rather
than decorative."

"Functional how?" Dhal asked.

"Some as a power source."

"How do they work?" Haradan asked.

Saan Drambe shook his head. "The source was known only
to the Ni-lach and it seems that only they are capable of trig-
gering its power. It's my opinion that such rings as Dhalvad
wears were a type of communications device. How they work
no one seems to know." Saan Drambe turned to Dhalvad.
"Unless you can tell us."

Haradan glanced at Dhal. "You think he activated the ring
somehow? That he was in contact with some of his own people
somewhere else?"

"It's possible. Dhal, the men you saw, you're sure they
were Ni-lach?"

"Yes. The old one's eyes were a light blue or gray and the
younger one had eyes that seemed to change color when he
moved his head. I remember him from before. He had—"

"You've seen the same person twice?" Saan Drambe interrupted.

Dhalvad nodded.

"Then you've used the ring before?"

"Yes. Once."

"Tell me, did the young Ni have a ring like yours?"

"I don't know. If he did I didn't see it."

"May I see your ring now?"

Dhalvad hesitated only a moment before he slipped the ring
from his finger and handed it over to Saan Drambe. The inspection took only a minute or so, then he returned it to Dhal.

"I believe the ring you hold to be one of the functional
type," Saan Drambe said. "I would caution you to take great
care in using it. It might be wise to have someone, one of us,
near if you decide to do some more experimenting with it."

Haradan peered down at the ring. "I'm not sure I understand
all you've said, Saan Drambe, but I agree with you concerning
caution. Dhal, perhaps it would be best if I keep the ring for
now, until we know more about it."

Dhal closed his fist on the ring and dropped his hand to his side. "No, I'll hold it. It's mine." Attempting to soften his refusal, he added, "I promise I won't do any more experimenting unless someone is near."

Chapter 10

THREE DAYS PASSED. HARADAN GREW RESTLESS. HE FELT IT WAS time to try to leave Annaroth. Dhalvad agreed, but Saan Drambe counseled them to wait until he could arrange for transportation north. Haradan and Dhal had decided upon Port Sulta as their destination after leaving the city; Saan Drambe was sure he could get them as far as Port Bhalvar without too much trouble, but from that point on they would be on their own.

Dhal watched Efan cross the room on his crutches. They had just finished eating their noon meal and were awaiting Saan Drambe's return.

The day before Efan had read to Dhal his father's report on the Ni-lach, and together with Haradan they had searched for details concerning Dhal's trancelike journeys into the ring world. Between the three of them, they left no questions unasked. But no real conclusions had been reached—the Ni-lach ring world was as much a mystery as ever.

As the boy left the room, Haradan spoke softly to Dhal. "Efan asks a lot of questions."

"No more than his father."

"They both seem overly interested in your ring. It bothers me."

"Why?"

Haradan shrugged. "I don't know. I can't put it into words. It's just a feeling."

"Are you saying that you don't trust them?"

Haradan looked at Dhal for a moment before answering. "Yes, but I can't tell you why. It may just be their Sarissa blood or Saan Drambe's delaying tactics, or it may be my own desire to get out of here as quickly as possible. Whatever the reason, I won't feel entirely safe until we leave Annaroth far behind us."

"Perhaps Saan Drambe delays because I haven't yet healed Efan."

"You offered."

"Once, yes, but we don't know if Efan said anything to his father about it. He said he feared for his father's safety should he suddenly become miraculously healed. It makes sense."

"Yes, I heard, but—"

"But what?"

Haradan shook his head. "I don't know, Dhal. There's just something about Efan and his father that bothers me, something that I can't put a name to. Perhaps I'm just being overcautious, but after all that's happened to us these past few weeks, I think it would pay us to trust no one but ourselves. If Saan Drambe wants us to try and heal Efan, we'll tell him that you'll make the attempt but only after we're safely out of Annaroth."

"Sounds wise. Haradan, has Saan Drambe said anything to you about the Mountains of the Lost?"

"No. Has he you?"

"Yes. Yesterday he asked me if I thought the mountains I saw in the ring world might not be the Mountains of the Lost north of Port Bhalvar. According to him, they are the only mountains in this area of the world that might possibly contain a hidden Ni-lach world such as hinted at by the Ni I saw in the ring."

"It's possible I suppose, but we haven't time now to go exploring. If we can make it to Port Sulta on the—"

The sound of booted footsteps coming quickly down the short corridor from the main tunnelway ended their conversation. When Saan Drambe strode into the room, one look at his face told them there was trouble.

Suddenly Efan appeared in the kitchen doorway. Dhal wondered if he had been listening to their conversation.

"What's wrong, Father?" Efan asked.

"They've taken Vahar! I couldn't stop them." Vahar, an old man with white hair and kind eyes, was Saan Drambe's only servant.

"Stop who?" Haradan asked. "Who's taken Vahar?"

"The Guard!" Saan Drambe snapped. "It was a mistake to use Janor's name that night we left the lower levels. Somehow word reached the regent that his favorite nephew was ill and when he sent someone to investigate, he learned that Janor wasn't sick, nor had he been in the main temple area in over a week. It didn't take them long to piece everything together. The last I heard they were trying to find the guard who gave us passage from the lower levels that night."

"And you think they've found him?" Dhal asked.

"Yes, why else would they have taken Vahar? They have my name but they have no proof. At this moment it's my word against the guard's. But once they have the truth from Vahar, they won't hold back. You must leave here now."

Turning to Efan, Saan Drambe began giving orders. "You know the secret way to the next level. You'll have to lead Haradan and Dhalvad to safety. I'll give you a fifteen-minute start, then leave by the main tunnelway and act as a decoy."

"Sir?" Efan said, his voice sharp and quick with fear.

"Everything is going to be all right, Efan," Saan Drambe reassured his son calmly. "There are guards loitering out in the tunnelway and I'm not sure of their orders. When I leave they may stay and continue to guard the door, or they may follow me. If they follow, I'll try to lead them away from you."

"And if they don't?" Haradan asked.

"It won't make any difference. By the time they decide to break in here you'll all be gone."

"Where am I to take them?" Efan asked.

"To the docks and our boat. You remember we talked it all over. When you reach the boat take it out immediately. Don't wait for me."

"But—"

Saan Drambe's hands closed on the boy's shoulders. "Efan, listen to me. The plans we made—you must follow them. It's what I want."

Efan's head dropped. "Yes, sir."

"Take the boat upcoast to the small inlet where we went fishing last year. You know the place. Wait for me there. I'll come as soon as I can."

Efan looked ready to protest again, but his father gave him no time. "You can do it, Efan. I know you can. Haradan and Dhalvad will help you with the boat. Go now. Show them the way. I'll be right along with the priest robes we used before. They should get you out of the warrens and down to the docks. From there on you'll have to improvise."

A few minutes later they slipped into the robes, then Efan opened a wooden cupboard in the kitchen and swung an entire shelf section out and away. Saan Drambe helped with the hidden door. "The way is narrow. I think it would be easiest if one of you would carry Efan down to the next level."

"I can carry him over my shoulder," Haradan offered.

As Haradan moved into position, Saan Drambe touched Dhalvad's shoulder and pulled him back a step or two. "There's food on the boat and extra clothing," he said softly. "I had a feeling that something like this would happen and I've been trying to think ahead. I've done much for you these past few days, Dhalvad, and you know what I want in return. If something should happen to me, will you give me your word that you'll take care of Efan? You know what I mean."

"Yes, I'll do what I can. I promise."

Nodding once, Saan Drambe then turned to Efan, who lay over Haradan's shoulder like a sack of dried grass. A whispered word of encouragement and a quick kiss, then Saan Drambe stepped back. "Go carefully, all of you."

Gi-arobi was the first into the darkness. Haradan, carrying Efan, went next. Dhal followed, with Efan's crutches and a lighted candle. The cupboard door closed behind them.

As they started down the flight of narrow steps, a whisper of sound swirled around them. "Wait no longer than three days, Green One. And remember your promise to me."

On the lower level, Efan led them through the winding corridors, swinging along on his crutches with practiced ease. Haradan carried him down each flight of steps, but he reclaimed his crutches when he reached level ground. Not once did he pause to speak to anyone. Every once in a while, Dhal could feel Gi's furred hand against his leg. Hidden again beneath Dhal's robe, the olvaar was finding it difficult to keep up.

When eventually they reached the end of the tunnelways and emerged from the semidark, Dhal felt a terrible heaviness lift from his heart. He was free—free of the darkness and the ever-threatening weight of rock, free to breathe fresh air again. Looking back into the dark cavern they had just left, he shuddered.

Haradan carried Efan down flight after flight of steps. Dhal followed with the crutches. By the time they reached the main docks, it was nearing the supper hour. Thankfully, there were few people about. Dhal looked skyward. Ra-shun was falling to the west, touching the clouds with gold, and Dhal wondered how much time had elapsed since they had left Saan Drambe's apartments. How much longer did they have before the regent's guards began looking for young Efan?

On the last and lowest tier of docks, Efan caught one of his crutches for the third time in a crack. If not for Haradan and Dhal, he would have fallen. The boy was breathing hard. His body trembled.

"Are you all right?" Dhal asked.

Efan nodded, but one look at his sweaty face and Dhal knew

that if the boy did not rest soon, he would collapse. He simply was not used to such strenuous exercise.

"How much further, Efan?" Haradan asked.

"Just a little ways, on the other side of the next wharf."

"Can you make it?"

For an answer Efan started off again, a determined look on his face. A minute later they turned onto a narrow pier leading out over the water and Efan indicated a small sailboat. "That's the one."

After helping Efan and Gi-arobi into the boat, Haradan and Dhal pushed away from the dock and raised the sail. As they slipped past the last boat docked at the wharf, someone called out to them. A man was standing at the railing of a fishing boat no more than ten boat lengths away. "You!" he called again. "You in the boat!"

Efan waved at the man but didn't speak.

"Late for taking your boat out. Wind is coming up."

"We're not going far," Efan answered.

When the man nodded and turned away, Efan cursed softly. "He'll remember us and they'll know that we took the boat."

"It can't be helped," Haradan said. Sitting down, he took the length of rope controlling the bottom of the sail and swung it to the left. The sail filled and billowed outward, and immediately they began to pick up speed. Holding Gi-arobi in his lap, Dhal watched the docks become smaller and smaller. Then, turning, he looked forward to the open water ahead and was instantly lost to the movement of the boat. It was exciting and beautiful and quickly soothed away all fears. He was free.

Dhalvad sat on the shore, gazing out over the inlet in which they had anchored the boat. It was late morning. Ra-shun was high overhead, her golden light reflected like scattered jewels across the water. The beach was peaceful, the air fresh and fragrant with the smell of kansa fruit. He turned and found Efan watching him thoughtfully. The stick the boy had been carving lay idle in his hands. "Something wrong?" Dhal asked.

"No."

"No?"

Efan frowned. "It's your eyes," he said softly.

Dhal faced Efan squarely. "What about my eyes?"

"They keep changing. When I look at them I feel . . . lost."
Efan shook his head. "No, that's not the word I want. I feel
pulled away from myself. Damn, that's not what I mean either!"
Efan's eyes dropped to the stick he held. He continued stripping
the bark with his knife.

Dhal threw a small pebble into the water causing rings of
ripples to move outward in ever-widening circles. Without
looking up at the boy, he asked, "Are you afraid of me, Efan?"

"No," Efan responded after a moment's hesitation. "I know
what they say about your people, but I'm not afraid of you."

Dhal looked up and smiled. "Good, because you have nothing to fear from me, nothing at all." He glanced at the boy's
legs. They were thin, the muscles grown soft with disuse.
"Efan, there is little chance that you will ever go back to
Annaroth now. While we wait for Haradan and your father,
would you like me to see what can be done about your legs?"

Efan shook his head. "No, I'll wait for Saan—for my father."

"All right, we can wait," Dhal agreed.

"Green One, do you think Haradan will be back tonight?"

Dhal flinched at the name "Green One." It had been Saan
Omna's favorite profanity. He turned to Efan and tried to answer his question without showing anger. "Haradan left early
this morning and he said it would take him eight hours to reach
the docks overland. Figuring the same time back and however
long it takes him to reach your father, I don't really expect
him before tomorrow evening."

"Do you think he'll be able to reach my father?"

"We can hope, that's all. Haradan still has a few old friends
on the docks. He was sure he could learn something from
them."

"What if my father has been arrested?"

"Pray that he hasn't. I've had a taste of Sarissa justice, one
I will never forget. I think in some ways your people are more
to be feared than mine."

A little while later Gi-arobi returned carrying two large, ripe
kansa. One look at his fruit-dribbled fur and Dhal knew that

while he and Efan sat talking, Gi had been happily gorging on the yellow fruit which grew on the low bushes near the rivulet where they had left their boat. While they tasted Gi's offering, the olvaar waded out into the water to wash the juice from his fur.

"I love to watch him," Efan said. "Green One, could you teach me more of his language?"

"Yes, if you will do something for me."

"What?"

"Please call me Dhalvad, or Dhal. It is my name."

As night closed, Gi-arobi entertained Efan with a story while Dhal repacked the leather pouches that contained their food supplies. Gi was a good storyteller, his lilting speech most pleasing to the ear. The story he told that night concerned a certain small but very wise olvaar named Re-sanar, who outwitted a gigantic ver-draak who was threatening an olvaar gathering. The hero of this story was suspiciously like Gi, though Dhal kept that to himself. The only draak Gi had ever tangled with were strictly in the "baby" category.

Efan was completely enthralled as Gi paraded before his knees, using gestures to emphasize how the hero killed the ver-draak with a silver lance. Suddenly Gi lunged forward and up into the air.

Then Gi stood quietly, looking down at a place before his feet. "Ver-draak dead. Deep safe for olvaar now." With a quick lift of his head, Gi looked at Efan. "Like story?"

Grinning, his white teeth bright in the encroaching darkness, Efan nodded. "It was a wonderful story, Gi. Is it true?"

"Lar-aval says is true," Gi replied promptly.

"When did it happen?"

Gi shook his head. "Long past."

Though Dhal knew Gi had probably made some additions to the story Lar-aval had told him, there was one point that caught his interest. "Gi, this lance that killed the draak—you said that it was silver light. Do you mean metal?"

"Lar-aval says."

"Was it a Sarissa weapon?"

"No."

"Not Sarissa. Where then did this weapon come from?"

"Gi not know, Dhal. Re-sanar lived before Sarissa come to Deep."

"Why do you ask?" Efan wanted to know.

"I've never known the olvaar to carry or make any kind of a weapon, so where would they get a metal lance?"

"Does he mean a sword?"

"No," Gi interrupted. "Lar-aval says silver light, like silver fire, burning."

"Who is this Lar-aval?" Efan asked.

"An old olvaar, a patriarch in Gi's family."

"How old?"

"I'm not really sure, but from what I've learned from Gi, Lar-aval is somewhere around three hundred years old."

"But that's impossible!"

"Is it? Who can say? No one that I know of has ever studied the olvaar."

"But—" Efan sputtered to silence, shaking his head in disbelief.

"Gi," Dhal said. "This weapon, does Lar-aval know what happened to it?"

Gi came and stood before Dhal. It was getting harder to see in the growing dark. "Lar-aval says silver fire given to Ni-lach. Safe them."

"The olvaar had contact with the Ni-lach?" Efan asked quickly.

"You never told me that, Gi," Dhal said, wondering what other gems of information lay inside that furry little head. "Gi, why did the olvaar give this weapon to the Ni?"

"Ni-lach friends. Lar-aval says Ni keep silver fire from others. Safe them."

"Others? What others, Gi?"

"Men not Sarissa. Men who kill and eat olvaar!" Gi declared with repugnance.

"These men were *not* Sarissa?"

"Not! Lar-aval says Ral-jenobb come before Sarissa."

"Ral-jennob, sun travelers," Dhal murmured aloud. He shook

his head. "There's something strange here. I wish I could speak to Lar-aval."

"Where is he?" Efan asked.

"Back in the Deep. But to go back there now would be suicidal. Still . . . there is something about Gi's silver fire that bothers me. I feel as if I'm looking into the dark, knowing there is something there, something important, yet not able to see it."

Reaching out, he drew Gi close. "Only recently did I learn about myself, Gi, and I've never spoken to you about my people. Tell me, what else do you know about the Ni-lach?"

"Gi know what Lar-aval says. No more. Gi young when Ni go away."

"All right, then tell me what Lar-aval says about the Ni."

"Say many things. Ni are singing people. Here before Sarissa, before Ral-jennob. Ni-lach are water folk. Kind, gentle. Wrong for Sarissa to kill Ni-lach."

"Gi, do you know if there are any other Ni within the Deep?"

"Lar-aval says no. All gone now."

"Gone where?"

"Gi not know. Lar-aval says Ni find new home maybe."

Chapter 11

*I*T WAS LATE AFTERNOON. *HARADAN HAD BEEN GONE THREE AND* a half days and Dhal was growing worried. Leaving Efan to his carving with Gi-arobi as an audience, he went down to the beach.

After a brief swim and a run up and down the beach, he moved into the blue-green depths of the uncut forest to gather some fresh kansa. A feeling of peace fell over him. How like the Deep this land is, he thought, green upon green, growing and ever watchful of the life within its embrace.

While he was sorting through his pile of fruit, he happened to glance down at his ring. The green stone caught the sunlight as it filtered down through the branches of the trees. Flaming to life, the invisible crack opened and once more he was looking down into a swirl of color. Forgetting his promise to Haradan, he looked deeper into the golden lights, wondering if they would change as they had before.

Seconds passed. He waited. Closing his mind to everything around him, Dhal pictured the face of the young Ni he had seen the last time and willed the colors to change. When it happened it was so sudden that he could not remember seeing the change: one second the swirling mist was gold, the next it was blue.

As the mist receded, Dhal found himself in the middle of a scene of great activity. Ni-lach male, female, and young were all busy by a lake, pulling at nets and splashing in the shallow water. And above their excited voices he could hear the thread of music unlike any sound he had ever heard before.

Startled by the appearance of so many Ni, he stood frozen, hardly daring to believe his eyes. Haradan had said that the Ni-lach had all been killed, that nowhere in Sarissa territory could any be found. Sarissa territory? Was that the answer? Was it possible that the scene he viewed was a place far from Sarissa lands? Or was he only dreaming it all, wishing for the impossible?

From the position of Ra-shun, low in the eastern sky, he knew it was morning. A light fog lay over the water. Above the lake rose a series of moss-covered cliffs, and up beyond the cliffs stood a great mountain with twin peaks reaching skyward. He had never seen such mountains and was awed by their size and closeness.

More and more of the Ni stopped talking and joined in the song. The music seemed to flow as a living thing across the openness of the water, beckoning. Though he could not understand the words, they seemed to pull at him. He felt himself move forward. Then he became aware of the echo of the song bouncing back from the cliffside, creating a strange harmonic effect.

Dhal watched as some of the Ni males began to swim out into the lake, dragging a portion of the great nets behind them. He saw a great roiling motion in the water, then suddenly something broke the surface—it was a water draak, the largest he had ever seen, its head high above the water on a long, thin neck.

He tried to yell a warning but no sound passed his lips. Those who were swimming seemed unaware of their danger. The singing continued. Dhal tried to run toward the people, to warn them of their danger, but movement was difficult, as if he were wading through hip-deep clingor grass.

One of the females stood up and pointed. Like most of the others, she was naked. Other heads lifted, but no one seemed unduly disturbed by the fast-approaching draak. Then Dhal saw the churning of water just ahead of the draak.

The men with the nets swam out and away from each other just as the draak closed on them. Whatever swam ahead of the draak had no time to escape the nets. As the men began swimming back inland, the Ni on shore began quickly pulling in the nets. The singing continued, but now it had changed to a slower beat. Then the draak slipped beneath the surface, and Dhal stood in gaping wonder as the full implications hit. The Ni had used the draak to help them with their fishing! Impossible! Yet he had seen it!

Several of the younglings turned away, splashing out of the water. One small male almost walked into Dhal before seeing him. When he looked up, his crystal eyes went wide in surprise, then suddenly he cried out.

Dhal lifted his hands in a gesture of peace, but his movement only frightened the child even more. Falling backward over his own feet, the little one rolled away, still crying.

Then three Ni males ran toward Dhal, all naked but armed with throwing spears usually reserved for fishing. Behind them came others, nets forgotten, singing ended.

Dhal panicked. Though he had neither meant nor done the child any harm, he did not think he could explain that to the angry-looking Ni coming at him. Lifting his ring hand, he quickly found the invisible crack and willed the stone colors back to gold and himself back to his own world.

He was aware of bodies and strange voices closing around him, but he kept his eyes on the stone, not daring to look away even for a second. Gradually the lakeside voices began to fade. The last thing he heard was a softly whispered word that sounded like "stay."

When he opened his eyes, all was quiet and he was back sitting on the sand. He was startled to find Gi standing at his left elbow, his golden eyes round with interest. "How long have you been here?"

"Small time. Gi watch for Dhal come back. No come. Gi find."

"Gi, did you see the people in the ring world? Did you hear them singing?"

Gi shook his head.

"You're sure you didn't hear any voices?"

"No hear anything, Dhal."

For long moments, Dhalvad sat contemplating the strange Ni-lach ring that had come down to him from his father. Confused by what he had witnessed and not a little afraid of the new forces he had stirred in the green stone, he unlaced the cording at the neck of his tunic, slipped the ring onto it, then carefully knotted the cording around his neck, letting the ring slip down inside his tunic.

"Dhalvad! Dhalvad!" It was Haradan's voice.

Dhal quickly made a sack of the front of his tunic and filled it with the fruit he had gathered. "Coming, Haradan!"

A moment later he was running back toward the beach. "Everything all right?" he called when he saw Haradan.

Haradan waited until Dhal stopped in front of him. "Saan Drambe is dead." His voice was dulled by exhaustion. His clothes were torn, his face streaked with dirt and sweat.

"Dead how?" Dhal asked.

"Come, let's head back to the camp. I'll tell you on the way."

As they left the beach and entered the woods, Dhal thought about Efan. "Haradan, what are you going to tell the boy?"

"He's been told the truth. There was no other way."

Haradan walked in front of Dhal on the narrow path. The very calmness in Haradan's voice told Dhal that his foster father was greatly disturbed and was trying hard to cover it up. "What happened, Father?" he asked softly.

Haradan stopped and turned. "You know, there were moments these past few weeks when I was sure I would never hear that word or your voice again. I know what's going through

Efan's mind right now, the emptiness, the pain. Only for him there will be no return of the dead to life."

"You're sure Saan Drambe is dead?"

Haradan started walking again. "I'm sure. It took me a full day to reach the docks and another half day to find my friend Entl sar Vlame. I've not seen him for almost ten years but he remembered me. We used to do some trading together. Entl knew I lived in the Deep and he knows I have a son, but that's all. When I asked him about the rumor of an escaped Ni, he willingly told me all he knew." Haradan took a deep breath. "According to Entl, Saan Drambe died within hours of our leaving the city. Following our departure, he tried to speak with several influential friends, probably hoping to forestall his arrest, but before he could make any headway, the Guard came for him. A short time later he heard himself accused of being a traitor.

"When Saan Drambe refused to confess, the regent ordered him to be taken to the torture cells. He tried to escape, and led his guards a chase through the warrens that Entl said would be remembered for many years. Finally they cornered him on the Trading Arc. Some witnesses say he was pushed from the edge, others claimed that he jumped. Whatever the truth, he didn't live to betray Efan or us."

"What are we going to do with Efan?"

"We'll have to take him with us."

"To Letsia?"

"The boat is too small for us to sail directly to Port Sulta. I think our best chance lies in sailing to Port Bhalvar and from there across the sea to Port Cestar, then on to Sulta."

"I remember hearing Saan Drambe speak of friends in Port Bhalvar, Haradan. The boy might be better off there than going with us to Port Sulta. After all, he is Sarissa."

"We'll ask him. The choice will have to be his."

"Agreed."

"While I was gone, did you have a chance to see what was wrong with Efan's legs?"

"No, he wouldn't let me touch him until his father was here. I think he's afraid of me."

"Damn," Haradan swore softly. "There's nothing for him to be afraid of! Do you think you *can* help him?"

"I don't honestly know, but I'll try as soon as he'll let me."

Upon reaching camp, Haradan ordered Dhal to ready the boat. The sound of muffled sobbing followed them down to the water's edge. By the time Gi and Dhal had managed to get the boat all the way into the water, Haradan had made two trips from camp bringing supplies. "Load them in the back under the seat," he said. "Make a place for Efan in front. I'll go get him."

"We're leaving now?" Dhal asked, lifting the first of the food pouches.

"Yes. By the time we clear the inlet it will be getting dark. Until we're closer to Port Bhalvar, we'll do most of our traveling by night to avoid Sarissa ships. It will be more dangerous than sailing during the day, but we have little choice. According to Entl, the regent has ordered a search of all small boats in Sarissa waters."

"Then they know about Saan Drambe's boat."

"Probably. There's nothing we can do about it but move as quickly as we can."

"Haradan, you said that we'll head for Port Sulta. Tell me truthfully, how do the Letsians feel about the Ni-lach? Will I be welcomed there?"

"I don't know, Dhal. But surely the Letsians can't be any worse than the Sarissa."

Gi and Dhal had almost finished packing everything away when Haradan returned carrying Efan. Wading into thigh-deep water, Haradan laid the boy down on the bottom of the boat on a pile of blankets Dhal had prepared. Efan was silent now, his eyes closed, his face puffy and red.

Morning found their boat tied to a half-submerged log in a small river inlet. The great aban trees that overshadowed the river provided them with perfect cover.

Walking the length of the log with the last of their food pouches, Dhal jumped across to the riverbank and climbed the rise to the spot Haradan had chosen for their campsite. As he moved through the knee-length ferns and wild grass, he was reminded of home in the Deep. Would he ever see it again? Would he ever call any place home again?

Upon his return Haradan put a finger to his lips, cautioning him to silence. He then pointed to Efan who lay flat on his back, his eyes closed to the beauty around him.

"Asleep already?" Dhal asked, moving away from the youth.

Haradan nodded. "Probably the best thing for him. That was a long haul last night and he did a damn fine job considering the circumstances. Crippled or not, that boy is going to make a fine sailor one day."

Looking out over the river inlet, Dhal voiced an inner fear. "Haradan, do you think Efan blames me for his father's death?"

"Do you blame yourself, Dhal?"

Dhal turned. "Yes and no. Everything just seemed to happen. I didn't wish Saan Drambe dead. Others yes, but not him. Yet he was the one who died."

"He died trying to protect his son, Dhal, and all that he did for you he did with a goal in mind. He hoped you could grant him a miracle. He wanted Efan to walk again and he was willing to take chances to get what he wanted."

"But what about Efan? Does he understand all that?"

"If he doesn't now, he will—when he has time to think about it. Come on, rest. After last night we all should get some sleep. If we're going to continue sailing at night, we'll have to do our sleeping during the day."

Chapter 12

SINCE THEIR DEPARTURE FROM ANNAROTH THEY HAD SEEN ONLY three ships, and those only at a distance. Sitting beside Haradan, Dhal was conscious of Efan's eyes on the back of his neck. Not one word had Efan spoken to him since learning of his father's death. Dhal tried to pretend that the boy's continued silence didn't bother him.

When they beached the boat on the fourth morning of their journey, Haradan was the first over the side, splashing into hip-deep water. After fastening the tow line to a convenient tree, he returned and began grabbing up their supply pouches, throwing them onto dry land. Dhal had just finished securing the sail and bent to help him. "Never mind," Haradan said. "I'll get these. You help Efan ashore." Without a backward glance Haradan turned and waded ashore. After a moment or two Dhal stepped over the side and into the water. He gave Gi a lift to dry land, then returned and pulled the end of the boat around until he could reach Efan. Leaning over, he put his arm around the boy. Efan stiffened, then relaxed as he felt Dhal's other arm slip under his legs. Efan was tall but thin; Dhal carried the boy's weight easily as he and Gi-arobi followed Haradan's path into the woods.

Haradan passed them on his way back. "Just a little farther," he said, pointing. "Go ahead, I'll bring the rest of the packs."

When they reached the place Haradan had chosen, Dhal put Efan down next to the pile of pouches. Still the boy's eyes avoided his. Afraid that Haradan's tactic had not worked, Dhal stood and took a step away, thinking to go after Efan's crutches.

But Efan reached up and caught Dhal's hand. "Please," he said, dark eyes lifting. "I'm sorry. I've been acting like a child. Forgive me."

Squatting, Dhal squeezed the boy's hand. "Is all well between us then?"

Efan nodded. "It wasn't your fault—my father's death. It was a mistake to think so. You and Haradan have been nothing but kind to me and I'm ashamed of the way I've been acting."

"You need not be ashamed, Efan. I understand."

"I'm forgiven?" The silent plea in the boy's eyes touched Dhalvad deeply, reminding him of his first meeting with Gi, and the delicate balance between wariness and trust.

"Forgiven," Dhal said. "Friends?"

There was only a moment's hesitation, then Efan smiled. "Friends."

When it was Dhal's turn to stand watch, Haradan woke him. It was midafternoon. Ra-shun was moving to the west, Ra-gar was still overhead. Before he lay down to sleep, Haradan told Dhal that he had counted five ships passing, the gold and red sails marking them as Sarissa.

"You think they're still searching for Saan Drambe's boat?" Dhal asked, carefully keeping his voice lowered so as not to wake Efan.

"I don't know. Regent Lasca is a very unpredictable man. It may be that he's already forgotten all about us, or it may be that he has even broadened his search. We won't know until we reach Port Bhalvar. We should be able to pick up some news there. Until then we'll just have to keep watch as best we can and pray that Regent Lasca has other things to take his interest. Personally, I can't see him worrying about one lone Ni very long, not with an entire nation to rule."

Leaving Haradan to get some rest, Dhal and Gi-arobi walked down to the shore where they searched the shallows for edible mollusks. As Dhal watched Gi wash the grit from several of the shellfish, he wondered if the olvaar regretted his decision to leave the Deep and follow them. Was Gi's sense of home less strong than his own?

Gi splashed up out of the water and deposited his offering on the pile. Reaching out, Dhal gently pulled at the fur on the back of Gi's neck. Instantly golden eyes locked on his. "Dhal wants?" the olvaar whistled.

"Gi, would you like to go back to the Deep?"

"Dhal going back?"

"No, I can't. It's too much Sarissa territory and they have named me enemy. Not so with you though. It's not too late for you to return home if you want to."

Gi cocked his head to one side. "Dhal unhappy Gi come?"

"No, little friend. Never that," Dhal answered, switching to Gi's native speech. "Dhal thought you like to go home now, before too late for turning back."

"Gi stay with Dhal, yes. Happy see new lands. Lar-aval knows."

"Lar-aval knows what?" Dhal asked.

"Gi with Dhal. Gi promise to take care of Dhal."

"Oh," Dhal said, smiling. "I didn't realize."

Ra-shun slipped below the horizon and Ra-gar was falling to the west as Gi and Dhal returned to camp. In a few hours' time darkness would begin to filter in from the east. Then it would be time to set sail once more.

All was quiet in camp. Haradan and Efan lay sprawled asleep on their blankets, Haradan in the shade, Efan in a pool of spotted sunlight.

Moving over to the boy, Dhal stood quietly a moment, then knelt beside him. With his eyes closed and his face relaxed in sleep, Efan looked much younger than his fifteen years. Sunlight accented the hollow of his cheeks and the soft curve of his lower lip. While letting his gaze stray from Efan's face down the length of his still-growing body, Dhal reached out and gently laid his right hand on the boy's forehead. Not until he actually touched Efan did he realize his own intentions.

Dhal wanted to enter the crippled body with that part of him that was a healing force, to seek out the injury, to heal. Up until that moment he had been forestalled, first by his own weakness, then by Efan's silent hostility. But now all that was changed. Dhal's strength had long since returned, and he and Efan had taken the first tentative steps toward friendship.

Should he try to heal Efan without his permission? In that moment of indecision, Dhal saw Saan Drambe as he last remembered him: dark eyes on his son as Haradan stepped into the dark tunnel. How he had loved his son and had wanted him to walk again.

Looking down at the boy, Dhal felt a sense of rightness touch him. You've not given your permission, young friend, he thought, but your father has.

Suddenly Efan's breathing changed. As the boy's eyelids fluttered open, Dhal laid his fingertips on Efan's forehead, willing him back to sleep.

There was a moment when Efan fought against that return to sleep, his lips moving soundlessly in protest. Then he relaxed and lay still.

Once assured Efan was deep in a dream state, Dhal gently turned him over onto his stomach, carefully positioning his head to the side so Efan could breathe freely. He was aware of Gi taking a position on the other side of Efan. Gi had seen him work before, so Dhal knew he would not interrupt or try to interfere. As a recipient of Dhal's healing gift, Gi would never deny that gift to another.

Dhal pulled the boy's tunic up and out of the way, and moved his hands gently over Efan's back, following the contour of the spine. He then slipped down Efan's pants and continued his search. As his fingers moved to Efan's lower back, down over the buttocks to his legs, Dhal sensed the "wrongness." There were several partially crushed bone pieces in the spine, two of them pinching the life cable. Dhal did not know the medical terms to describe Efan's injuries, but in his mind there was a picture of the tissues, muscles, nerves, and bones that were there — he could "see" what was and knew what should be. It was only a matter of rebuilding.

Closing his eyes to better picture the healthy body he would gift Efan, Dhal concentrated on becoming one with the boy, giving him of his energy in the only way he knew how.

Slowly, carefully, Dhal tried to undo the damage, but the injuries were old, the body cells slow in responding. Closing his mind to the fear that Efan was beyond his help, Dhal tried even harder. Time lost all meaning. He became deaf and blind to the living world around him. Bathed in an aura of green, Dhal moved into a gray and boundless world where he had no voice, no hands, no body. All was energy, flowing around him as freely as the air he breathed. *Come fight with me, Efan. Together we can make you whole.*

Dhal woke to semidarkness and the rolling motion of a boat upon water. The stars above were fading quickly in the haze of green light that edged into the sky. Morning?

The last he remembered was Efan. Lifting his head, he looked back along the length of the boat. First he saw the shadowed and bulky form of Haradan, and beyond him, Efan sitting at the tiller. Both were intent upon their jobs, and judging from their low murmured conversation, Dhal guessed they were headed inland again.

His eyes were heavy and the effort to keep them open was too much. Letting his head down, Dhal relaxed back on the mound of blankets and pouches beneath him. Each thought or movement was countered by an overpowering wave of drowsiness. Sleep claimed him once more.

The motion of the boat had quieted when Dhal stirred to full wakefulness. The sky above was mint green; the stars and the darkness were gone. Pushing himself to his elbows, he was surprised to find himself alone on the boat. Then he heard the splash of water. "Haradan?"

The splashing sound grew louder. "Dhal, you awake?" A

moment later Haradan's head and shoulders appeared. When he saw Dhal's eyes open, he smiled. "About time you woke. You had me—us—worried." Reaching down, he took Dhal's arm and pulled him to a sitting position. "Are you all right?"

"Yes, I think so. The last I remember is sitting down by Efan. Haradan, how is Efan?"

"He's fine. Whatever you did to him, it worked. His legs are weak and it'll be some time before his muscles return to normal, but he's walking. When I found you lying beside him yesterday, I knew what you'd tried to do. I was angry at first. You should have wakened me. Someone should have been on watch."

"I'm sorry. You're right. I thought about waking you but everything just happened. I couldn't seem to stop myself."

Haradan shrugged. "Well, no harm done anyway."

"Haradan, is Efan happy?"

"Happy isn't word enough, Dhal. You should have seen his face when he woke and found he could move his legs. He was ecstatic. When I helped him up and steadied him while he walked, he began to cry. I don't think he'll ever look upon you as enemy again—you or any other Ni."

Chapter 13

TWO DAYS SLIPPED INTO FOUR. THEN SIX. BEFORE THEY SET SAIL once more. Dhal was pleased to see Efan happy again— the boy's smiles and laughter were more than adequate reward for the quiet days Dhal spent trying to regain his strength. Four days later, they docked at Port Bhalvar in the early afternoon. They hoped to buy supplies here and leave for Port Cestar by nightfall. "You stay with the boat, Dhal," Haradan said. "Keep your head covered. One look at that head of hair and anyone with eyes will know you for Ni."

"How long will you be gone?"

Haradan stepped up onto the dock. "We shouldn't be gone more than several hours. Efan wants to try to find a friend of his father's, an old merchant who's done business with his father."

Gi and Dhal watched Haradan and Efan head down a side street. Their pace was slow, as Efan was still getting used to his legs; day by day there was a marked improvement. Haradan had easily convinced the boy to stay with them for a while.

With his father gone and his position among his own kind in doubt, Efan had turned to the only people who seemed to care what became of him: one old dockworker turned wilder, one very small olvaar, and one member of the dreaded Ni-lach.

Dhal glanced around the wharf. A good number of boats had already returned with their morning catches and buyers were beginning to arrive.

Port Bhalvar lay nestled between two hills at the base of an inlet. Cutting the city in half was the river Argan. The seven bridges that spanned the deep, narrow ravine between one portion of the city and the other were marvelous to see, their metal and wood structures painted bright red and yellow.

From the old wharf Gi and Dhal could see the clusters of slate-roofed buildings as they rose, tier upon tier, up the hillsides. Here and there, among the rows of buildings, they could see open gardens and parks with bushes and trees blooming in great abundance.

Gi sighed deeply. Dhal smiled at him. "It would have been fun to have gone with them, wouldn't it?"

"Fun yes. Dhal safer here."

"I suppose. Still . . ."

As the time passed, Dhal found his thoughts wandering back to the last time he had looked into the ring. He pulled the cording from around his neck and lifted the fire ring from its resting place against his chest. A moment later, he had the ring on.

Gi-arobi immediately moved closer. "Gi see?"

For long moments Gi sat and stared into the fire stone, then he lifted his head. "Dhal make fire ring live now?"

Dhal was reluctant. The last time he had stirred the mysterious life force within the stone, those who peopled the ring world had not been very friendly. Remembering the spears they had raised against him, he was of a mind to leave well enough alone.

But he was too curious. If he could only find a way to speak to those people, he could ask so many questions. But how? Was it even possible?

As he looked down at the ring, he was possessed by an

irresistible urge to return to that Ni world. He took a moment
to make sure no one was looking his way. Settling down on
the pile of pouches next to Gi, he leaned over. "Ready, Gi?"

Gi nodded enthusiastically.

"Watch for the change in color and listen close. The last
time I did this, I could hear the Ni speaking."

"Gi listen."

Moments passed as Gi and Dhal shared watch over the green
stone. Then, swiftly, the colors began to shift. "Do you see
the colors, Gi?" Dhal whistled softly.

"Suns' light gone. Water colors come now."

The blue and green colors began to fold one into the other
in a mesmerizing pattern. For a moment Dhal felt as if he was
falling forward, then he felt Gi's small furred hand clamp tight
on his wrist.

"No like, Dhal," came the olvaar's shrill whistle. "Gi leaving."

For a moment Dhalvad thought to follow Gi-arobi's example
and break the pull of the stone's power, but then he noticed
another change in the layers of color. A picture was forming,
just as it had before—this time he was looking at a great
building of red-black stone, with a long, slanting roof tipped
to the north and a single, triangular turret to the south. The
open windows to the east were large enough for a man to enter
standing. The building was so unlike the round, squat buildings
erected by the Sarissa that for long moments all he could do
was stand and stare.

Then his eyes went to the magnificent aban tree that sheltered the building. The girth of the tree was easily the size of
twenty men standing in a tight circle. Its topmost branches
cleared the height of the cliffs to the west. Dwarfing all the
other trees around it, the giant aban stood as a lone sentinel at
the throat of an open valley. To the northwest was the same
lake he had seen on his last trip to the ring world.

Looking back at the building, he saw movement in front of
a pair of great wooden doors that stood open. Dhal approached
cautiously, reluctant to leave the safety of the trees. Upon
reaching the last row of bushes, Dhalvad paused, gathering his

courage, then stepped out into the open. Something had changed this time—he was actually walking, not gliding.

Dhal was two hundred paces from the building when several Ni appeared in the doorway. He continued walking, keeping his pace steady. He counted thirteen people in and around the doors.

He was within twenty-five paces of the Ni when one of them spoke. He did not notice which one, nor did he understand the words spoken. "I don't understand," he said. Again his words had no sound.

From the looks on their faces, Dhal knew the Ni could see him. Several spoke at once. He listened and tried to make sense of the babble.

The voices died away, then two of the females held their hands out in a gesture of peace and moved toward him, their crystal eyes never once leaving his. All were silent now. Dhal looked to the others standing near the doorway. He was thankful that no weapons were in sight.

The female on the left spoke. Dhal shook his head. The two females exchanged glances, then the first one tried again. "Do you speak the trade language, outlander?"

Though the accent was strange, he understood and nodded. "Your name, outlander?"

Dhal looked closely at the female nearest him. He could see the wind move the loose strands of her hair, but this time he could not feel the air. It was as if he was there, yet not there. Was he dreaming it all? Were the people real or only images of the past locked into the stone? And what of Saan Drambe's theory of communications?

"Can't you speak, outlander?" the other female asked.

Suddenly a tall Ni appeared at the open portal. As he approached, one of the females spoke. "He seems to understand the trade language, Donnal."

The male nodded as he stopped before Dhal. His eyes were light blue, not crystal, but his hair was a deep, rich green. He nodded and spoke softly. "It has been long and long since last there was a Seeker in Val-hrodhur. Only the older ones remember such as you. If you will stay a few moments, our leader will come and speak with you. He's on his way."

Stay? In a world that was more dream than reality?

"Seeker, won't you talk to us?" one of the females asked.

Would that I could, thought Dhal. He wondered what she meant by naming him Seeker.

"Is he the same one Fantar saw?" the female asked.

The Ni male nodded. "Yes, I think so. Fantar described him as Ni dressed as outlander. He was out in the hills the first time he saw him. The second time was on the trail here. Then many at the Gathering saw him too."

Val-hrodhur? Was this then the place Fantar and the old one had spoken of as their destination? Val-hrodhur Gathering to gift the Tamorlee—that was how Fantar had described it. Was he finally to learn the truth behind the legends of the Tamorlee?

"Danner comes," someone announced from the crowd. Dhal looked past the three who had confronted him and was surprised to find that as many as thirty Ni had gathered, most of them male. Their silent appearance made him uneasy.

The crowd parted as the old Ni stepped forward. His hair was white with age, but his eyes were Ni.

Stepping forward, the old one looked Dhal over, then bowed his head. "Greetings, Seeker. I am Danner of the Gathering of Val-hrodhur. I'm pleased to have lived long enough to have one of the Seekers return to us. How can we serve you?"

"He won't answer, sir," the first male said.

"Will not or cannot?" Danner asked, stepping closer. The old one reached out to touch Dhal, but his hand moved toward Dhal's arm—and through it. Dhalvad felt nothing.

Startled by the unreality of it all, Dhal was sure now that all he was seeing was part of a dream. Suddenly he heard a shrill piping whistle. At the sound of Gi's alert, Dhal felt a wrenching pull back to reality. Like a wave of rain, a veil of blue-green mist dropped around him.

He could no longer see the Ni-lach of Val-hrodhur, but still he could hear their voices. A female: "Look, he's fading!" Then the old Ni, his voice thundering in Dhal's mind: "Seeker, strengthen your projection! Speak to us. I feel you are in need!

Tell us what we can do to help you. Please, come back! Tell us—"

There was a moment of disorientation as Dhal stirred from his strange dreaming, then Gi-arobi was there repeating his whistled warning. Before Dhal could ask him what was wrong, Gi dove under the seat.

"Gi? What's wrong?" Dhal demanded, leaning down to see where the olvaar had gone. "What are you—"

"You!" The harsh voice came from behind him. "You there!"

Dhal turned just as a big man stepped down into the boat, rocking it with his weight and throwing Dhal a little off balance. The man was Sarissa. On the dock behind him stood two more men, their dark tunics decorated with the emblem of the Sarissa Guard of Annaroth.

"What are you, deaf?" the man growled, reaching for Dhal's shoulder.

Dhal tried to evade his grasp but fingers caught in the hood of his tunic as he ducked under the man's arm. He heard cloth tear, then he was jerked sideways and thrown against the gunwale.

"What's wrong with you?" the man bellowed angrily, reaching for him a second time. "All I asked you was . . ." The man's voice trailed off, his eyes widening in disbelief.

"It's him!" the man cried, lunging forward.

But this time Dhal was faster. Pushing away from the gunwale, he dove for the dock. He heard the splash of water as the large man lost his balance and went overboard. A moment later Dhal was on his feet and running, the other two guards fast behind him. Jerking his hood up and over his head, he ran the length of the dock, jumping piles of fish and dashing around the fishermen who had stopped their work to watch the chase.

He headed straight for the side street where he had seen Haradan and Efan disappear. He had just cleared the last of the wooden docks when he rememberd Gi-arobi. Praying that the olvaar would have sense enough to remain hidden in the boat until all was clear, he ran up the cobble street and took the first turn he came to, startling several women who were coming from the other direction.

Before he could reach the other end of the street, the cry of "Ni-lach" echoed in the air. Gone in that moment were all thoughts of finding Haradan and Efan. Hide first, he thought, search later. At the end of the narrow lane, Dhal came to a street that climbed up in a long flight of steps. He was almost to the top when two men ran out from the lane below him. Once again the cry went up. "Ni-lach! Stop him!"

Dhal remembered little of the twists and turns he followed those next few minutes. The streets were narrow and littered with refuse. The clutter of buildings, the dark shadows created by high stone walls, all were alien to him. It was so unlike the free openness of the Deep that he could not understand why anyone would choose to live so crowded together. It was almost as bad as the underground tunnels in Annaroth.

In the next ten minutes he finally managed to outdistance his pursuers. Though he could hear the clamor of voices coming up the streets behind him, he slowed his pace to a fast walk, to call less attention to himself. Carefully keeping his hood around his face, he threaded his way through several open markets until he located another flight of stairs. Moving upward once more, he noticed that the crowded buildings started to give way to several open parks where trees and grass had been allowed room to grow. The trees were trimmed and kept small; the grass was cut short. Here the streets were wide, the buildings less crowded, and there seemed to be fewer people moving about. Twice passersby looked at him strangely, but it was not until he heard a comment from a man sitting on a bench in front of a prosperous-looking inn that he realized what was wrong.

"Out of your depths, aren't you, fisherman?" the man said, glancing down at the water stains on Dhal's tunic and pants.

Dhal looked down toward the bay. Realizing his mistake and hoping it was not too late to do something about it, he quickly passed down the street, searching for a way back down to the lower levels. Fifteen minutes later he was still searching, the walled-in upper reaches becoming a maze that led nowhere.

Finally he arrived at a large marketplace similar to the one he had seen in Annaroth. One glance told him that here the

Sarissa classes mingled, the sellers coming from the docks and lower city, the buyers from the upper levels and other side of the river. There was a good-sized crowd in the marketplace. Fresh flowers, fruits, and vegetables were in abundance, as well as unusual trade items from Letsia and Annaroth.

Fearing the crowds yet realizing that dressed as he was he would only be one among many, he forced himself to move into the stream of buyers, taking care that his hood was up and that no one came too close. But everyone seemed to move in and around one another with such unconscious ease that he soon lost his fear and began to take an interest in some of the goods being sold and traded. There were foods and clothes, jewelry and perfumes and weapons in such variety and description that he could not have named all their makers.

An hour later he was still looking for a possible place to hide when he almost walked into two Sarissa guards. They looked like the same two who had chased him from the docks, but he could not be sure. Neither man seemed to see him, their eyes wandering over the heads of the crowd in front of them.

Carefully Dhal turned to the side. Realizing that to run would be to call attention to himself, he kept a slow pace, moving off around a group of people who were haggling over the price of a bolt of cloth. It took several minutes to maneuver out of sight and he had almost completed the process when he saw five or six men moving through the crowd in his direction. They were peering at faces and asking questions. Several of them were obviously dockworkers; the others looked more official.

Angling off to the right, Dhal headed for a stand of trees he could see beyond the marketplace. But he was stopped by a shoulder-high stone wall. The lush green beyond the wall called to him, promising safety. He followed the wall, hoping to find a place to climb over without being seen.

As he passed several buyers standing and talking together, he heard one of them ask about the unusual number of Guard in the area. Walking slowly, Dhal caught the other man's reply.

"I understand they're looking for a Ni who escaped from Annaroth."

"I thought they were all gone."

"So it was reported. It's probably one of the half-bloods still wandering about."

"Probably. I don't know why we didn't get rid of them the same time we got rid of the full-bloods. They've been nothing but trouble since the end of the war."

"That's what Connar said just the other day. I remember hearing the entire subject discussed in council some years ago and I believe it was decided that . . ."

Dhal moved off. He continued to follow the wall, leaving the marketplace behind.

Soon he came upon a large, open gateway. Beyond the gates lay a well-tended park where bushes were trimmed and flowers grew along the stone pathways. The trees overhead were aban and vellvine. There were only a few people moving through the park, but as he walked toward the center he found more visitors around the flowered gardens, some sitting on the cut grass, others on wooden benches along the pathways. Farther on he passed several food booths, and as he sniffed the air he was reminded that he had not eaten since morning and then only dried fruit, a hard bun, and water.

Next he came to a long, rectangular walkway paved with large slabs of smooth stone on which four men sat, drawing pictures with chalk. Haradan had once told him of such artistry, but he had never before seen it. He lingered to watch an old man draw, then turned away and moved along the path.

He was nearing a small crowd when he first heard the music. Someone was singing. Curious, he worked his way around the edge of the crowd and moved in for a better look. The singer was another chalk artist.

Dhalvad stood with the others, caught up in the soft magical chant. The song was not loud but it carried clearly, each word and note building to create a picture in sound.

Dhalvad looked down at the stone to see the picture the artist was drawing while he sang. Words, music, and chalk flowed together in a strange, mesmerizing pull. Slowly he lowered himself to the ground, watching the chalk artist continue to work, song and chalk blending, creating a living picture of a world that could not possibly exist, yet which was haunt-ingly familiar, as a remembrance from the past or from a time before birth.

How long he sat staring at the picture he did not know. The song ended. He reached out, knowing he could touch the picture and make it his. But before his fingers could touch the stone, another hand shot out and caught his wrist in a firm grip.

Dhal looked up at the chalk artist. For long moments they watched each other. The people standing around them drifted away, several tossing coins into a cloth pouch that lay unfolded near the artist's leg.

The artist appeared to be about Dhal's age. He wore his dark hair long and free. A cheaply woven headband kept it out of his eyes. His tunic and pants, not much better than Dhal's, were dark, a greenish brown that would allow the singer to blend in with his surroundings.

At first Dhal thought the man's eyes were blue, then they seemed to change, to lighten, but Dhal could not be sure—the artist held his head in such a way that he looked up through dark eyelashes, shielding his eyes. He had nice features, a straight nose, hollow cheeks, well-molded lips. He looked a little sad, Dhal thought, as if he longed for something that was beyond reach. His song and picture told that to Dhal.

Slowly the singer released Dhal's wrist. "Tell me, stranger. What did you see in my picture?"

Startled by the singer's speaking voice, Dhal looked closer. "You're a woman!" he exclaimed softly.

A half smile touched the singer's lips. "I most certainly am. Does that shock you?"

Dhal shook his head. "I don't know. I've never seen a chalk artist before, though Haradan told me about them. I thought they all would be men."

"Most of them are, but one earns a living where one can." Her smile faded. "You're new to Port Bhalvar?"

"Yes."

The singer looked down at her picture, then back at Dhal. He saw that her eyes were blue with flecks of gray in them.

"Tell me, stranger, what did you see in my drawing that made you want to touch it?"

Carefully keeping his head tilted down, shielding his own eyes as best he could, Dhal answered. "It seemed real. Alive."

The singer's eyes narrowed in suspicion. "How do you mean that?"

For a moment Dhal was at a loss to explain. "It was your singing, I think. It seemed to do something to the picture. I felt that I could reach in and touch what I saw."

"And what did you see?" the woman pressed.

Dhal looked down at the chalk picture. It was not as he remembered it. It had become flat and lifeless, just a sky and mountains, a lake of green ice and something in the lake. "What's that supposed to be?" he asked, pointing at the object in the lake.

"A water draak named Ba-lee. According to Ni legends, she was supposed to have been the first to serve the Green Ones."

"Have you ever seen a water draak?"

"A few, but only small ones. You?"

"Only in my dreams. There are no water draak in the Deep. The streams in the marshlands are too shallow for them."

A few moments of silence passed as Dhal studied the chalk picture. The artist leaned closer, trying to probe beneath the shadow of his hood. "Why do you hide your face?" she asked.

Dhal started to his feet, then out of the corner of his eye he saw several men moving into the artists' square. One was a guardsman. Dhal lowered himself back down. He swore softly as he glanced around, trying to locate another way out of the garden. When he turned back, he found the chalk artist watching him intently. Almost imperceptibly, she motioned for him to slip behind her and into the bushes.

He did not question the escape route offered, especially since he had no better plan himself. He moved over to sit beside her, then when assured no one was watching, he lay down and quickly rolled under the lower branches of the bushes that circled the square.

The bushes were dense and there was no escaping through them, so he found a small, open space deep within the growth and lay quietly. A few moments later he heard the chalk artist begin to sing.

Chapter 14

IT WAS NEARING THE SUPPER HOUR. DHAL HAD DRIFTED OFF TO sleep. A hand gently squeezed his leg, waking him. "It's time to go."

It took him a moment or two to remember where he was. Then he glanced at the chalk-smeared fingers on his leg and the day's events came rushing back. "All clear?" he whispered.

"Yes, for the moment," the woman replied. "Come out and we'll leave the gardens together. If the guards look for one alone, they may overlook two together."

As he stood up, she handed him her pouch full of chalks. "Here, you carry this. It may help to disguise you. By the way, my name is Pocalina-fel-Jamba. My friends call me Poco."

She looked at Dhal expectantly, her eyes on a level with his. He realized that she wanted his name. "I'm called Dhal."

"Doll?" she asked, making a rocking motion with her arms.

He grinned and corrected her, spelling out his name. "No. D-H-A-L."

"All right, Dhal, let's go."

As they passed down the stone walkway, he tried to thank her for her help. "Not many would have done what you did for a stranger, fel-Jamba."

The woman shrugged. "Perhaps not; one never knows."

"Why did you?" he asked bluntly.

The daughter of Jamba hesitated, then replied. "There are several reasons. One being the honest fact that I don't like the Guard. None of us do. They represent authority without a conscience. They harass us, they levy fines if we're found in Upper Bhalvar too early or too late, and they are quick to punish without trial or hearing. We of Lower Bhalvar have learned to tread lightly when the Guard appear. We've also formed a pact to look after each other or any who fall prey to the Guard and their cruel games."

As they moved out of the garden, Poco turned and looked at Dhal. "Hungry?"

"Yes."

"Well, we'll find a—" Suddenly Poco threw an arm across his shoulder and smiled at him, whispering quickly. "Pretend we're good friends. Guards ahead!"

Dhal saw the two men standing outside the entrance to the gardens and felt shivers run up his spine. Poco started to talk about her pictures and the parkgoers that day and about anything else that came to mind as they walked past the guardsmen. A few minutes later she turned into a small side street. Slipping her arm free, she grinned. "Way free. Come."

"Come where?"

"Down. Once past the middle towers we should be safe for a while."

Falling into step beside the singer, he asked, "Poco, you haven't asked me why I hide from the Guard. Aren't you curious?"

She laughed. "Yes, I'm curious, but while you've been sleeping, I've been listening, and I think I know why you were running." When he failed to respond, she continued. "According to the rumor I heard this afternoon, there's a Ni running loose in the city, a killer by all reports. It's said that he arrived by boat this morning and with him two others, a boy and a man. With your face hidden in that hood, you might be any one of the three."

Dhal glanced at his companion but found her eyes straight ahead as they walked. "None of the three have been caught?" he asked, trying to keep his voice neutral.

"Not the last I heard. Look, the towers!"

The stairway down to Lower Bhalvar was alive with tradesmen making their way home after a successful day in the upper city. Five or six guards watched the flow of sellers, but none took interest in the pair of chalk artists that kept to the center of the wide stairway.

At the next level Poco steered Dhal off to the left down a narrow street that wound north, then down another side street, heading east. She stopped when they came to another set of stairs leading down. They were quite alone.

"I think we should talk before we go any farther," she said.

"What do you want to talk about?"

"You," Poco replied. There was a tremor of excitement in her voice, though she tried to hide it. "*Are* you the Ni they search for, or only friend to him?"

Dhal hadn't expected so direct a question. He hesitated.

"I admit that I am one of the three," he finally answered. "I ask that you take it no further."

"Fair enough . . . for the moment. Next question. Where do you want to go? Did you come to Upper Bhalvar for a reason or by mistake?"

"I was being chased. I had no choice in the matter. As for where I want to go, I want to return to the docks to look for my friends."

"Possible, Dhal, but not very wise. The Guard will be watching the docks and all strangers will be stopped. If your friends have their wits about them, they'll stay away from the docks."

"Even after dark?"

"Even then."

"Have you any suggestions to make?"

"Several," she answered promptly, "if you will trust me."

"Trust you how?"

Pocalina looked into the shadow of his hood, her gaze never

wavering as she answered. "I know a place where I'm sure you'll be safe from the Port Guard. I can take you there, then go to the docks myself and look for your friends."

Dhal shook his head, incredulous. "You would do this for me, a stranger to you?"

"Why not? I've told you how we all feel about the Guard. Are you afraid I will betray you?" There was silence then. "Yes, I think you are, and I can't really blame you. Well then, where do we go from here? To the docks?"

"Yes. I think it best for now."

Poco nodded silently. Turning, she led the way down the narrow lane to the stairs. The shadows were growing long, arching out over the streets. Fifteen minutes later she announced that they were on the lowest tier, two streets west of the main dockside marketplace. There was still some activity in and about the selling stalls, but most of the buyers were packing their goods to return home. All the fish booths were closed, as were most of the fruit and vegetable stalls.

Pocalina pointed out six guards loitering on the fringe of the marketplace. "They work in pairs for their own protection. It's unusual for so many to be here this time of day. It doesn't look good for your friends."

Silently, Dhalvad agreed.

"Dhal, I think it would be wise for you to reconsider my offer," Poco said softly. "Let me find you a safe place to stay, then I can come back and look for your friends. If they haven't been taken already, I'm sure I can find them. Trust me?"

It did not look as if he had much of a choice. The six guards were not the first he had seen—he had counted ten others in a space of fifteen minutes. "All right, Poco. Your way."

An hour later he found himself on the other side of the river Argan, three levels above the docks and still climbing. As they climbed, they talked. Remembering Efan's hopes of finding his father's friend, he told Poco about Donar sar Frenzel.

Poco had heard the name and thought the man would not be too hard to track down. As they cleared the last steps on the fourth stairway, Dhal looked to the west where Ra-gar was falling into the sea. "It will be dark by the time you get back to the docks," he said, thinking how little he would care to thread such a winding maze at night.

"Do you worry about me?" Poco asked, surprised.

"Shouldn't I?"

"No. Port Bhalvar is my home. I know it well and have friends in many places. Don't be afraid for me. Come, we still have a ways to go."

"More stairs?"

"No, this is the last tier before reaching Upper Bhalvar. This section of the city is older than the rest and many of the buildings have long been abandoned. I used to live here before I started working as a chalk artist, and every once in a while I come back to visit some old friends."

Poco led Dhal around and over a maze of jumbled rock where buildings were fast becoming engulfed in a wild growth of tree and vine. At last they came to a row of stone buildings that were partially standing. Some had collapsed roofs, most were without windows and doors.

Stopping at a cavelike opening, Poco indicated that they now went down. After descending into the dark about ten steps, Poco paused at a wooden door. "In here lives a very special friend, Dhal. He may be home. He may not. Whatever you do, don't act surprised and don't make any quick moves. Understood?"

Dhal nodded, hoping that all of this was not some elaborate plot to trap him.

Poco knocked, then slowly pushed the door open. Dhal stood quietly in the doorway, listening to her move around the dark room. A few seconds later there was a spark of light. Poco was squatting in front of a cooking pit, touching a match to some dry tinder.

As the flame caught, she turned and waved him into the room. "It isn't much, but Screech has made it his home."

"Screech?" Dhal repeated.

Picking up a branch from the fire, Poco crossed over to the table and lighted a candle that stood in a niche in the wall. As the light chased the shadows back, she turned and went to rummage through a box cupboard behind the door.

"His real name is Ssaal-lr but I call him Screech because of the awful noise he makes when he's angry." She shrugged. "It looks as if he's gone wandering again. Nothing much to eat here. Salt, a few bites of dried fruit, a handful of tea leaves, and a box of spice. I'll have to bring something when I come back. I hope you can wait to eat."

"I can wait," he assured her. "How long do you think you'll be gone?"

"I'm not sure. Much will depend upon luck and how well your friends have hidden themselves from the Guard."

He looked around the room. "What if your friend returns?"

"From the looks of things, Screech has been gone some time. Like most of his kind, he's a hunter. He likes to prowl the wildlands to the north. It wouldn't surprise me to learn one day that he's ranged as far north as the Mountains of the Lost."

"What do you mean by 'his kind'?"

A half smile touched Poco's lips. "Friend Dhal, have you ever seen a derkat?"

"No, but I've heard of them. Furred creatures with long tails and large eyes. Less than man, more than beast."

"A good description though somewhat inaccurate. I myself have found Ssaal-lr more man than beast, but there are many who would glady argue that point with me. I met Screech five years ago, up here in this crumbling section of buildings. At that time I was still using this place as my home. It was all I could afford. One day, while I was out picking up wood for my fire, I heard the rumble of falling rock followed by a strange, screaming cry. To make a long story short, I found Ssaal-lr half buried by a partially collapsed wall. He was hurt and unconscious. You can imagine how nervous I was at first, never having seen a derkat before, but he was unconscious and offering me no harm so finally I began digging him out. Once clear of the rock I carried him back here."

"Carried? I thought they were large animals."

"Not animals!" Poco shot back instantly. Then, she shrugged. "Sorry, I just don't like to hear them called animals. Anyway, I could carry Screech because he was only half his adult weight. He had been half starved by the trader who had hoped to sell him in the exotic animals market. Somehow Ssaal-lr had managed to escape the trader's ship after docking and had made his way into the middle tiers where there was some cover. It took me five weeks to get him back on his feet, and during that time we learned a lot about each other. Screech told me about his home and family and he—"

"The derkat can speak?" Dhal asked, surprised by the thought of communicating with such supposedly dangerous animals.

"Yes and no," she answered. "They don't speak as you and I are right now. Something about the position of their tongue prevents that, I think, but they can communicate by a type of sign language and certain noises."

"Does this Ssaal-lr understand you when *you* speak?"

"He didn't at first, but he does now, at least most of what I say." Poco moved toward the door. "Well, time for talking later. Let me see what I can do about finding your friends for you. And I'll bring some food back when I return." She paused and turned on the first step leading out of the cellar. "One more thing. Earlier you asked me why I chose to help you and I said it was because of the Guard. That was true. But there is one other reason. My father was Ni. I am half-blood."

Startled, Dhal stood silently as Poco ascended the steps and disappeared into the murky twilight above. Half-blood Ni? She doesn't look it, he thought, yet why would she claim it if it were not true? Was it possible that she had lied just to make sure he would stay where she had left him?

Fearing to fully trust Pocalina-fel-Jamba, Dhal spent the night huddled in a narrow covert between a line of bushes and a stone wall that had once been the south side of a building. Wrapped in a blanket he had taken from the cellar, he watched the rubble-filled street before the cellar entrance, waiting for the trap to spring shut.

But his vigil went unrewarded. Morning arrived and Pocalina had not returned. The growing feeling that he could trust the chalk artist gave him courage to return to the cellar. Had she planned to betray him, he reasoned, surely the Port Guard would have been there already. He went directly to the pallet of straw and grass. Sleep came quickly.

* * *

The smell of meat cooking nudged Dhal awake, but when he opened his eyes, the room was empty.

"Poco?"

The silence made him freeze, his hand going to his belt sheath. But his knife was gone! He was sure he had not taken the knife from its case before lying down. His eyes were drawn to the fire. The coals at the edge of the pit were glowing red. Hanging on a spit over the fire was the carcass of a nida, a small, tailless dog.

Sitting up, Dhal quickly glanced around the cellar. But all was quiet and he was alone—or so he thought until he saw a shadowed form sitting on the floor just beyond the table and chairs.

Slowly Dhal untangled his legs from the blanket. "Poco? That you?"

He froze as the shadow moved. Suddenly eyes appeared within the shadow, like two beacons of yellow light. He had never seen such eyes before. They were huge, at least twice the size of a man's eyes, and as round as the twin suns.

In one fluid movement the shadow form stood and stepped into the firelight, revealing the coat of short, gray fur that covered it from head to toes. Derkat! Poco's friend, Screech. It had to be him!

As Dhal looked up at the derkat he was of two minds. One half told him to run for the door, while the other half kept reminding him that this creature was Poco's friend and, therefore, not an enemy.

Slowly he pushed to his knees. The derkat took another step closer, placing himself directly between Dhalvad and the doorway. You don't need to speak to make *your* thoughts known, Dhal thought. Am I your captive then? Do you see me as an intruder, or are you just curious about my presence?

He remembered that Poco had claimed that the derkat understood man speech. It was worth a try. He had no wish to tangle with this taller-than-man creature whose raking claws could disembowel a man in a single stroke.

"Poco said that she had a friend named Ssaal-lr," he began,

keeping his voice low and enunciating each word carefully. "Are you Ssaal-lr?"

A low rumble came from the derkat's throat. Dhal took a deep breath and tried again, pausing carefully between each sentence. "Poco brought me here to wait. She said I would be safe from the Port Guard. She went to look for my friends. Understand?

Again that rumbling sound.

Now what? Dhal thought. Gazing deep into the derkat's eyes, he wondered about Poco's claim that the derkat was more man than beast. Was it only wishful thinking on her part?

The derkat's face was long, his two fur-tufted ears set high and back on either side of his head. The fur around his eyes fluffed outward, dark gray overlain by lighter gray, and came to a point just over his mouth. If there was a nose it was lost in fur. The skin of the derkat's lips was black and smooth and showed clearly; Dhal saw a glint of white teeth and remembered the story he had once heard about a derkat that had hunted men instead of its usual prey.

Deciding he would be much safer waiting outside for Poco, Dhal took a step to the right. Then another. At his third step, the derkat moved to intercept him, the four-fingered hand clamping down around Dhal's wrist.

Instinctively Dhal pulled back. The derkat growled deep in its throat. Heart racing, Dhal stepped to the side, trying to twist his arm from the creature's grasp. "Let go," he said, trying to keep his voice calm.

The derkat did not respond as he had hoped. He was jerked to the side, and before he could recover his balnce, Ssaal-lr was behind him, clamping a long arm over Dhal's shoulder and across his chest. Crushed up against the derkat's body, Dhal was held immobile. The rumbling sound in his ear grew monstrous.

One of the most important lessons Dhal had learned in the Deep had dealt with courage in outfacing a superior enemy, such as an adult draak or a hungry gensvolf. To run was to be chased. To stand quietly was to instill wariness in your opponent or, if you were lucky, to cause it to lose interest in you completely.

Praying that he was not making a mistake, Dhal let his head fall forward and relaxed, going limp. For a moment or two there was no change in the crushing force that held him, then he felt a shift in the derkat's arms as Ssaal-lr took all of his weight.

The growling ceased abruptly. A moment later Dhal's arm was released and he was being lifted. Keeping his eyes closed, his body relaxed, he became aware of the derkat's breathing as it lowered him to the floor.

As much as he wanted to open his eyes he somehow managed to keep them closed, even when soft, padded fingers brushed across his cheek and mouth. The minutes passed. Twice he felt a warm breath on his face. The derkat was definitely curious and not about to lose interest quickly.

Dhal felt the derkat's hands move up and down his body, from shoulder to legs, patting at him as if trying to nudge him back to consciousness. Then the creature was breathing in his face again. Go away, he thought. Forget me and go back to your meal.

Suddenly he heard a knock, then the squeak of unoiled hinges. "Ssaal-lr! What—what are you doing to him? What happened here?"

Dhal almost turned over at the sound of Poco's voice, but the derkat was still leaning over him and he dared not move.

"What in the name of—"

Recognizing Haradan's voice, Dhal cautiously opened one eye. The derkat was rising. Dhal looked past Poco to Haradan and Efan. Poco brushed by the derkat and quickly knelt beside Dhal. She saw that his eyes were open.

"Dhal are you all right?"

"Yes," he assured her, "now that you're here. When your friend tried to stop me from leaving I decided it was easier to play dead than to fight with him."

The worried look slowly faded from her eyes. "You're sure you're all right?"

"Yes, I'm fine." Dhal looked past her shoulder. "But I think

Haradan is going to be in trouble unless you speak to your friend."

Poco turned and saw the derkat facing Haradan, his claws unsheathed, his eyes on the sword Haradan held in his hand, point up. The growling noise in the derkat's throat had risen. With one effortless bound Poco placed herself between the two, her face to the derkat.

"Glad I am that my friend Ssaal-lr has returned," she said quickly. "I'm sorry I wasn't here to greet you and explain the presence of a stranger in your home."

Sitting up slowly, Dhal looked to Haradan and Efan. The boy shot him a worried glance. Haradan's eyes stayed on the derkat.

Reaching out, Poco touched the derkat's right arm. "Ssaal-lr, look at me."

The long, furred tail of the derkat twitched nervously back and forth, a sign of his agitation. But at the sound of the woman's voice, his ears had pricked forward and Dhal knew he was listening to her. When she repeated her request, the derkat's eyes dropped from Haradan to Poco, who stood a full head shorter. His growling died. After a moment of silence, he made a soft coughing sound, which Poco quickly imitated.

Poco spoke again, using hand signs to reinforce her words. "These men are friends, Screech. They need our help. The Guard look for them, just as years ago they looked for you."

The derkat brought his hands up. Though familiar with the rudiments of sign language, Dhal was not able to follow the intricate weaving of hands and clawed fingers that followed.

Poco began translating out loud. "Ssaal-lr says that he meant the Green One no harm." Poco shot him a side glance, then resumed speaking. "You are the first of the water folk he has seen in a long time. He saw that you were afraid of him and didn't want to frighten you away. He was very upset when you collapsed.

"We understand, Screech," Poco reassured him. "It was all a misunderstanding. Wasn't it, Dhal?"

"Yes," he agreed, rising.

The derkat's hands moved, signing. Again Poco translated. "The Green One is not ill, he asks."

"No, Ssaal-lr. I am fine. I only feigned illness to ensure continued health."

Ssaal-lr looked at Dhal a moment, then those big eyes closed and he made a strange "humphing" noise that Poco explained was derkat amusement.

Dhal turned to Haradan. "Good to see you again."

Haradan returned his smile and carefully put the sword away. "The same goes for us. If not for the young lady we would still be searching for you. When we found out that—"

Poco interrupted. "Ssaal-lr, I think your nida is burning. Come on, everyone, let's sit down. We can talk while we eat. I know Dhal is hungry and I'm sure the rest of us can find room for a few bites."

"Sounds good," Dhal agreed. "Wait, I forgot! Did any of you get a chance to go back to the boat? I left Gi there."

"Easy, Dhal," Haradan said. "Your little friend is all right. Gi?" Turning, Haradan looked back toward the still-open doorway. A small furred head poked out from behind the large door.

A whistle click of greeting was followed by a run through the tangle of long legs. Leaning down, Dhal offered his hand to Gi. A moment later the olvaar sat perched on his shoulder.

"We didn't find him," Haradan explained. "He found us. He must have stayed in the boat until dark, then started looking. How he was able to separate our scents from all the fishy smells near the docks is really remarkable. We were about ready to set out looking for you next when Poco found us and explained that you were safe. We would've come right then but Donar sar Frenzel recommended we wait and finish gathering the supplies we would need."

Dhal saw Poco smile at the olvaar. Her eyes caught his. "It seems that we both have unusual friends, Dhal. I've heard of the olvaar but had never seen one before yesterday. Do you understand his singing?"

"As easily as you understand Ssaal-lr."

Suddenly Ssaal-lr was standing beside Dhal, his hands moving in speech once more. "What did he say?" Dhal asked, noticing that Ssaal-lr's eyes were fixed on Gi, who at that moment was using Dhal's hair as a shield.

"I'm not sure," Poco answered. "But I think he wants to know if the little-fur will be joining us for dinner." Poco grinned. "Either that or—can he cook him for dinner?"

Dhal smiled as Gi-arobi whistle-clicked his indignation. "I think you have your answer," he said. "Gi says that friends do not eat friends."

Chapter 15

THEY MADE A STRANGE COMPANY, TWO SARISSA, TWO NI-LACH, one olvaar, and one derkat. For five days they sheltered together in Ssaal-lr's cellar home, talking, sleeping, planning. Early each morning Poco would leave them and climb to the upper levels to ply her trade as a chalk artist. By listening to the daily gossip, she was able to keep them abreast of the Port Guard. It was their hope that the Guard would eventually tire of the search, but by the end of the sixth day, Dhal realized that it was a false hope. Each day the search drew closer.

The cellar steps were dark in shadow. Night was fast approaching. Leaving Haradan, Efan, Ssaal-lr, and Gi in the room below, Dhal went to look for Poco, who had excused herself from their company several hours before, complaining of a need for fresh air.

Poco had not gone to work that day but had stayed and helped the others plan. Because they had little chance of retrieving their boat, they had talked about going overland through the Mountains of the Lost to Janchee, a small port town farther north, where they hoped to find a ship to Port Sulta.

Poco's failure to return made Dhal uneasy. Poco herself was an enigma. One moment she was friend and fellow conspirator, the next moment she was a stranger and as mysterious as any Deepland flower growing in the shade of the pepperbole trees. Dhal delighted in her laughter, which was deep and throaty, and marveled at her wisdom and her outlook on life. Orphaned at a young age, living by her wits and her skill at drawing, Pocalina-fel-Jamba was a survivor and a dreamer. It was not in her to surrender to anything or anyone—too long had she stood alone. Yet there were moments when Dhal had felt her eyes on him and, turning, had seen a warm and happy look that promised fulfillment to anyone who could win past her spirit guard.

Love? Was he in love with Poco? In truth, he did not know. So he remained silent, keeping his thoughts to himself.

Walking down the long-abandoned street, he climbed a partially destroyed stairway and paused on a stone landing that had once been part of the street pointing east. From there he could overlook Lower Bhalvar. Beyond the third-tier bridge, lights had begun to appear along the waterfront. All looked peaceful and quiet.

Deciding Poco had gone another way, he turned around and followed a different street heading north. When he reached the end of the street, unsure which way to try next, he heard a voice. It was soft and seemed far away. He stood quietly a moment, listening. It was Poco. He could never mistake her voice for another, its hollow, haunting sound weaving pictures of indescribable wonder, of heights and depths, of lands lost in shadow, of people long ago and those yet to be born. There was a sadness in her singing, a longing that touched the heart and made it feel empty yet full at the same time.

Dhalvad followed the brooding melody. Moving down the dirt lane then up around the corner of a still-standing wall, he climbed another stairway and moments later found himself confronted by an old tower. The singing came from above.

It took a moment to find the door to the tower. Inside, the

shadows were growing darker by the second and he could just
make out the winding stairway. Drawn by Poco's singing, he
wound his way upward, carefully keeping to the outside wall
where the steps were more likely to be secure. Up and up he
went. He lost count of the stairs. Twice he passed small windows, both open to the air. The stone wall was rough and cool
against his hand, the warmth of the sun's heat slipping away
as night closed in.

He saw the end of the stairway above and an open portal
to the sky. Poco's song was clear now, her words building
mind pictures only dreamers might understand.

Silently he climbed those last few steps, then moved out
onto the small, round roof. To his left the wall that had once
encircled the roof was gone. Poco sat before the opening, her
face turned to the north. He followed the direction of her gaze
and for the first time saw the green-black chain of mountains
called the Mountains of the Lost, named for the many men
who had tried to tame the wilderness and who had never been
seen again.

Suddenly Dhal became aware of the silence of the night.
He looked at Poco, wondering if she was finished with her
singing. The moments passed. Finally he closed the distance
between them, speaking her name softly so as not to startle
her.

He saw her shoulders twitch at the sound of his voice but
she did not turn. He stopped, thinking his presence might not
be wanted. "Poco, may I join you?"

Still without turning, she lifted her hand and held it out.
"Be welcome, Dhalvad sar Haradan."

He clasped her hand and lowered himself to the roof. "You
were gone a long time. It was getting dark and I grew worried."

Poco squeezed his hand gently. "How did you find me?"

"Your singing."

Profiled against the darkening sky, Poco's face was statu-
esque, serene, patient, all emotions in balance. "Did you like
it?" she asked.

As her lips moved, he felt a flutter of excitement course
through his body. That the statue should live and choose to

speak to him . . . "Yes," he said softly. "I liked it, but I thought it sad."

Gently Poco withdrew her hand. Still facing the mountains, she said, "Not sad, Dhal, only searching."

"Searching for what?"

"You know. I've seen how my songs touch you. Some hear but do not see. Others see but will not listen. Only a few are so made that they both see and hear. You are one. The others are lost in the past. One was my father. Another, an old man who used to sit and beg in the marketplace near the wharf. There were several more, but they are all gone now. It has been seven years since I last "touched" anyone with my singing. There were times when I wondered if it was all my imagination. Then you came and sat down in front of me and you saw the picture live."

Poco turned. "For a long time now I've dreamed strange dreams. I sing to free them, to make them live, if only for a few moments. You've seen my world. I ask you, is it real? And if real, where does it lie? I sing because there is a longing within me to be one with that world. It is my hope that some day I will meet someone who can tell me where my world is and how I may reach it."

"Have you ever thought of going to look for this world yourself," he asked, "rather than wait here for someone to come and tell you where it is?"

"Yes. But which way do I go? North? South? East or west? The world is large and my knowledge of it very small. If I left Port Bhalvar in search of my dreams, it would be my luck to be going away from rather than toward. So I stay and wait and talk to tradesmen and sailors, hoping that one day one of them will be able to tell me what I want to hear."

"This world, what if it's only in your own mind?"

Poco shook her head. "No, it's real. It must be real! I won't think otherwise. I've lived with it too long now to deny it. My mother often told me that my father sang of strange lands. Had he lived he might have understood my dreams and helped me with some answers."

"You said he was Ni."

"Yes. We lived in a small settlement south of Port Bhalvar. I don't remember it. I was young when my father was killed. They were killing all of the Ni. They called it a war but it was nothing but a slaughter of the innocent. Afraid that the Sarissa might do something to me because of my half-blood, my mother brought me to Port Bhalvar for safety, but her family wouldn't take us in. So we lived up here, in the old sector of the city, because it was all mother could afford. Every day we would walk to the sixth tier where my mother worked in one of the inns. I was ten when she died in the mudslides that hit this part of the city. It seems a long time ago. There are moments when I can't even remember what she looked like."

"Do you remember your father at all?"

"No. He was part of the Draak Watch and was gone much of the time."

"Draak Watch?"

"You've never heard of the Draak Watch, and you a Ni?"

"My home was in the Deep for twenty-four years, Poco. I didn't even know I was Ni until just recently. I know very little about my—about our people. I would like to know more."

Poco nodded. "Very well, a history lesson then. Long ago the Sarissa learned that the Ni had a strong empathy with the draak, that they could control the great reptiles with song. Such of the Green Ones who had this power were quickly hired to help secure farmlands and villages against attack. These Ni were known as the Draak Watch. Perhaps you yourself might have been a part of it if the war hadn't destroyed us as a people. Do you sing?"

"To draak, no," he answered, smiling. "I usually run."

"As do most people with a brain in their head. Still, if you knew the right songs, perhaps even you could control a draak."

"I think not. But tell me, after the war and the killing, what was done to replace the Draak Watch?"

"Nothing. That's why so many villages have been abandoned down through the years. In some of the more populated areas watchfires have served to keep the draak away, but only at night. The rest of the time people run."

"Tell me more about the Ni."

"I wish I could, Dhal, but there's little more that I know. I was young when the war came, a year or two older than you were, perhaps, but still too young to remember much. There are a few things I can pass on, things I've heard from others, but whether they are true or false is something that only the legend makers would know."

"Such as?" he prompted.

"Such as how our world was named. Did you know that Ver-draak is man's name for our world?"

"What did the Ni call it?"

"Our people called it Lach and we are the Ni, the People. Ni-lach, People of Lach. It's said that the Ni had three home sites, Jjaan-bi, Hrod-hur, and Tre-ayjeel. Few have ever heard of them. In fact, I doubt anyone today could even tell you where one is located. They seem to be as lost as our people."

"Do you think one of them might be the place of your dreams?"

"It's possible, I suppose," Poco admitted.

"Tell me more about the Ni."

"Well, from all I've gathered, the Ni were originally a wandering people, curious about their world and always on the move, at least until the finding of the Tamorlee."

"Tamorlee?" he echoed, a chill skittering down his back.

"Yes. You've heard of it?"

"Just recently. Tell me, do you know what it is?"

Poco shook her head. "No, not really. All I can tell you about the Tamorlee is that when it came into existence, our people changed somehow. When I first heard about the Tamorlee, I thought it had something to do with the coming of man to Lach, but Varcal said that the Tamorlee was before the coming of man. He spoke of it as a gift from the gods."

"Like a treasure of some kind?" Dhal suggested.

"I don't know what he meant. He never explained. All he would ever say was that the Tamorlee was gift to the Ni-lach and the Ni-lach gift to the Tamorlee. I think he repeated something he had heard others say rather than something he knew for a fact."

"Who is this Varcal?"

"A half-blood like myself. He was on old man when I knew him and not always aware of what was going on around him. He lived in his own world most of the time. He died while I was still living with my mother."

"You spoke about the coming of man to Lach. Do you believe then the legends that say the Sarissa came from the stars?"

"Why not? Anything is possible. Of course it may be that the Sarissa only use the legends to make themselves feel more important, but I think not. The legends are too many."

Dhal shook his head. "But if man had wisdom enough to travel the stars, why did he forsake it all to come and live here? What about his own world? Why did they leave it? What happened to the vessels that brought them here?"

"Ships."

"What?"

"They were called starships. Our ancestors—I mean man's ancestors—were said to have come in great metal ships that could carry as many as a thousand men. One of those ships is said to be half buried in a place called Barl-gan."

"Where is that?"

"No one seems to know."

Dhal looked long at Poco, wondering if she was teasing him, "Poco, is it true about the starships?"

"Trass said it was true. He was another old friend, a sailor. When I was much younger he used to tell me about the first men, about their strange tools and weapons. He once told me about a sword of light that could cut through solid rock."

"I've heard of such a weapon." Dhal said. "Gi told me about it."

"The olvaar? Where did he hear about it?"

"From a story one of the older olvaar was telling."

"Stories. It seems that is all we have left, stories about the People, stories about man . . . and where I wonder is the truth?"

For long moments Poco sat quietly. Dhal was about to ask her about her life in Port Bhalvar and her plans for the future when suddenly she spoke. "It *is* the only way to go," she said softly.

"What?"

"North to the mountains. It's the only way left open to you now," she explained. Darkness had closed around them. Far to the north he could just make out the line of the mountains. "With Annaroth to the south, and the Port Guard watching the docks and the western flatlands where you would be easily seen and captured, you are left with no choice but to go north into the mountains."

Reaching out, he took Poco's hand once more. "We were talking about the Ni," he reminded her.

"We have talked about the dead long enough," she said flatly. "It's time we started thinking about the living and how best to keep *you* out of the hands of the Port Guard."

Chapter 16

. . . *And so I still think it worth a try," Haradan argued.* "If we can't get to our boat then we go overland."

"And if we try for the docks and are picked up?" Efan came back quickly. "What then? With you and I in the hands of the Guard, how long do you think it would be before they would force us to tell them where Dhalvad is hiding?"

"He has a point," Pocalina said. "Perhaps it would be better if we returned to our first plan and you all go together. I think . . ."

Dhal's mind wandered from the argument. He had heard it all five or six times already. Haradan was for trying to reach Port Sulta by boat, Efan for going overland. Poco simply counseled caution, and Ssaal-lr and Gi remained silent.

Dhal looked down at his ring, which he had taken to wearing again. It seemed to wink at him, catching the firelight and reflecting it back into his eyes.

Unconsciously, he brought it up toward his chest, gazing down into the green stone. He thought of the world Poco had tried to capture with song. Were they both only dreaming or were their worlds real? And did their dreaming have something to do with their being children of the Ni?

Looking deep into the invisible crack of gold that lay at the heart of the green stone, Dhal felt himself withdrawing. Gradually the voices of his friends dimmed. Gold gave way to blue then green and he felt a sense of excitement sweep over him.

One moment all was blue shadows, the next moment he was sitting in a green light. Looking up, he saw high overhead what appeared to be a piece of windowlike glass tinted a delicate jade green. Though he strained his eyes he could not see beyond the glass.

Then he heard the pad of naked feet on stone, approaching from his right. They seemed to come closer, then they were moving away. When all was silent again, he looked around him. In the shadowed darkness beyond the green light, Dhal could discern several large columns and two or three darker spaces that looked like portals.

Beneath him, the stone floor was cool. He looked down and saw a portion of a circle carved in the stone. There were intricate patterns all along its outside edge. Reaching out, he traced several lines from the outside of the circle toward the center.

Then he stood up to get a better look at the pattern. Bathed in green light, the carved circle took on a luminous quality, the twin sun shapes at its center seeming to absorb the light. A large, seven-pointed star surrounded the suns. Irresistibly drawn, he crouched at one side of the carved circle and tried to make sense out of the shapes and lines that were positioned about the two inner circles. Several of the symbols were easily read—water, sword, flame—but in the center of the innermost sun there was a replica of a hand, palm up. Peace? Friendship? A request for aid or worship? It could have meant any of them.

Dhal placed his right hand down flat on the stone floor, matching his fingers against those carved in stone. The fit was almost perfect. Filled with surprise, he smiled, pleased by this strange find yet not sure why.

But when he tried to draw his hand away, he could not. It was as if his hand was stuck to the stone. A flutter of panic spread outward as he tried again and again to free his hand. Nothing happened.

Dhal stopped struggling and frantically searched the shadows, looking for help. It came to him then that this passage into the ring world was different somehow. Again he tried to free his hand. Nothing happened.

"Damn!" As that word reverberated through the chamber, a coldness settled over him. He had spoken aloud! At last his voice was audible in the ring world! Why? Had he done something different this passage?

Fearing that he might just have trapped himself in a strange world with no way home, he leaned down to gaze into his ring stone, willing himself back to Poco's cellar. Long minutes passed and nothing happened.

"Please," he called, lifting his voice. "Someone—anyone, help me!"

As his cry echoed around the stone walls, he felt a sudden warmth steal into the palm of his captured hand, a glow of heat that tingled into each finger and up through his hand to his arm. Afraid, he threw himself to the left, hoping to break the seal that had melded flesh to stone. It was no good—all he managed to do was wrench his shoulder with the force of his fall. The seal remained unbroken.

The warmth that had invaded his hand now flowed freely into his arm and upper body. Sprawled flat on his stomach, he pleaded with the empty room, praying that someone somewhere would hear him. "Please, let me go! I didn't mean to touch the stone! Please, help me!"

The warmth touched his spine like a flash of lighting, then instantly leaped to his brain. There was a moment of pain followed by a feeling of heaviness over his eyes, as if something was pushing at his mind from inside.

Dhal shook his head, trying to rid himself of the pressure. It would not go away. Somehow he managed to push himself to a sitting position, his right hand still caught on the stone. As he lifted his head, he caught a flicker of movement off to his right. He turned to find four naked men standing just within the outer edge of the circle of green light. Two were young, only boys, the other two were older, their muscles accented by the unusual light. Formidable-looking yet wary, they stood watching him.

Their green hair caught and reflected the green light from above, and he saw that they were Ni. "Please," he begged of them, "help me."

He watched as the two Ni approached and looked down at him. Their faces were unreadable. One of them turned and spoke to the boys. Dhal did not understand the language he used, but assumed it to be the language of the People.

As the two boys ran away, Dhal saw the movement of other bodies in the shadows beyond the pillars. The pressure over his eyes was growing stronger. He closed them, trying to will the pain away. A moment later it ceased.

When Dhal looked up again, the two Ni were kneeling just outside the stone carving. "Please, help me. I didn't mean to do wrong. I didn't know what would happen. I'm a stranger to your world. The ring brought me."

The two Ni looked down at his hand. It was obvious that they understood what he was saying. One started to reach out, but before he could touch Dhal, the other snatched his arm back. "No, Avak! You would do more harm than good. Wait for Danner."

The Ni named Avak turned crystal-gray eyes to Dhal. "E-ev is right. We can't help you without ourselves becoming caught. Danner will be here soon. He'll release you from the Tamorlee."

"Tamorlee?" Dhal echoed.

Avak gestured toward the green light overhead. "It is above you. Your ring wakened it."

Dhal looked up at the green glass, then back down at his hand. He noticed then that the green stone in his ring was actually glowing with the same colored light as above. "What is the Tamorlee?" he asked Avak.

The Ni looked surprised. "You do not know the Tamorlee?"

Dhal shook his head.

"But you are Ni. Surely you have only forgotten," Avak offered.

A sudden surge of pressure over Dhal's eyes caused him to wince. Avak noticed and put out a hand, but a soft voice stopped him. *"Ne, Avak, nev qual saba."*

Avak jumped at the sound. Rising, he turned and gave a half bow to the old one who moved out of the shadows. Her hair was gray with age, her crystal eyes sunken yet alert. She was dressed in a shapeless, floor-length tunic and her feet were bare.

Stopping before the carved circle, she looked at both males, who stood calmly before her. "He speaks the trade language, Malil Thura," Avak said.

The female nodded, then motioned the males back. "Clear the hall. I'll see to our guest."

Thura looked down at Dhal. Though aware of the shuffle of feet and the whisper of voices beyond the circle of light, Dhal could not take his eyes from the old one. Something about her commanded his full attention: she radiated an inner power that even the most insensitive could not miss.

Kneeling down outside the circle, she spoke. "I see questions in your eyes, child. I too have questions. But best they wait until we have you free."

Quickly she slipped a ring from the middle finger of her left hand. It looked to be a duplicate of the one Dhal wore. She held the ring between thumb and first finger, rose, and made a passage around the circle, touching the seven star points. It looked as if the stone of her ring fitted each small indentation in the design. When she came back around, she smiled. "Only a moment longer, child. Hold still."

With her ring she touched Dhal's, and the pressure that had pushed into his mind began to flow away like a river in flood. He closed his eyes in relief, still confused but thankful that the pain was gone.

"Lift your hand, child."

Opening his eyes, Dhal looked at the old one. She nodded. "It must be your own action, child. I have redirected the power source, so you are safe. Lift your hand and be free."

Dhal looked down at his hand and willed his numb fingers to move. Slowly he leaned back, pulling his hand free. The moment it came away from the stone floor, a strange weakness washed over him. He felt himself falling forward. Hands caught him, dragging him away from the stone carving.

A few seconds later he lay propped against the old one, held upright by her thin arms, his head resting against the softness of a sagging breast. He tried to sit up but found he had no strength.

"Rest child, the weakness will pass." After a few moments of silence, the old one spoke again. "Only the very wise or the very foolish dare touch the Tamorlee, child."

When he failed to reply, she let his head slip down onto the crook of her arm, then she forcibly turned his head to look into his eyes. "Did you come then to give—or to take?"

"Take what?" he asked.

The old one frowned. "Something is wrong here. Your accent is so strange, even for an outlander. What is your name, child? How did you pass the watch without anyone stopping you? Where did you come by the ring you wear?"

A male voice suddenly broke in. "I believe I can answer one of those questions, my dear Thura."

Startled, Dhal looked up to see the same Ni male he had seen before, outside the wooden building, the one who had named him Seeker. The old one acknowledged the male with a nod. "Danner."

Danner squatted down and placed his fingers at Dhal's throat. "Was he hurt?" he asked, speaking trader.

Thura answered. "He was weakened, but he seems alert."

Dhal lay quietly and listened.

"You said you could answer one of my questions," the female said.

Danner nodded. "Yes. I don't know his name or how he came by the ring, but I can guess how he got in here."

"How?" Thura asked impatiently.

"Transfer, my dear. In your arms you hold a Seeker."

For a moment the old one looked incredulous. "This is the same outlander you saw earlier?"

Danner smiled and nodded. "He is, and the same one who frightened the people at the lake. Each time he's been seen the transfer was incomplete—all we received was an image without substance. It frightened everyone until we figured out what was happening. It's been a long time since we've had a Seeker come to Val-hrodhur. Was it you who found him?"

"No," Thura answered. "Avak and E-ev were taking their class to the lake. Passing the hall, they heard someone cry for help and came to investigate. Avak sent one of the boys to find me."

"Shall I take him?" Danner offered.

Thura shook her head. "No, he's all right."

Danner looked down at Dhal. "A few moments ago I heard you speak. You seemed unable to do so the last time we met. Was it the weakness of the transfer that prevented you from speaking before?"

"I don't know," Dhal answered truthfully. "What do you mean by transfer?"

Danner frowned. "Before I answer that, would you tell us your name please?"

"Dhalvad sar Haradan."

"Ni named linked with an outlander name," Thura observed.

"Half-blood perhaps," Danner suggested.

"No Seeker was ever half-blood!"

Dhal did not care about his name or bloodline at that moment. All he wanted to know was what had happened to him. "Please, will you tell me where I am?"

"You are in Val-hrodhur," Danner replied. "The home of the Tamorlee. But as a Seeker you should know that."

Dhal hesitated. "What is a Seeker?"

There was a hiss of an indrawn breath, and Thura's eyes narrowed. "If you don't know that, then you are not a Seeker!"

"But if not," Danner put in, "what is he?"

"A stealer of rings, perhaps," Thura responded distastefully.

"No!" Dhal protested. From somewhere he found strength enough to roll out of the female's arms. Pushing to a sitting position, he closed his hand into a fist, fearing they might try to take his ring, his only contact with his own world. "The ring is mine! I didn't seal it!"

As Danner made a move toward him, Dhal scuttled back a

pace or two. "Be not afraid, Dhalvad," Danner said calmly.
"We do not accuse. We only wish to learn. Come, tell us how
you came to be here and how we may help you."

"But if he isn't a Seeker, Danner, it would be inappropriate
to—"

Danner held up a hand to stop the protest. "Thura, he is a
Seeker, else he wouldn't be here now. It's obvious that he is
untrained, yet he had the strength to activate the stone and each
passage brought him closer and closer to the Tamorlee until at
last he reached the source of the ring's power. In innocence,
he entered this chamber and charged the ring without taking it
from his finger. That one act alone convinces me that he didn't
really know what he was doing." Danner looked at Dhal. "Have
I guessed right, Dhalvad?"

Dhal nodded. "The stone pattern was so unusual. I just
wanted to touch it. I didn't mean to do anything wrong." He
shook his head. "I'm confused. I don't know what is real or
unreal at this moment. You—this place—am I just dreaming
it all? Am I here or am I sitting with my friends back in Port
Bhalvar?"

"Port Bhalvar," Danner repeated. "I've never heard of it.
It must be far. Perhaps that is why it took you so long to
complete a proper transfer."

"Are you saying that the world I see in the ring stone is
real? That I am *not* dreaming it all?"

The frown on Thura's face slowly faded as she explained.
"The fire stones retain and reflect, they do not create, child.
The Seekers use them to heighten their own powers so they
can transfer to whatever destination they desire. That place
which you visualize in the fire stone is open to you through
the power of the Tamorlee. How you were able to use the stone
without understanding it is something of a mystery to me."

Danner shook his head. "I don't know, Thura, perhaps not
so much a mystery. Though I haven't the talent of a Seeker,
I once knew one and he told me that if one activated the fire
stone and failed to give it proper visualization, the stone would
do either of two things: either it would reflect the thoughts and
place of another Seeker who was at that precise moment using

his own powers, or it would reflect its source, the Tamorlee. From what I've been able to piece together these past few weeks, for Dhalvad it has happened both ways. The first two times he activated the stone, it must have picked up on Fantar."

Suddenly Danner's eyes went wide. "Damn! That would mean that Fantar has the talent to be a Seeker! I'll have to get someone to reach him before he starts home. It's been years since we've had a Seeker come from among us." Eyes sparkling, Danner continued. "This might mean a resurgence of our gifted blood types, Thura! I wish that Ympath was here now. He should know what has happened. He could—"

"There will be time enough to tell him later," Thura interrupted. "We have our own work ahead of us now. If this youngling is what you think he is and is unknowing of his power, then best we find a way to help him before he makes another and more serious mistake."

"Yes. Yes, you're right," Danner agreed quickly. "Dhalvad, are you strong enough to stand now? Come, try. Here, lean on me."

"Where are you taking me?" Dhal asked.

"To someone who can answer your questions better than I."

Chapter 17

*B*Y THE TIME THEY HAD WALKED THE LENGTH OF TWO SHORT COR-
ridors and climbed a flight of steps, Dhal's strength had
begun to return.

Danner noticed. "Feeling better?"

"Yes, thank you."

"We haven't much farther to go, at least for our first stop,"
Danner said, steadying Dhal with his hand.

Thura turned at a huge carved stone portal. As they passed
through the large doorway, Dhal hesitated, fear and disbelief
churning inside. The cavernlike room before him was glowing
with green light, its source a giant crystalline boulder that lay
in a slightly recessed portion of the floor. The crystal was dark
green in some places, lighter green in others. As he watched,
he thought he saw a pulsating movement pass through the
crystal, like a wave of green-gold light shimmering through
water.

He felt Danner pull on his arm. "Come," he said, leading

Dhal forward. The crystal grew larger and larger as they approached. Unconsciously Dhal pulled back.

"Come, Dhalvad," Danner coaxed. "The Tamorlee won't harm you."

"That is the Tamorlee?" he asked, unable to take his eyes from the shimmering crystal.

Thura had stopped at a scattering of loose rock that lay near the crystal. When Danner and Dhal approached, she turned and spoke to Dhalvad. "You are in awe of the Tamorlee, child. I can see it in your eyes. It is well you should be, for the Tamorlee is like no other that has ever been before . . . at least to our knowledge."

Tearing his eyes from the crystal, Dhal looked at the woman. "What *is* it?"

"It is what you see, a giant, centuries-old crystal."

"Why does it glow?"

"It is its nature."

"You speak as if it were alive."

"It is, in its own way."

"It's alive?" Dhal gasped, turning again to the crystal.

"Yes, we believe so," she answered. "It doesn't breathe. It doesn't eat. Yet it changes size, parts of it breaking off so it may increase its dimensions. The process is slow, its growth judged in hundreds of years. The shards at your feet are proof of its growth. The stone you wear in your ring is also a part of the Tamorlee. Every once in a while one of the shards that break and fall off is different. Like the Tamorlee, it glows and shows life. Such a shard is taken, polished, and placed in a protective setting much like the one you wear, though yours is more ornate than any I've ever seen before."

Thura looked intently at him. "It's an honor to carry one of the fire stones, Dhalvad. They are given only to the wise and very trusted."

Silently Dhal finished her unspoken thought: And so what are you doing with such a treasure, stranger-child?

Having denied stealing the ring, Dhal refused to deny it a second time. "How often do you find fire stones? Are they common?"

Danner answered. "Some years we find one or two, other years none."

Dhal looked at the huge crystal and thought of the green glass surface he had seen above him only minutes ago. "The green light that entered the room where I was found, does it come from here?"

Danner nodded. "Yes. From the sun chamber a small portion of the Tamorlee is visible."

"You said that when I touched my ring to the stone pattern on the floor, I activated the Tamorlee. What did you mean? What happened? Why couldn't I move?"

"The Tamorlee releases a type of energy we call 'polu,'" Danner started to explain. "It's a force that can both repel and attract. It's how we communicate with the crystal."

"Communicate? You mean talk, as we are now?"

Thura interrupted. "Before we answer any more of our guest's questions, Danner, I think it would be wise for him to stand before l'Tamorlee and have him tell his story. Let l'Tamorlee judge the truth behind his appearance here. If all is well, his questions will be answered. If not..."

Choosing to ignore the old one's threat, Dhal looked at the giant crystal once more. "I can understand your discomfort at my unannounced presence and your reluctance to answer my questions. Perhaps it would be best if I just returned from whence I came."

"No," both said quickly. "Not before you have spoken to l'Tamorlee," Thura added.

Dhal frowned, uneasy. "You would have me speak to the crystal?"

"No, Dhalvad," Danner answered. "L'Tamorlee is our Speaker. He has empathy with the crystal. It is through him we learn from the Tamorlee."

"By 'him' do you mean a Ni?"

"Yes, he is one of us. As a child he was chosen by the crystal. When he dies, another will be chosen."

"The Tamorlee is a crystal and is also one of the Ni."

"Yes, and I think I now see your confusion. The Tamorlee

is the crystal life form, l'Tamorlee is a Ni. Together they form a working unit. Do you understand now?"

"Yes, I guess so."

"Then you will come and speak to l'Tamorlee now?" Danner asked hopefully.

Dhal looked at the crystal once more, his mind seething with questions. How did the fire stones work? Why had his stone brought him to Val-hrodhur?

"Will you come?" Thura prompted, growing impatient.

"Yes, if you will answer one more question."

Danner and Thura exchanged glances, then Thura nodded. "Ask your question."

"The Ni named Fantar told me that he was going to the mountains to gift the Tamorlee. And another man from my own world once said he believed the Tamorlee lay in the Mountains of the Lost, north of Port Bhalvar. Is that where I am now?"

"I have never heard of your Port Bhalvar or the Mountains of the Lost," Thura answered.

Danner shook his head. "Nor I."

"But the Tamorlee does lie in the mountains?" he pressed.

"It does."

It was suddenly terribly important for Dhal to know exactly where the Tamorlee lay. "Do these mountains have a name?"

"Cer-an-dargal, the Mountains of Learning."

Dhal was disappointed. He had never heard of Cer-an-dargal. Surely the Tamorlee was far from his homeland.

"Where are we going?" he asked as he walked beside Danner. They crossed around and behind the crystal, heading for another portal.

"Outside," Danner replied, "then down to the Learning Arc. We'll find l'Tamorlee there."

"Does he have another name?"

"He does," Danner answered without hesitation. "But it's only used by those who know him as blood kin. To the rest of us he is l'Tamorlee." As they passed through the darkened portal and down a short curving tunnel out into the light of late afternoon, Danner continued speaking. "When you are pre-

sented to l'Tamorlee, speak the truth at all times. He will know
if you do not. It is a gift with him, rare among the People."

"Is he old?"

"In years, no. In knowledge, yes."

"You said we would find him in the Learning Arc. Is he a
teacher then?"

"Yes, but he is also a student, as are we all. What he learns
from the Tamorlee he teaches to us."

Thura cleared her throat and Danner fell silent. He did not
look at Dhalvad again until they began winding their way down
a series of stone steps carved out of the cliff.

As they descended, Dhal was able to get a good look at the
valley below. He instantly recognized the great aban tree with
the triangular building sheltered under its spreading branches.
And off to the left of the cliffs lay the lake where he had
watched the Ni call a water draak to aid them in filling their
fish nets.

It took several minutes to reach the base of the cliff. Beyond
lay a beautifully kept garden and a stone path formed of interlocking slabs of shale. Along the walk, flowers were growing. It was late in the year for such flowers to bloom, he
thought, but perhaps here in the valley of the Ni they were
protected from the cool mountain winds. It came to him then
that if the ring world was real and that if he had somehow
managed to transfer himself to another part of his world, then
these mountains could be anywhere on Ver-draak, in another
climate where the cool months were shorter or there was no
winter at all.

Dhal shook his head. So many questions. He hoped l'Tamorlee would be more cooperative than Thura.

As they approached the front doors of the building known
as the Learning Arc, they were met by a group of younglings
accompanied by an adult. "One of our classes," Danner murmured softly.

The children watched curiously as Dhal walked past, their
crystal eyes alive with interest, their whispers like wind through
tall grass. Just as he reached the open doorway, he paused and
turned to look once more at the children.

"Is something wrong, Dhalvad?" Danner asked.

"No," he answered. "It's just that I've never seen so many Ni all at once." One of the children, bolder than the rest, lifted his hand and waved. Smiling, Dhal returned the silent greeting.

"What do you mean?" Thura asked, glancing at the children.

"In my part of the world, the Ni have all been killed or driven away. I was the last."

Thura's eyes narrowed. "Where did you say your homeland was?"

Dhal looked at Danner. He too was frowning. Dhal sensed a sudden hostility. Why? Rather than answer Thura's last question, he asked one of his own. "Twice you have referred to me as outlander. What did you mean?"

Thura glanced quickly at Danner, then back at Dhal. "Outlander—the Ral-jennob. Don't tell us you've never heard of the sun travelers. Their history is taught to every Ni child as a lesson in the dangers of becoming overly involved with the outlander's internal wars. I can't believe any Ni has gone without such learning, no matter his homeland!"

Dhal shook his head. "I have heard of the sun travelers, but only through stories. My life in the Deep wasn't touched by them. They were only—"

"The Ral-jennob touch everyone eventually. It is their way," Thura said. "They came to Lach and they brought their ways with them. They are an aggressive people, a fighting people, and we have learned to walk wide of their path."

"Do you believe these sun travelers come from another world?" he asked.

"Yes," Danner said, nodding. "That is what the Tamorlee tells us. It speaks of knowledge of a distant world, one that can be found in the stars at night."

"There is a legend that the Sarissa came to Ver-draak—I mean Lach—from the stars, but not many believe it. I wonder if they are kin to the sun travelers."

"What do these Sarissa look like?" Danner asked.

"They are tall and strongly made. Most have dark hair and dark eyes. They are arrogant and greedy, and some of them cruel."

"And these Sarissa warred on the People?"

Dhal nodded. "Haradan told me that the Sarissa were afraid of the Ni. He said that they tried to use them and when they found out they couldn't control them, they killed them. Very few escaped."

"I must admit that your words distress me," Thura said. "I don't like the thought of Ni being slaughtered, no matter their homeland. L'Tamorlee will be no less disturbed, I am sure."

"It sounds to me as if these Sarissa may be blood kin to the Ral-jennob, Thura," Danner said.

"It's possible," Thura agreed. "But we can discuss that later. Come, Dhalvad, it is time you meet l'Tamorlee."

Chapter 18

MINUTES LATER DHAL FOUND HIMSELF STANDING WITH DANNER in a wide corridor outside l'Tamorlee's teaching room. Thura had gone inside and closed the door behind her. They waited. Five minutes. Ten.

Finally, Dhal heard the sound of footsteps in the entrance-way. Suddenly two Ni appeared, each wearing over their tunics a curious harness whose straps crossed in front and ran up and over the shoulder. A knife sheath was attached to the harness at the right hip; the hilt of a sword stuck up behind the left shoulder. These were the first armed Ni Dhal had seen among the People, and he knew a moment of panic when they stopped in front of him.

He had been trapped! Gone was his desire to meet the Ni-lach Speaker. All he wanted at that moment was a return to his own world, to sanity and things he could understand. It was then he remembered his ring. There was more than one way out of that building . . . or so he hoped.

Dhalvad looked at Danner. The old Ni's eyes were on the

floor, his hands clasped in front of him. The two guards stood seven or eight paces away, watching Dhal.

Slowly Dhal brought his right hand around in front of him, tipping his fist up so he could see into the fire stone. It took only a moment to find the glowing crack.

Suddenly a hand fell on top of his and the fire stone was hidden. Dhal looked up. Danner shook his head. "I know what you're trying to do, Dhalvad, and must refuse you such action. It's imperative that you speak with l'Tamorlee. I know he can help you."

Dhal nodded at the two guards. "Are they here to help me too?"

"You are a stranger to us, Dhalvad sar Haradan. It would be unwise for us to admit you into the presence of l'Tamorlee without taking some precautions. Please, don't feel yourself threatened. You will not be harmed."

Danner started to say something more but the door behind them opened then, and Thura beckoned them inside. Danner went first. Dhal followed. The guards stayed three or four paces behind him as he crossed a stone floor laid with interlocking, oddly shaped pieces of colored stone. On a slightly raised platform at the far end of the large, circular room sat a Ni-lach. His hair, a much lighter green than any Dhal had ever seen, was worn in two loose braids that reached his lap. Sitting crosslegged on a large, cushioned mat, the Speaker silently watched Dhal's approach. There were four other Ni standing off to Dhal's right; he wondered if they had been in the room when Thura entered.

As Dhal stopped before the platform, l'Tamorlee stood and stepped down. For the first time since entering that strange Ni world, Dhal realized that his smaller stature was average among the Green Ones.

For long moments l'Tamorlee didn't speak, his dark, crystal-gray eyes moving in a careful study of Dhal's features. When their eyes met, Dhal felt cold sweep through him—for a moment there was a frightening sense of emptiness or unimaginable depths.

He quickly closed his eyes, protecting himself against—

against what? Power? Physical harm? No. No, it wasn't that. It was more a feeling of loss—but loss of what? Of his world? Of self? Dhal shivered, remembering old Gragdar's accusation that the Ni-lach were soul stealers.

A voice, soft and deep, came to him out of his self-imposed darkness. "Open your eyes, Dhalvad sar Haradan. All is well."

Slowly he lifted his head, eyes open.

"Why is it that my eyes frighten you?" l'Tamorlee asked. "They are little different from your own."

Steeling himself, Dhal again locked eyes with the Ni Speaker. Crystal ice . . . cold . . . knowing, but now there was a stillness there, a shielding of power that reinforced the spoken words.

"You are among friends, Seeker. There is no need to fear. Do you know who I am?"

Dhal nodded, unable to find his voice.

"Thura has told me what happened in the sun chamber. She spoke of your boldness in touching the Tamorlee. She isn't sure you knew what you were about. Is this true?"

"I meant no harm to you and yours, sir. If I did wrong in touching the stone pattern, I beg your pardon. I do not wish to be your enemy."

"The word enemy is a trade word. We do not use it here. Perhaps it would be best if you sit down with me and talk a while. Thura, Danner, please join us."

As they all took seats on the raised mat, l'Tamorlee looked to the two guards, silently ordering them to another part of the room. They moved to stand quietly next to the wall, but their eyes remained fixed on the platform. The four other Ni were asked to sit but were not introduced.

Dhal tried to show a calmness he did not feel. When l'Tamorlee asked him about his world and how he had come to Val-hrodhur, Dhal found he could not lie. In truth there seemed no reason to: He had nothing to hide.

When Dhal had finished his story, l'Tamorlee shook his head slightly. "You say you are a Healer. That you should be both Seeker and Healer is most amazing."

"More dangerous than amazing, sir," Dhal answered. "At

least from my point of view. If I hadn't used my power to heal, I never would have been chased from my home."

"Perhaps, perhaps not," l'Tamorlee said softly. "One never knows." He looked at Danner and Thura, then back to Dhal. "I grieve for the loss of the Ni in your birthland. I knew them not yet still they were a part of us through the Tamorlee. It's sad that you don't know your father's name, for surely he was a Seeker. But with information you have given me now and the memory impressions the fire stone can give the Tamorlee, perhaps we can learn more about your parents and your homeland. Your accent *is* different. As a Seeker, your father must have traveled far from Val-hrodhur, perhaps even to the other side of the world. That might account for the accent and your speaking only the trade tongue."

Dhal nodded. "It's possible."

"It's been a long time since any of the Seekers have returned to us," l'Tamorlee continued. "Thura believes your coming to be a portent; whether of good or evil will depend upon the knowledge the fire ring carries."

Dhal suddenly realized the full meaning behind some of Thura's earlier comments. "The ring carries information?"

"Yes. It is a part of the Tamorlee. It learns from the Seeker, then passes its knowledge back to the Tamorlee, which in turn gives that information to me and through me back to all the Ni-lach. Nothing is ever forgotten, no knowledge ever lost, if it is with the Tamorlee."

Dhal was stunned by the magnitude of such a network of information and learning. He looked down at his ring, an eerie feeling creeping up on him. While living in the Deep, he had seen certain plants that grew from other plants, parasites unable to live without a host. Was this Tamorlee like those plants, absorbing energy and information through the Ni-lach Seekers?

"Your ring, Dhalvad." Dhal looked up to find l'Tamorlee holding out his hand.

Though he disliked the thought of being an unwitting host to a mysterious crystal, neither did he like the thought of giving up his ring. It had belonged to his father. Also, it was responsible for bringing him to Val-hrodhur and he suspected he could not return to his own world without it.

He let his hand drop to his side, fingers closing into a fist. No one was going to take his ring! Danner nudged him gently and, with his eyes, silently bade Dhal to give the ring over.

Ignoring him, Dhal turned sideways off the cushioned mat and stood up. "The ring is mine," he said, taking a step back from the platform.

"No one has said that it is not," l'Tamorlee stated firmly.

Dhal saw Thura glance behind him and he cursed silently. For a moment he had forgotten the two Ni-lach guards. He heard their naked footsteps approach. He stepped to the side, turning so he could see the two guards. "I wish to return to my own world now," he said quickly, "to think about what you have said."

"No," l'Tamorlee said, rising. "You must stay and speak to the Tamorlee. Please, give me your ring. I promise that it shall be returned to you."

"Give it to him, child," Thura prompted. "Did you not come to us for help? We can't help unless you allow it." Something in the old one's voice made Dhal want to trust her. Even the eyes of l'Tamorlee seemed softer, reassuring. Almost... almost he gave the ring over.

But he had hesitated too long. The two guards moved in. As a hand fell on his shoulder, he dropped and spun around, all thought of obeying l'Tamorlee erased in that single touch. His ringed fist drove into the stomach of the first guard. The Ni doubled up and fell as Dhal leaped away from the platform to face the second guard. In one fluid motion the guard's right hand reached back over his shoulder and from his chest harness he drew a sword—a sword such as Dhal had never seen, with a blade of glaring, white light.

As the guard swung the sword at Dhal, l'Tamorlee yelled at him to stop, but by that time Dhal had ducked the first swing and had bolted for the door. He reached the other side of the room five steps ahead of the guard. As he flung the door open, he saw out of the corner of his eye a flash of light coming at him. Instinctively he raised his left arm to deflect the blow, at the same time lunging through the doorway. A stab of fire laced through his left shoulder and he cried aloud.

Dhal turned as the guard came through the door. Whipping his knife from its hidden leg sheath, he went to his knees as the Ni guard overran him. Pushing up quickly, he caught the guard off balance, heaving him up and over onto the floor. Danner, l'Tamorlee and the other guard came running through the door.

Dhal lifted his knife. "Stay back! I'm leaving!" He did not wait for an answer, but started backing away. While the Ni guard heaved to his feet and groped for his sword of light, Dhal turned and ran.

Bursting through the main doors, he headed for a nearby copse of trees. He turned once to look behind. L'Tamorlee, Danner, and one of the guards stood in front of the building watching him. L'Tamorlee's hand was on the guard's shoulder, as if restraining him.

Breathing hard, his shoulder a fiery torment, Dhal stopped to look at his wound. Fearing to use his healing powers lest he tire himself and have no energy to use the ring, he settled for numbing his back and shoulder muscles. Then he raised the fire ring. He had had enough of l'Tamorlee and the strange Ni who lived in Val-hrodhur. He was going back to his own world—if he could.

As the swirling colors flowed before his eyes, he pictured Haradan and the cellar where he had left his friends. He concentrated as he never had before. There was a sudden clearing of the colors as blue-black shadows formed into shapes. He saw the glitter of firelight, then felt a momentary lurching sensation.

A gasp of surprise came from Poco. "Look, it's Dhal!"

Haradan moved out of the shadows. "Dhalvad, how did you get in here?" he demanded, dropping down beside him. "Where have you been? We've been worried."

"He appeared," Poco said, her voice shaking slightly. "He just appeared. I was sitting there near the fire, wondering if Screech was having any luck in finding him and then—then he just appeared. There was a strange flicker of light and then he was sitting there. I've never seen anything like it before."

Poco was looking at him with wide eyes. Slowly she approached and put a hand to his shoulder as if to reassure herself that he was really there. Dhal flinched at her touch, then renewed pain flooded through him and he felt himself falling. Hands caught him and lowered him to the floor.

"Damn! He's been hurt," Haradan snapped. "Build up that fire, girl! We need light! Efan, go get some water. Lay quiet, Dhal. Let me see what's wrong."

". . . so I decided not to take the chance. When I'Tamorlee demanded I give him the ring, I broke away. That's when the Ni guard attacked me with his sword. His first stroke missed. His second didn't. After I reached the hall, the guard overran me and I managed to knock him down, then I escaped. When I was safe in the woods above the building, I used the ring to come back."

Dhal looked from one face to the next. Ssaal-lr had returned from his search and had heard all but the beginning of the story. His yellow eyes were close lidded as he looked at Dhal. Dhal wondered what he was thinking.

For a moment or two all were silent, then everyone started talking at once. "Wait!" Haradan said, raising his voice. "If we're going to make any sense out of this, let's ask our questions one at a time, please."

Haradan then turned to Dhal. "Do you feel up to answering some questions, Dhal, or would you like to rest a while?"

"Ask. I'll try to answer."

For more than two hours they talked. Dhal answered their questions as best he could and had some of his own to ask, the most important concerning his physical presence in both worlds. His leave-taking had gone unnoticed in the semi-darkness of the cellar. Everyone had believed that he had simply slipped out to attend to personal needs, and only when he failed to return did they become worried. It proved to him that the transfer to the other world had been complete.

Finally, swallowing nervously, Efan asked about the loca-

tion of Val-hrodhur. "Do you think it's in the mountains north
of Port Bhalvar?"

"I don't know, Efan," Dhal answered. "When I spoke of
Port Bhalvar and the Sarissa, the Ni-lach didn't seem to know
where or who I was talking about. I don't believe they could
live so close to Port Bhalvar and not know of its existence."

"But the Mountains of the Lost are wild and uncharted,"
Efan argued. "Could it be that the people you met live in some
secluded valley where they guard the Ni-lach treasure?"

"Treasure?"

Efan frowned. "My father heard stories about it."

Dhal shook his head. "I saw no treasure, not unless you
consider the crystal itself a treasure, but what one would do
with such a large stone is beyond comprehension. Personally,
I don't think I'd like to tamper with it. There was something
eerie about that whole place, almost unreal."

"But it was real," Haradan said quietly, "because illusions
and dreams do not physically harm. Dhal, I think it would be
best if you let me have your ring for the time being, lest you
be drawn back to that world and hurt again."

Dhal looked down at the ring. He did not want to give it
up. Haradan saw his hesitation. "For twenty-four years your
ring was in my keeping, Dhal. Trust me still?"

Looking at the ring one last time, Dhal slipped it from his
finger. He watched as Haradan placed it in a small leather
pouch at his belt.

Two days later Haradan and Dhal decided it was time to
leave. Having determined that their boat was lost to them, they
had finally chosen the overland route through the Mountains
of the Lost to Janchee, where they hoped to find transportation
to Port Sulta. Efan, Poco, Gi, and Ssaal-lr all agreed that it
was the only way left open.

Chapter 19

THE NEXT MORNING POCO AND EFAN LEFT TO GET SUPPLIES FOR
the trip. Poco was sure that by going up and around the
search pattern set by the Port Guard that day they would have
no trouble reaching the docks. Dhal hoped she was right.

Dhal had come to like Pocalina-fel-Jamba very much, her
brisk manner, her teasing ways. He had met few women while
living in the Deep and was at a loss for comparison; still, he
thought she would outshine most women her age. Poco was
lively and self-confident, yet shy and modest. Though she was
one woman among three men, she did not ask to be treated as
other than one of them. Dhal spoke of his feelings to Haradan.

"It had to happen eventually," Haradan said, smiling.

"What had to happen?"

"Man, woman—what we were talking about earlier this
fall."

Startled, Dhal sat quietly, staring at the shaft of daylight
that filtered down the cellar steps. Did he really love Poco?
Did it matter if he did? Soon they would be gone from Port

Bhalvar and Poco would go back to her singing. They would never meet again. If what he felt for Pocalina-fel-Jamba was love, it was a thing that could not be.

Efan and Poco returned before nightfall, carrying leather pouches filled with dried foods. The boy looked tired, and Dhal wondered if he might not have changed his mind about going with them. Donar sar Frenzel had offered Efan a place in his household, so Dhal was surprised when Efan had announced that he still wanted to go with them, no matter their destination.

Over the days they had spent together in the cellar, Dhal had noticed that Efan had become extremely quiet and had taken to pacing restlessly. Though the boy used the excuse of exercising his legs, Dhal felt it was more than that. Something was bothering Efan, but until he felt like talking it out there was nothing any of them could do to help.

"Any trouble?" Haradan asked, as he helped relieve Poco of her burden.

"No, everything went fine," she said. "We even have a map of the old trail through the mountains. Donar sar Frenzel gave it to Efan before he left."

Haradan and Dhal exchanged quick glances. Could they trust Efan's friend with their planned route to Janchee? Was it too late to change their plans?

By the time darkness had fallen, they were ready to go. Slinging a waterpouch over her shoulder, Poco led the way up out of the cellar. She was to accompany them to the old north gate, then Ssaal-lr would guide them as far as the fishing village of Canna, near the foothills of the mountains. Beyond that they would be on their own.

They reached the old gate in half an hour. There was no passing of the Port Guard there. Long abandoned for an easier route to the northwest, the stone roadway was all but buried in bush, vine, and weeds. The heavy gate tilted outward under the leverage of the roots of a fast-growing cara tree.

In the murky twilight the gates looked like the swollen eyes of an old man, once proud but now grown fearful in his loss of strength and youth. A portion of the gate had cracked at the bottom. Poco pushed a section of boards to the side and slipped through a V-shaped opening. One by one, the others followed.

A short distance beyond the gate the trees grew tall once more, and clingor vines running tree to tree formed a canopy overhead. Looking down the black tunnel that was all that was visible of the old north road, Dhal felt a flicker of uneasiness. And he was not the only nervous one: Efan was looking back at the old gates as if they were his last link with civilization.

Dhal turned to find Poco standing beside him."Changing your mind?" she asked softly.

He knew what she meant. "No, it's too late for that. Had we remained with the boat we probably would have been picked up before we left the harbor. By going overland we should put an end to the hunt. There's no reason for the Sarissa to continue their search now. We have nothing they want and I can't see them chasing us for revenge alone."

"It should take you no longer than a week to reach the foothills," she said, slipping the shoulder pouch off. "Trust Screech and you should have no trouble finding the old trail through the mountains."

"Poco, I want to thank you for all you've done for us."

"You are entirely welcome, Dhal."

There was something else he wanted to say but the words became tangled in his mind. "I want to . . . it's been . . ." Damn, he thought, get it out! "Poco, I'm going to miss your singing . . . and I'm going to miss you."

It was getting darker by the minute. Poco's face was so shadowed that Dhal could not see her eyes, but suddenly there was a flash of white teeth and he heard a low chuckle. "I wondered if you'd ever get around to that." Her lips brushed his cheek, but when he reached for her, she stepped back. "Take care, Dhal, and know that you always have a friend in Port Bhalvar."

She moved to stand before Ssaal-lr. "You know the wildlands better than most, Screech, but be careful. I want you returning in one piece."

Ssaal-lr answered with a soft coughing sound, which Poco imitated. Then, like a cloud shadow, she was gone.

Silently Dhal turned and followed Haradan, wishing there was some way to stay in Port Bhalvar and, at the same time, wondering if he had made a mistake in not asking Pooo to come with them to Letsia. But would she have come? Would she have given up all she had known to trek through the mountains with almost strangers? And to what end? To mate with a Ni who might be as much despised and unwanted in Port Sulta as he was in Annaroth? To resume life as a chalk artist in Port Sulta?

"You were wise in your choice, Pocalina-fel-Jamba," Dhal said softly into the night air. "May the next man you meet have more to offer you than I."

After the first night, they traveled by day through farmlands abandoned since the growing season had ended and the harvesting was done. On the morning of their eighth day, they took a small roadway heading northeast toward the coast.

Dhal looked down at the cloth sling he wore over his shoulder. Gi-arobi lay asleep inside, tired after walking all morning beside Dhal.

The wound he had received while visiting Val-hrodhur was no more. A few minutes of self-healing, after he had regained his strength, had erased all sign of the burn made by the light sword.

Efan walked ahead of Dhal, Haradan behind. Ssaal-lr was some distance ahead, cutting at obstructing vines and routing his companions around such obstacles as fallen trees and bogs, where a man could sink out of sight in a matter of seconds. That morning they had entered a section of the flatlands where moisture was squeezed out of the ground by each step.

Efan's pace—though he tried his best—slowed them down. The muscles in his legs were growing stronger by the day but it would be weeks, perhaps months, before he would regain full strength. Dhal saw Efan misstep and was close enough to catch his arm to prevent a fall. "Want to stop?" he asked.

Efan nodded. "Can we?"

"I don't know why not. I'll go ahead and ask Ssaal-lr to find us a place to stop where the ground is dry."

During the days they had spent in the cellar and on the road, Dhal had pushed himself to learn more of the derkat's form of speech. Already he could read a good many of Ssaal-lr's hand signs if the derkat made them slowly. Suddenly Haradan's voice came from behind them. "Keep walking and don't do anything when I drop out of line."

"Something wrong?"

"I think we're being followed. Twice I've seen something moving down our backtrail, but it was too far away to see it clearly. Go ahead, catch up with Ssaal-lr and find cover off the trail."

Dhal looked back through the trees behind them. "What if it's a draak? You may need help."

"Don't worry. If I need help, I'll yell."

"Do you think it could be the Port Guard?" Efan asked, a worried frown creasing his forehead.

"We'll know soon enough. Go on, both of you. I'll catch up."

Dhal hurried ahead to alert Ssaal-lr to the possibility of hunters on their trail. Gi-arobi woke up and poked his head out of the sling as Dhal whistled to get Ssaal-lr's attention. "Why running, Dhal?" he asked, peering along the trail as if a gensvolf might pounce on them at any moment.

"Haradan thinks we're being followed. He's gone to check."

Ahead of them Ssaal-lr had stopped and was waiting. Dhal had finished explaining their situation by the time Efan approached, breathing hard. With a jerk of his head, Ssaal-lr indicated that they should follow him uptrail. He directed them off the path where, crouched down behind a fallen aban tree, they waited.

The wait was not long. Ssaal-lr's ears pricked forward. Rising slowly, he peered through the tangle of vines before them. Before Dhal could ask him what he saw, he made his coughing sound and took several gliding steps out and around the foot of the tree. Gi, who was almost invisible in the undergrowth, was only a few steps behind the derkat and it was he who announced Haradan's coming—with Poco.

Dhal's heart jumped at the sound of Poco's name and, though

his mind was seething with a hundred questions concerning her sudden appearance, he could not keep from smiling. Then he saw her and his smile disappeared.

She looked exhausted. Her face was streaked with dirt and sweat, her hair was uncombed, and her eyelids were puffy from lack of sleep. Her arms and hands were marred with scratches and dried blood. Her tunic was torn.

With an arm around her waist, Haradan led her up the trail. "We've got trouble," he announced. "We *are* being followed."

"By who?" Efan demanded quickly.

Poco shook her head. "I'm not sure who's leading them. Let me rest and I'll tell you what I know." Sitting down right where she was, she continued. "After you left that night I went back to the cellar. I was tired and decided to stay there rather than go to my place. In the morning I got up early and was about ready to leave for the park when I heard voices. They were arguing. Thinking about you and the Port Guard, I went to find out what was going on. After leaving the cellar, I walked down the path above Old Street and found myself looking down on a large group of men. I counted twenty."

"Port Guard?" Haradan asked.

"No, not all. Five maybe. The majority of them were dressed in long, dark overcloaks. They wore no insignia on their clothes, at least none that I could see. Each of them carried a backpack and weapons enough for three. At first I didn't know what they were about—they seemed to be pointing this way and that—then it came to me that they were probably volunteers helping the Guard search for you." Poco's eyes found Dhal. "But I was wrong."

"What happened?" Dhal asked.

"While I watched from cover, one of them spoke to a man I couldn't see. His face was turned away from me. A few minutes later that same man led out, heading straight up Old Street toward the north gate. I followed them. When I saw them break through the gate, I knew we had been betrayed."

Out of the corner of his eye, Dhal saw Efan lower his head and instantly he knew what Poco was saying: Donar sar Frenzel, who had given Efan a map showing the route north to Janchee,

was the only man in Port Bhalvar who had any inkling of their
intended escape route.

Poco watched Efan as she continued. "I went back to the
cellar to collect some things, most of which I've lost along the
way. I managed to stay just behind them all the first day. I
intended to circle around them at night and come ahead to warn
you, but things didn't work out. The flatlands can be dangerous,
especially at night. I don't know how many times I walked
into mudboles and hidden streams. I finally gave up and waited
for morning, by which time the men had moved uptrail. It
wasn't until early this morning that I was able to pass around
them. They went into Breon, the closest fishing village, probably checking to see if you had passed that way."

"How far behind us are they?" Dhal asked.

"Four hours, maybe a little more. I've been running off and
on for the last six hours just trying to put some distance between
myself and your friends."

"Did you recognize any of them?" Haradan asked.

"No."

"Could they be Sarissa from Annaroth, Haradan?" Dhal
asked.

"It's possible, I suppose, but what would drive them? It
seems to me that they would just be glad to chase you out of
their territory. Why do I suddenly feel that we are being pushed
rather than chased? And pushed in a certain direction?" Haradan
looked at Efan. "Boy, do you think your father's friend gave
us away?"

Efan's eyes snapped up. "I—I don't know, sir."

"It would seem the obvious answer," Poco said.

Efan looked down. "I'm sorry. I thought Donar could be
trusted."

Haradan squeezed the boy's shoulder. "We all make mis-
takes, Efan. The wise learn from them. What's happened has
happened. Don't blame yourself. We have other things to think
about right now—like how we can lose our escort." Turning
to the derkat, Haradan asked, "Ssaal-lr, do you know what lies
ahead? Is there a place where this trail divides, or another route
we can take into the foothills?"

Ssaal-lr thought a moment then began weaving his fingers in intricate gestures. Pocalina translated. "He says that there'a a fishing village northwest of here. It's situated on a river that leads to the sea. It's called Sar-ruel." Poco looked at Screech, her eyes narrowing. "Screech, isn't that the village where they had so much trouble last year?"

"What kind of trouble?" Dhal asked, as Screech made an affirmative motion with his hand.

"People disappearing, reports of strange deaths and mutilations. It was reported that an evil spirit in the form of a giant sea draak was haunting the river. According to what I heard, the village folk were so frightened they abandoned their town for safer shelter along the coast."

"Sea draaks," Haradan said, shaking his head. "It's been a long time since I've heard of any being seen in the Enzaar Sea. They are said to be shy creatures, seldom seen and never captured. Some claim they are only legendary."

"But who is to say that what is legend to us now was not once reality?" Poco said. "Witness your foster son. The true-blood Ni were no more, yet there he stands, proof that legends can live."

"You have a point," Haradan agreed. "But a sea draak couldn't be responsible for dead or mutilated bodies. Like any other draak, they eat what they kill—meat, bones, and blood. There would be nothing left."

"True, but their appearance may have been all that was needed to spook an already frightened people into flight."

"This village is abandoned?" Haradan asked Ssaal-lr.

"Yes."

Like Dhal, Haradan had been trying to pick up some of the derkat's speech. "What lies beyond the village?"

"Small hills growing larger. Dark forest. No road. Animal trails along river."

Dhal watched Ssaal-lr's hands move and listened to Poco translate. What would she and the derkat do once they reached the village? Hide in the area until the hunters had passed them by? Or try another route back to Port Bhalvar? At the thought of leaving Poco behind a second time, a strange warning whispered through his mind, a foreknowledge that hinted at death should he let the woman out of his sight again. Her death or mine? he wondered.

A thought suddenly bubbled up from that portion of the mind that is all animal wariness. Poco had claimed to be trying to warn them of hunters on their trail, but what if she was lying? Was it possible that she was the betrayer and not Donar sar Frenzel? Instead of following the hunters, was it possible that she led them?

No, he thought, if she has betrayed us, she would not have come ahead alone. You're letting your imagination run wild. Judge not your friends wrongly. You have all the enemies you need!

"Our map shows two roads out of Breon," Haradan said. "One straight north along the coast to Janchee, the other northwest through the mountains. If the men who follow believe we are headed for Janchee, they'll probably head straight north and we can lose them there. The only problem will be that if they do take the coast route, they'll be ahead of us eventually and in a position to set a trap somewhere outside Janchee."

"If we lose them now and they realize that they are following a false trail, perhaps they'll give up and go home," Poco suggested.

"It's worth a try. The northwest route is somewhat longer, but if we want to lose those who follow us we'll have to try something." Haradan looked at Ssaal-lr. "How much farther to this abandoned village?"

"Two hours walking."

"All right," Haradan said. "Let's get started. I want to make sure we stay ahead of our friends. With any kind of luck we can be up into the foothills before dark, just in case our trackers decide to split their forces and some of them come our way."

Chapter 20

SAR-RUEL WAS DESERTED. TRAILING CLINGOR VINES HAD WOVEN a net of green leaves over and around most of the buildings, and where doors and windows had been left open by fleeing village folk, the vines had made themselves at home, crawling across wooden floors and up and over homemade tables and benches.

After peering into several of these deserted homes, Dhal was touched by a strange feeling of timelessness, as if the homes were not forever abandoned, but only waiting expectantly for the return of their owners. Furniture, drapes, plates on the tables, a piece of clothing thrown or dropped onto the floor, all seemed waiting, as if the people of the house had stepped out only for a moment.

The air was still—too still. Where were all the birds? Poco dropped back to walk beside Dhal. As her arm brushed his, she looked at him, her features dark with worry. "I knew it would be empty," she said softly, "but not like this."

"You used the word haunted back on the trail. Do you believe in such things?"

"Had you asked me that last week or even yesterday, I probably would have said no, but now I'm not so sure. I believe that we are more than just blood and bone, that there is a spiritual essence to all life . . . but whether that essence can exist in our world without bodily form . . ." Poco shrugged. "Feeling is not seeing."

"Poco?"

"Yes."

Dhal hesitated, afraid to ask the question that had been on his mind since seeing her on the trail. She was waiting. Damn it, ask her, he thought. If she says no, she says no—you'll live.

"Poco, have you thought about what you will do next? I mean, are you going back to Port Bhalvar?"

"It matters to you, Dhal?"

"Yes. It matters."

"You wouldn't mind if Ssaal-lr and I tagged along to Letsia with you?"

"No. No, I'd love for you to come. Will you?"

Poco smiled. "Yes, I think so. I always did want to travel and I think now is the time."

"It'll be getting dark soon."

Poco and Dhal turned at the sound of Haradan's voice. They were standing on a long wooden dock in front of a deserted inn, watching a series of small whirlpools that had suddenly appeared in the center of the river slightly downstream. Dhal thought there was something odd about those whirlpools, a feeling a wrongness.

Haradan joined them on the dock. "Find anything or anyone?" Dhal asked him.

"No. You?"

"No. Poco went through that section over there," Dhal replied, pointing west along the dock, "and I just finished going through these buildings behind us. If anyone is living here now they are in hiding."

"Have you seen Screech or Efan?" Poco asked.

"No, but they should be along," Haradan said. "We agreed to meet here. While we're waiting we could—"

"Look, there's Screech," Poco announced, pointing to the bank of the river. "He must have circled around."

"I wonder if *he* found anything," Haradan murmured.

Suddenly Ssaal-lr started running toward them, letting out an ear-splitting yowl that etched itself into Dhal's brain like a knife across heartwood.

Covering his ears, Haradan cried, "What's wrong with him?"

That high-pitched scream was repeated as the derkat raced toward them, a wicked-looking blade clutched in his right hand.

Dhal heard the sucking sound of water as he whirled around. For a second or two he could not believe what he was seeing. A water draak—the largest one he had ever seen—was rising up out of the river, its narrow head, long neck, and heavy shoulders silhouetted against the sky.

"Draak! Run!"

Grabbing Poco's arm, Dhal cleared the dock in one bound, almost jerking Poco off her feet. Behind them he heard the crunch of wood splintering, then a cry. Still running, Dhal looked back and saw Haradan flung into the water. The draak lunged against the wooden pilings, heaving itself up out of the water.

"Run!" Dhal yelled at Poco, pushing her ahead. As soon as he released her, he stopped and turned, drawing his knife. As he started back toward the dock, a gray form flashed by him, shrieking defiance. Ssaal-lr was on the attack.

Poco screamed for them to come back, but at the sight of Haradan swimming free of the wreckage of the dock, Dhal kept going. If they could distract the giant reptile long enough, Haradan might just have a chance.

Ssaal-lr caught the draak's attention first, his darting movements and ear-splitting cries enough to antagonize an entire herd of draak. Mouth open, teeth snapping, the draak's head dipped down toward the derkat. Ssaal-lr jumped to the side, avoiding the draak's first lunge.

Haradan was still in the water, swimming hand over hand

away from the draak. Suddenly the draak's tail flashed up and down. "Haradan, look out!" Dhal yelled. The draak's tail came down with a terrible splash—and Haradan was gone.

A hissing sound reminded Dhal of his own very precarious position. He turned just as the draak's head swung around. He heard Poco yell as he threw himself out of the way. Rolling over and over, he felt something brush his leg, then he was up and scrambling away from the dock. The hissing noise followed. The next few seconds became a nightmare of running and falling, the teeth of the draak only a snap away. Then, suddenly, Ssaal-lr was there, pushing him out of the way.

Slamming hard against the ground, Dhal rolled over and looked behind him. The derkat slashed at the snout of the draak. Faster then the eye could follow, the draak tipped its head sideways and knocked Ssaal-lr from his feet. Before the derkat could recover, the draak had reached down and fastened on Ssaal-lr's left arm and shoulder, dragging him into the air.

The draak started shaking Ssaal-lr. Frantic, Dhal looked around for the knife he had dropped in his mad scramble to get out of the way. He could not find it!

Horror-stricken, Poco stood where Dhal had left her, her eyes on the draak and her friend. Dhal could see her mouth moving but could not hear her cries above the noise of the battle.

The derkat screamed his rage, and with unbelievable ferocity, he swung at the draak's eye. Ssaal-lr was fighting for his life, all instinct and rage. With a mighty thrust, Ssaal-lr drove his knife into the draak's left eye.

Like any wounded thing, the draak tried to jerk away from the pain and in doing so caused the knife to rip down through the eye. One moment Ssaal-lr was dangling from the mouth of the draak, the next he was falling free to the wreckage below. Thrashing in pain, the draak threw itself back into the water, and seconds later it had disappeared beneath the surface.

As soon as the draak was gone, Poco and Dhal raced toward the broken dock to the place where they had seen Ssaal-lr fall. Dhal was first to reach the still form. Ssaal-lr lay face down, his shoulder and arm soaked with blood, raw flesh laid back to the bone. Groaning in pain, the derkat lifted his head. When Dhal saw the splinter of wood that stuck out from the derkat's right eye, his stomach turned.

"Gods!" Poco gasped.

Swallowing his revulsion, Dhal let himself down into the wreckage of wooden pilings and planks and, after some maneuvering, got into a position where he could touch the derkat.

"Be careful, Dhal," Poco whispered. "He's in pain and may not recognize you as friend."

Poco knew the derkat. At Dhal's touch, Ssaal-lr growled and threw himself over onto his back, the claws of his good hand up in a threatening position.

"Keep your eyes on the water, Poco," Dhal said. "Warn me if the draak shows again. And watch for Haradan. The last I saw, he was swimming for the riverbank. I don't know if he made it or not."

Dhal turned his attention to the derkat. "Ssaal-lr, can you hear me? It's Dhalvad. I want to help. Poco is here with me. We have to get you out of there before the draak comes back. You're hurt badly. Let me help."

For a moment Ssaal-lr didn't respond, then slowly his clawed hand dropped. Keeping up a running monologue, Dhal moved in. The derkat flinched at his touch but did not fight or resist. Once Dhal had him on his feet, Poco helped guide the derkat away from the ruined dock to safe ground.

By the time they led Ssaal-lr into the shelter of the nearest building, Efan and Gi-arobi had found them. Both had heard the noises coming from the riverfront, but neither had arrived in time to witness Ssaal-lr's heroic battle with the sea draak. Standing to the side of the doorway, Efan looked down at the derkat who lay on a straw pallet taken from another room. "Are you going to try to heal him, Dhalvad?" he asked softly.

Dhal looked up at the young man and nodded. "Yes, I'll try."

"Can I watch?" he asked timidly.

"I would prefer it if you and Gi would go and look for Haradan. He was thrown into the river when the draak appeared."

"We look, Dhal," Gi piped up. "Come, Efan."

Efan looked down at the olvaar, hesitating, then he nodded and followed Gi to the door.

"Be careful that you don't rouse that sea draak again," Poco called after them.

Dhal knelt beside Ssaal-lr. The derkat was still losing blood, his arm and shoulder torn so badly that death would soon follow if Dhal did not heal him. Dhal reached out and laid his fingers on the derkat's forehead. Ssaal-lr moved under his touch, then stilled.

"Dhal, what are you going to do?" Poco asked softly. "What did Efan mean when he asked if you would heal Ssaal-lr? Can you really help him?"

"There's no time to explain, Poco. Just trust me. Ssaal-lr sleeps now and is in no pain. I'll do what I can for him, I promise."

The derkat's body was different, yet still there was a knowing of its form, a vision of rightness of each muscle and bone and the complexity of eye and brain tissue. Dhal could feel the energy flow out of him as he willed Ssaal-lr's body to rebuild itself. Gradually he ceased to be aware of his surroundings, becoming one with the living form beneath his hands.

"I don't believe what I have just seen," Poco breathed softly. "How? How is it possible? What are you, Dhalvad?"

"He is a Ni-lach Healer," Haradan's deep voice answered.

Dhalvad roused from his peaceful trance. He opened his eyes. Poco sat beside him. Beyond her stood Haradan and Efan. Everyone was watching him. He was tired, yet his body felt light. His eyes found Haradan. "You made it."

Haradan grinned. "Yes, thanks to you and Ssaal-lr."

"Thought the draak got you with its tail."

"I dove just in time, then swam downriver a ways." Haradan's hair was still wet and plastered to his head. His clothes clung to his body. He nodded at Ssaal-lr. "Are you finished?"

"Yes. He'll be weak from loss of blood, but he will live."

"You look tired. Why don't you lie down for a little while?"

Fighting off a wave of sleepiness, Dhal shook his head. "We should be leaving soon, in case someone comes this way."

"You haven't the strength to do any walking right now. I've seen what healing does to you." Haradan stepped around Poco and, taking Dhal by the arms, forced him backward onto the straw pallet. Dhal had no strength to resist. "You lay down right here beside Screech. Poco, Efan, Gi, and I will share watches. If we leave before first light tomorrow morning we should be into the foothills before our friends even realize that they're on the wrong trail."

Dhal was having difficulty keeping his eyes open. "Do you think anyone will follow us?"

"Only time will answer that, but don't worry about it now. Close your eyes and sleep. We'll wake you when it's time to go."

Dhal woke to the sound of voices. Next to him, Ssaal-lr was breathing easily, still sound asleep. Haradan and Pocalina were sitting side by side in the doorway, silhouetted in the early morning light. Poco was beautiful, her features accented by the morning shadows.

". . . and so that is why we had to leave the Deep," Haradan was saying. "His gift is beyond my understanding. I don't think Dhal even understands how it works. He just seems to 'know' how to heal."

"You love him though he is not your own," she said. "I can hear it in your voice when you talk about him."

"You have your own gifts, Pocalina-fel-Jamba. I think you two are well matched."

"Matched?"

"You love him, don't you?"

Suddenly another form appeared in the doorway. For a moment Dhal did not know who it was, then Efan spoke. "We tried to follow the glowing lights, sir," he said to Haradan, "but they disappeared too quickly. Do you want us to keep looking?"

"No, it's almost daylight. We'll be leaving soon."

"What do you think the lights were?" Efan asked.

Haradan did not answer for a minute. "Ghosts perhaps, but more likely it was some night creature, such as a veegar moth which lures other insects near by producing a flickering light in its tail."

"But these lights didn't flicker, sir, and they were larger than any insect would produce."

"I know. I saw them. I was just making a comparison."

"It wasn't a veegar moth then," Poco said.

"No."

"Then what?"

Haradan shrugged and stood up. "You said the village was haunted."

"Do you really think those lights were some kind of ghost?" Efan asked seriously.

"Anything is possible, Efan, but until we know for sure let's not frighten ourselves with untested theories. Anyway, we'll be leaving soon. If the lights we saw were ghosts, they should be satisfied with our departure."

Chapter 21

AT EARLY LIGHT, THEY LEFT THE ABANDONED FISHING VILLAGE and followed the river north, into the foothills. Because Ssaal-lr was weak from the loss of blood, their pace was slow with many stops to rest.

The derkat had been startled to wake and find himself whole once more. But for a patch of missing fur on his shoulder and a swelling around his one eye, Screech looked quite normal. It was Poco who explained to him how his healing had taken place. Whether or not the derkat fully understood all that had happened to him, he accepted his miraculous return to health in silence, his yellow eyes studying his healer with a calmness Dhal found unsettling.

Night closed in. They sheltered back in the trees beside the river. They had hoped that whoever followed them would give up upon reaching Sar-ruel, but a speck of firelight in the hills below signaled that such was not the case.

Poco turned to Dhal, frowning. "How did they find our trail so quickly?"

"Does it matter?" Dhal said, turning away. "Somehow they've followed us, and it means that they aren't ready to give up."

"What do we do now?" Poco asked Haradan.

Haradan pulled out Donar's map and laid it in front of them. Carefully pointing out the way, he said, "If we cross the river here and go east toward this mountain pass, then north, we should gain time and, if we're lucky, we might just lose those who follow us. It's entirely possible that they have the same map we do, but if we're careful not to leave them any sign of our choice of trails, they'll probably take the one that stays west of the river and, we hope, not learn of their mistake until it's too late. Even if they continue on and try to cut us off where the two trails merge, we should arrive at least a week ahead of them. A quick run to Janchee, then on to Port Sulta."

"You make it sound easy," Poco said, studying the map. "But from all I've ever heard about these mountains, no man or party of men has used these trails in a long time. There must be a reason. I think that whichever trail we take, our passage will not be easy."

Haradan looked up. "Dhal?"

"I was thinking about those who follow us. I can't understand what drives them. Will nothing but my death satisfy them?"

"Don't talk that way!" Poco snapped.

"She's right," Haradan agreed quickly. "There's no good in talking of death. We're all alive and healthy, thanks to you, and if we keep our heads and don't panic, we'll come out of this."

Efan remained silent.

Late the next morning they forded the river, linked one to another by rope that Haradan had found in one of the abandoned homes in Sar-ruel. The river was wide but shallow, except for a narrow channel on the far side where they were forced to swim. Gi-arobi rode Dhal's shoulder all the way, whistling encouragement as they plunged into the deep water.

Haradan was the first across. He was followed by Poco,

then Ssaal-lr, then Efan. Dhal was the last to cross and was thankful for the towline around his chest, for the water was swift in the channel and for every stroke forward he floated three or four downstream.

They were able to keep their packs reasonably dry by carrying them over their heads until they reached the channel, then throwing them across to the other riverbank. All but one reached the shore safely; the other was lost to the current.

They were thankful that the air was warm, for they dared not delay to dry their clothes. At noon they stopped to rest and eat, then they were climbing once more. Ssaal-lr took the lead. In the late afternoon, Dhal looked back to see Efan struggling up a narrow trail between two large boulders. The boy's face was red, and Dhal knew he needed to rest.

A little farther uphill Dhal managed to catch Haradan's attention and called for a halt. Everyone was grateful for the stop. After sharing water from one of the hide flagons Haradan carried, they sat and talked, eyes directed at the climb still ahead of them. The trail was all but obscured in places, overgrown with trees and bushes. Ahead the ground rose steeply. Large boulders scattered here and there showed signs of a recent rock slide. Haradan cautioned his companions to watch their footing when they started out again.

Dhal turned to talk to Efan. But a sudden growling noise alerted him. He looked up to find Ssaal-lr perched on a large rock slab to his right, pointing downtrail. In a moment Dhal had scrambled up to join the derkat. Haradan was right behind him.

"Damn," Haradan muttered. "How did they know?"

Dhal had no answer. Staring at the small specks of black that were crossing the river, Dhal felt a moment or two of panic. Then he remembered the long hard hours of climbing that separated them from the river valley, and his heart slipped back into place.

Haradan slid down from the rock. "They must have an excellent tracker with them. I was sure we left no tracks."

"What's wrong?" Efan wanted to know.

"We're still being followed," Haradan answered. "Come on, pick up the packs. We've got to keep moving."

Accepting the news in silence, Efan looked at Dhal, then turned to do Haradan's bidding. Dhal helped the boy with his pack. "They're far behind us, Efan. No need to worry. They'll get tired of all this soon enough. We have nothing they want. Revenge can't drive them forever."

"What if it isn't revenge they want?"

"What else could it be?"

"A reward?" Efan said softly.

"You mean a bounty?"

"That, or some other kind of reward. Isn't it possible?"

"It would have to be an awfully large reward to draw so many men. I have a feeling there's something else at work here, something that we've overlooked. I can't explain it, but it's there."

Efan looked at him strangely, his expression suddenly unreadable. For a second Dhal thought Efan was going to say something, but then Haradan interrupted.

"Come on, let's move. You can talk later."

It was their sixth night in the mountains. They were all tired. Twice the first day they saw their pursuers far below, then the trees grew taller and thicker and they lost sight of them. Whenever they came to a fork in the trail, they were careful to obscure all marks of passage.

They chose their campsite prudently that night, using a tall rock ledge to guard their backs. Before them burned two fires. For the last three nights they had been plagued by gensvolf— bold, long-legged, sharp-fanged creatures that slipped up on a camp as quietly as windseed in spring.

Dhal looked across the fire and saw Pocalina watching him. She smiled, her eyes bright, her expression mischievous. "What are you thinking, Dhal?"

Forgetting the gensvolf, he turned his thoughts to Poco and the love he had been unable to express until that moment. Perhaps now is the time, he thought. He returned her smile. "I am thinking that you are quite beautiful."

Tilting her head in a nod of casual acceptance, Poco's smile widened. "And is that all that you are thinking?"

"At the moment, yes."

Dhal heard Haradan chuckle and turned to look at him. He was sitting near one of the fires massaging his legs. Sometimes Dhal forgot that Haradan was that much older than the rest of them; the climbing must have been hard on him.

Haradan winked at Poco. "Have a care, Singer. You are the first woman he has ever really known and I think he's in love with you."

Poco's smile faded as her blue eyes fastened on Dhal. "True, Dhal?"

Dhal nodded, unable to speak.

For long moments she just looked at him, then she came to kneel in front of him. Leaning forward, she kissed him, her hands pulling his head up. As he reached out to draw her closer, she released him and sat back on her heels, her smile gone.

"It's said that love is a gift from the gods, Dhalvad sar Haradan, but it is also said that love is a form of madness. It's long been my belief that waiting brings wisdom and patience builds strong bonds. I want you to know that I am your friend— and more than friend if you would like—but stay uncommitted until you are sure it *is* what you want."

"And if I say that I *am* sure?"

A warm smile lighted Poco's face. "Then I say that you won't easily be rid of me, Green One."

"What was that?" Haradan asked, unable to hear those last whispered words.

"Never mind," Dhal said, pulling Poco to a seat beside him. "I'll tell you later—maybe."

Dhal had first watch that night. Gi-arobi followed, then came Haradan, Poco, and Ssaal-lr. Efan was the last one on watch. When Dhal woke at morning light, he saw Efan seated between the two fires, carving on a small branch. His fingers moved nimbly; the pattern he was working on looked quite intricate. Dhal watched him for a few minutes.

Finally Dhal got up, rolled his blanket, then went over to

the fires. Efan looked up. "All quiet," he said. "Should I call the others?"

"I'll do that," Dhal said. "You freshen one of the fires and start some water boiling."

Efan nodded and put down the piece of wood he was carving.

"What are you making?" Dhal asked, bending down to pick up the branch.

"Nothing." Grabbing the branch before Dhal could look at it, Efan stuck it into the fire. Dhal watched the wood burn, then turned and looked at the boy.

"It wasn't any good," Efan explained, as he picked up several more sticks and added them to the fire.

Since leaving Port Bhalvar, Dhal had noticed a change in Efan. No longer did the boy smile and, though never much of a talker, he had become absolutely laconic. As Efan stood up, Dhal laid a hand on his shoulder. "Efan, is there something wrong?"

"No," the boy snapped. "There's nothing wrong. I just don't like the mountains! I wish we could have gone another way— across the sea. Then—then no one could have followed us."

"Haradan thinks we've lost the men who were behind us."

Efan was silent.

"You don't think we have, do you?"

Efan shook his head, his eyes downcast.

"Is that what you're afraid of? The men who follow us?"

Efan looked up, his dark eyes moist with unshed tears. "Not for me! I'm not afraid for me!"

Damn, Dhal thought, something is wrong! The only time he had seen Efan cry had been at the news of his father's death. Efan was shaking now. Embarrassed, he pushed Dhal away, then turned and ran from the camp.

"Efan!" Dhal called after him. "Efan, come back!" He turned to Haradan. "Haradan! Get up! Efan's gone. I'm going after him."

Haradan woke quickly, throwing his blanket off as he sat up. "What?"

"I'm going after Efan. Wake the others."

There was no sign of the boy among the nearby trees, but Dhal could hear him breaking through the tangle of dead wood and vine, and followed the sounds.

When Efan saw Dhal, he stopped and turned. "Go away! Leave me alone! You're better off without me! I don't want to go any farther! I'm going back!"

"You can't go back," Dhal snapped, closing on him. When Efan tried to break to the left, Dhal caught him by the arms. "Alone, the gensvolf would have you in a night! And there are still those men behind us! What do you think they'd do to any stragglers they pick up? You made your choice days ago, Efan. You'll have to live by it!"

Efan fought, his eyes wide in the frightened realization that he did have no choice, that there was no going back.

Suddenly Haradan was there, stepping in between them. He took Efan and tried to calm him down. Then Efan's tears came as he clung to Haradan, his words incoherent. With a nod of his head, Haradan told Dhal to go back to camp.

Later that day while continuing their climb, Dhal dropped back beside Haradan. Efan was ahead, walking in front of Poco. Everyone knew about Efan's flight that morning, but no one had spoken openly about it.

"How is the boy doing?" Haradan asked, keeping his voice down.

"He's quiet but he's climbing," Dhal replied.

"Do you know what set him off this morning?"

"No, not really. But something's bothering him."

"Well, we'll keep an eye on him and ease up on the pace a little. Could be he's just tired. We're nearing the ridge. By tomorrow night we should be on the other side of the mountains and starting down. Personally, I'll be glad to get out of these mountains. The gensvolf are too bold here, and for two nights running I've seen ghost lights under the trees."

"You have?" Dhal asked, surprised. "Anyone else see them?"

"No, only me. They're similar to the ones we saw in Sarruel and there's something eerie about them. They make you want to follow them. I have actually had to fight the urge to leave camp and go see what they are."

"You think they're dangerous?"

"Physically, no. But what if a man tried to follow the lights and became lost out there—alone?"

"Should we double the watch?"

"Might be a good idea. It will mean shorter nights for all of us but it might also ensure everyone being here when we wake up. Go on now. Stop worrying about Efan. He'll be all right. He's young and he's city raised. He'll get over his fears after a while. It's still a good trek to Janchee. By the time we reach the port, Efan should be as good a forester as any man who ever walked the Deep."

Chapter 22

THE NIGHT AIR WAS CALM BUT COOL. THEY HAD WALKED WELL into the twilight hours, so by the time they set up camp and ate, it was quite dark. The warmth from the fire felt good against hands and faces.

They had just finished eating when Poco cried softly, "Look!"

They all turned. Off to the west was a line of bobbing ghost lights. There were five of them and they were just as Haradan had described. They seemed to be floating above the ground, weaving as if in some ritual dance.

Without taking his eyes from the dancing lights, Dhal stood up. "How far away are they?" he asked Haradan.

"I'm not sure," Haradan answered, joining him. Peering into the darkness, they watched the silent globes of light float and waver in the field below. "Do you feel their pull?" Haradan asked.

"Yes, especially if you try to watch them all."

"What *are* they?" Poco asked.

Haradan shook his head. "I don't know, girl, but something

tells me that whatever they are, they aren't friendly. Efan, Dhal, put more wood on the fire. If those dancing lights are night creatures, there's a good chance they'll stay away from our fire."

As Efan and Dhal turned to do Haradan's bidding, Dhal noticed that Ssaal-lr was missing. "Poco, where's Screech?"

Poco turned to look. "He was here just a few minutes ago. Over there, near the packs." Poco moved across the camp, calling the derkat's name. "Screech? You here, Screech?"

"What's wrong?" Haradan demanded.

"Screech seems to be missing," Dhal answered. Suddenly the derkat's yowl shattered the stillness of the night air. It came from the direction of the dancing lights.

"Damn!" Haradan swore. "The fool's gone after them!"

"Them?" Poco echoed.

"The lights! The damn light things!"

At Ssaal-lr's second cry, Haradan turned to the fire and grabbed up a lighted branch. Before Dhal could ask him what he intended doing, Haradan was gone, the burning brand he carried bobbing up and down erratically as he headed straight for the ghost lights.

"Stay with the fire!" Dhal yelled to Poco and Efan. He took another branch from the fire and started running. A shout from Haradan spurred him to a faster pace. Twice he almost lost his footing; it was too dark to be running over unknown ground at breakneck speed.

As he neared the lights, he caught sight of Haradan using his firebrand to keep something at bay, something that was hovering over his head making strange sucking noises. Dhal heard the hum of fast-beating wings, then there was a trilling noise that overshadowed the derkat's screams. Something brushed his head. He looked up to find one of the ghost lights right above him. Instinctively he raised his firebrand, poking it upward at the descending globe of light. As the night creature bobbed up and away, Dhal had the distinct impression of long spider legs dangling either side of the light.

"Dhal, over here! Help!" Haradan was trying to fight off two of the light dancers. Ducking left then right, he started running, then he stumbled and fell. One of the light creatures dropped onto him before Dhal could move.

Suddenly a dark shadow hit the light dancer, knocking it away from Haradan. As Dhal ran toward Haradan, Ssaal-lr's challenge rang through the air. A high-pitched whine followed the derkat's cry. The sound was almost deafening. Then it ended abruptly.

Haradan was getting up by the time Dhal reached his side. "Look," he cried, pointing. "They're leaving!"

Dhal glanced up at the bobbing lights, then turned back to Haradan. "Are you all right?"

"Yes, I think so—thanks to Screech. Damn thing had something around my neck before I could do anything."

"Let me see." Dhal raised his torch and checked Haradan over. There was an odd-looking red mark around his neck, but he seemed to be all in one piece.

"If Ssaal-lr hadn't chased that thing away, I'd be—"

"Not chased," Dhal interrupted. "Captured. Listen."

They heard a strange clicking noise off to their right. It was followed by a soft growl. "Over there," Dhal said, "Let's see what he's got."

As their light found Ssaal-lr, he looked up and coughed a greeting. He was standing quietly, licking at a wound on his right forearm. He stepped aside, letting the light fall full on the night creature he had torn from Haradan's back.

Dhal felt his stomach heave as he saw the mass that had once been a light creature. There were long tangled legs, thin and spidery, and torn wings that were as black as the night. A large glutinous sack that must have been part of the creature's body lay partially deflated, a strange glowing fluid pouring out onto the ground. A head was attached to the sack. It was black and furry with a pair of multifaceted eyes glinting red in the torchlight. The eyes were still alive. As Dhal watched, the creature stirred, a long, thin, cordlike tongue flicking out. They all stepped back a pace or two, even Ssaal-lr, who growled a warning. Then the thing shuddered twice and lay still.

A few moments passed. "Think it's dead?" Dhal asked.

"Let's hope," Haradan replied.

"What is it, Haradan? I've never heard of anything like it."

"Haven't you, Dhal? Think back to the swamp. What is it that comes each fall and lights the marshlands at night? Think small."

"Small?"

"Insect size."

"You're not talking about feeders, are you?"

"Yes. Don't you see it? They're much the same except for size."

"But feeders don't grow this big."

"Not in the Deep, they don't," Haradan said, "but we aren't in the Deep any longer. I've never heard of feeders this large, but that doesn't mean they don't exist. If this isn't a feeder, then I'd say it's a distant cousin. And knowing how feeders kill, I'd like you to take another look at my neck. If the skin is broken anywhere and it managed to pump some of its poison into me, we're going to need some frenza root and quickly."

Fortunately, they did not need the antidote for feeder poison. The burn around Haradan's neck was surface only, and the cut on Ssaal-lr's arm had come from Haradan's knife when the derkat had jumped the feeder.

In the morning the body of the giant feeder was gone. Haradan and Dhal were not surprised. Insect feeders were known to eat each other.

On their fifteenth day in the mountains they reached the deep V-shaped gap Haradan had pointed out days before. For the next six hours they followed a dry streambed downward. Suddenly the ground leveled off and they found themselves in an open grassy area. There were trees here and here, but not like the towering giants they had passed under during their climb upward.

Ssaal-lr found a clear patch of stone that seemed to be a wedge of a very old and narrow walkway. "The legends say that once there was a Ni-lach city in the mountains," Poco said. "A city would need roads."

"Forget roads for a minute," Haradan said. "Look at the land. Doesn't it look to you like a crop field? See how square it's cut. It's overgrown with bush and vine, but you can still see where the forest was pushed back."

"Do you think someone might be living up here?" Poco asked.

"It's possible," Haradan replied. "But not likely. These fields haven't been used in a long time. It would take years for some of those bushes to grow as big as they are. And when you consider the number of gensvolf we've seen, and those giant feeders, who in their right minds would want to live up here?"

They were halfway across the field when Dhal heard Gi's whistle. He looked past Efan, who was walking just ahead of him. He could not see Gi but he could see the tall grass moving as the olvaar ran toward them.

"Something wrong?" Haradan asked as Gi whistled again.

Efan, who had not said a word all morning, answered. "Gi says something about a draak."

Dhal glanced at Efan, a twinge of jealousy flitting through his mind. The secret language of the olvaar was a secret no longer. But he knew that he had no one to blame but himself: Efan knew the olvaar language because Gi and Dhal had taught it to him.

Dhal's thoughts were quickly pushed aside as Gi ran up, his whistle-clicks shrill in the air. Dhal translated. "Screech has found a draak lair. A big one. Tracks all over. Many draak! Hurry! Run!"

They wasted no time talking—they needed to find cover quickly. They were almost across the grassy field when they heard from Ssaal-lr, his high-pitched yowl making the hairs on the back of Dhal's neck stand upright. There followed the hissing roar of an aroused draak. They all started running again, toward a stand of trees straight ahead.

Again they heard the derkat's cry. Turning, Dhal saw Ssaal-lr running across the field. Right behind him ran the largest land draak Dhal had ever seen. Dhal heard Haradan whistle softly. The size of the creature was unbelievable. It had to be at least the size of the sea draak they had seen in Sar-ruel, and for a land draak, that was large!

The draak was fast and was closing on the derkat. Objects

that Ssaal-lr had to go around, the draak simply crushed out
of his way. Ssaal-lr was running head up and tail curled around
his body.

"Come on, Screech," Poco cried softly. "Run! Run!"

Suddenly the derkat swung east. Somehow he managed to
stay just ahead of the angry draak. "He's leading it away,"
Dhal cried.

"Damn fool," Poco said. "He's going to get himself killed!"
She turned and looked at Dhal. "We've got to help him!"

Haradan and Dhal traded glances. "What do you suggest?"
Haradan asked the girl. "We have no weapons with which to
fight such a monster. It looks to me as if Screech is doing the
only thing possible. We'll have to trust him to know what he's
doing."

"Gi said that there are other draak around," Dhal said. "We
had best keep our eyes open. I also think it might be a good
idea to move away from this open field. It's probably in the
draak's home territory. After Ssaal-lr outruns the draak he'll
come looking for us. We can leave him a trail by marking the
trees. I think he'll understand and follow."

"*If* he outruns the draak," Poco said.

"He will," Dhal assured her.

"I don't want to leave here without him," she protested.

"It will be getting dark soon, Poco," he explained. "We
won't go far, just up this hillside into denser cover."

Twenty minutes later they had located a reasonably secure
place overlooking the valley. There was a rock wall at their
backs and several climbable trees to either side of them.

While the others set up camp, Dhal climbed one of the trees
to see if he could locate Ssaal-lr or the giant draak. But when
he reached the top branches he found the field empty, the
shadows of the trees beginning to crawl across the grass. Turning, he looked downvalley, then something caught his eyes.

He climbed a branch or two higher and found a place where
he had a full view of the valley below. There was a building
there, shaded deep rust and orange by the last rays of daylight.
Dhal sat clutching his perch, afraid to close his eyes lest the
vision fade. It was not possible!

As Ra-gar slipped below the horizon, shadows engulfed the building. Raising his eyes, Dhal drew in a shaky breath. When he looked back down, all was darkness in the valley below. He could no longer see the building, but he knew it was there—waiting for him.

A voice came up from below. It was Haradan. "Dhal, have you gone to sleep up there? Ssaal-lr's back. Come down."

Looking one last time toward the darkened valley, Dhal turned around and began his descent, feeling his way carefully from branch to branch. Haradan waited below, a frown creasing his forehead. The reflected light of the small campfire had turned his face brown and shadowed. Suddenly he looked old to Dhal, old and tired.

"You said Screech was back?" Dhal asked, swinging down.

"Yes," Haradan answered, spotting him. "He outran the draak and left it wallowing in a mud bog over on the other side of the valley." He started back toward the others. "You were up there long enough."

"Yes."

"Yes?" Haradan knew something was wrong. "Did you see something up there, Dhal?"

"Yes."

"What?"

Ssaal-lr's ears pricked forward as Haradan and Dhal approached. He coughed a greeting to which Dhal replied, imitating the sound as best he could.

Poco smiled. "Thought we lost you up that tree," she said, eyes twinkling. "What did you do, take a nap when you reached the top?"

"No."

Poco's smile faded. Haradan caught his arm, turning him around. "What's wrong, Dhal? What did you see up there?"

"The men who were following us?" Poco asked, alarmed.

"No. It was something else."

"What?" Haradan demanded impatiently.

"Val-hrodhur—the ring world."

Haradan's hand shot to the pouch at his waist. "But I've got your ring!"

"I know. I didn't need it this time."

"I don't understand."

"Haradan, it's in the valley below us. I saw it from the top of the tree. It's the same building I saw before, the teaching center of Val-hrodhur."

"Are you sure?"

Dhal nodded.

"Perhaps it only looked like it, Dhal;" Poco offered.

"No, I don't think so. The building is very unusual. You'll understand when you see it."

For long moments they all just stared at each other. "When you told us about Val-hrodhur and the people who lived there, I got the impression that it was more than a small community of Ni," Haradan said finally. "Yet we've seen few signs of life and all of them old. Surely we would have come upon a few of your people by now if they were still living in the area."

"Not if they're in hiding," Poco said. "The Ni were hunted out of Sarissa territory years ago, Haradan. You couldn't blame them if they failed to greet wandering strangers with open arms."

Ssaal-lr asked a question. "Dhal tell us again about ring world Ni. Friends? Enemies?"

"Friends, I think," Dhal answered. "But after what happened to me the last time I saw them, I could be wrong."

Sitting down near the campfire, Dhal went over all that he could remember of the Ni-lach he had met in Val-hrodhur. By the time he had finished answering everyone's questions, full darkness was upon them and it was decided that they would leave the mystery of Val-hrodhur until morning. They kept a double watch that night.

Chapter 23

*D*HAL WOKE THE NEXT MORNING WITH A TINGLE OF UNEASINESS stirring in the back of his mind. He had thought about Valhrodhur and the Tamorlee long into the night. Torn between wanting to know more and wishing it all was a dream, he had gone over each of his brief journeys into the ring world, trying to piece the momentary fragments into a complete picture.

But there had been something missing, some piece of information that gnawed at the edge of his mind, some feeling of wrongness he could not interpret. Exhausted, he had finally fallen asleep, the mystery of the Tamorlee fading into dreams.

They shared a breakfast of dried soma bread, garval cheese, and hot herb tea. Speaking with his hands while he chewed on the hard bread, Ssaal-lr suggested that they split their forces. "Gi and Ssaal-lr go to valley, look for Ni-lach. Rest stay here."

"No, Screech," Dhal said. "If anyone goes to see what lies in the lower valley, it should be me."

"Not alone," Haradan and Poco said at the same time.

"I think it's best we all stay together," Haradan added. Poco nodded in agreement.

"All right," Dhal said. "Together, then."

Within minutes their things were gathered and packed. Ssaal-lr led off, Poco and Haradan right behind. Gi rode Dhal's shoulder, his soft, furry body brushing against Dhal's ear, his small hand twined in Dhal's hair to give him balance.

Efan followed last. Dhal had gone no more than several hundred paces when Gi turned and looked behind them. "Efan not coming," he whistled.

Dhal turned and saw that Efan stood in the shadow of the trees where they had camped. "Something wrong?" he called back.

After a moment's hesitation, Efan shook his head.

"Well, hurry up then," Dhal hollered. "This is draak territory and no place to find yourself alone."

Efan's head turned toward the open grassland to the east, then he started after them. Dhal waited. "Keep your eyes on him, Gi," he said softly. "See that we don't leave him behind."

"What wrong with Efan? Sad his face."

"I don't know, Gi. Just keep your eye out for him, all right?"

It took them over an hour to reach the lower valley and the ruins of the building he had seen while climbing the tree. "Well," Haradan asked, "is it the same one?"

They stood in front of the large doorway situated on the east side of the building. It was just as Dhal remembered it except for the vine and bush that had formed a woven barrier across the opening. Gone were the wooden doors that had barred the entrance. The vines did not reach the great triangular stone peaks that formed the support for the roof, so much of the top portion of the building was visible.

"Dhal?" Poco said softly.

Turning from the building, he let Gi down from his shoulder and looked south across the valley to the line of trees. They had followed a draak run through the woods that separated the upper valley from the lower. The wild tangle of vine and branches had proved that it had been a very long time since anyone had harvested firewood in either valley. This was not Val-hrodhur. It was empty of life and had been for many years.

"Dhal," Poco repeated, touching his arm. "Is this the place you saw in your dreams?"

He shook his head. "I don't know. The building looks the same except for the vines. But over there"—he pointed southwest toward the cliffs—"there should be a giant aban tree unlike anything you've ever seen before. I forgot about it last night."

"Dhal, has it occurred to you that the Ni-lach may have built more then one community such as Val-hrodhur? More than one building just like the one you see here?"

"It's possible, but—"

"But what?"

Dhal could not explain. This was not Val-hrodhur and yet . . . The uneasiness that had stalked him since waking coursed through his body in unseen tremors. He turned back to the building. "Let's try to get inside. I'd like to look around."

The building was empty, the roof caved in and rotted. Only the stone walls remained standing. Haradan and Dhal poked around inside the ruins, then they went back outside where Efan and Poco were sitting in the shade of some bushes.

"Find anything?" Poco asked.

"Nothing but rotting timbers," Haradan answered. "It's been abandoned a long time."

"How long?"

"Hard to tell, Poco. Judging from the timbers we found, I'd say fifteen to twenty years, maybe longer."

"About the time of the Sarissa war against the Ni?"

"Could be."

Dhal looked at Haradan. "You think the Sarissa came this far into the mountains after the Ni?"

Haradan shrugged. "I don't know. Efan, do you know anything about the Sarissa attacking the Ni-lach up here?"

Efan nodded. "Yes, a little. I was once told that over five hundred Sarissa marched into the mountains near the end of the war. Most of them never returned. The Ni turned out to be fierce fighters when cornered."

"I don't understand why the Sarissa would come all this way into the mountains," Dhal said.

"They believed there was a treasure hidden here," Efan explained. "Personally, I believe that's what started the war. Isn't that what starts most wars? One group wanting what another group has?" Efan's voice was tinged with disgust.

"You spoke about a treasure once before, Efan," Dhal said, squatting down so he was eye level with the boy. "Regent Lasca said something about it too. That was the first time I ever heard about the Tamorlee. Think back. Did your father ever say exactly what this treasure was supposed to be?"

"No."

"Did he ever say anything about the Tamorlee?"

Efan hesitated, then shook his head. "No, not that I remember."

Dhal looked at Efan a moment longer, then stood up. "I admit that this place looks something like the Val-hrodhur I visited, but it can't be. There are no people here and the building is in ruins and the—"

Suddenly his gaze fastened on the cliffs to the west. The sheer rock wall was vine-covered like everything else, but to the left and slightly above tree level the rock ledges were exposed.

"Dhalvad, is something wrong?" Haradan asked.

"There was a stairway clinging to the side of the cliff and above it a tunnel that led into a cave. I don't see it but—" He looked at Haradan.

Haradan understood. "Want to take a look?"

"Yes."

Dhal and Haradan set out for the cliff. After they had cut their way through the tangle of vine and bush at the base of the cliff, they searched for the place where the rock wall was broken by fissures.

Dhal was about ready to give up when Haradan found a piece of rock that was squared off on one edge sticking out of a loose pile of shale. Brushing the shale away, Haradan bent to take a closer look. When he stood up he was smiling. "It's a step, Dhal."

Dhal pulled back the vine that covered the wall. Haradan stepped up beside him to help. Within minutes they had cleared a small section of vine away and were peering up into semi-darkness where a network of vines formed a canopy over the crevice. Haradan brushed the rubble away to find two more steps.

The steps were so littered with dirt, rock, and old leaves that it was more a ramp than a stairway. Dhal felt his way up through the darkness, his hands sliding along the damp walls. Shortly, they reached the top of the crevice where they cut through the tangle of vines. Some of the vines were as thick as Dhal's wrist; cutting them was hard work. When they pulled the last vine down, light blazed through. Finally they climbed up through the last barrier and stood on a flat ledge of rock overlooking the valley. A sense of timelessness slipped over Dhal. How long had those vines been growing? How long since any Ni had passed that way?

He looked down onto the green valley below. Once that land had been home to Ni, then it belonged to gensvolf, draak, and feeder. Where the Ni-lach now? he wondered.

"Is it like you remember?" Haradan asked.

"Yes and no. The trees are different. And the building was in good condition." Dhal turned, trying to remember. "I was talking to Danner some of the time," he explained, "and I didn't pay attention to where he was leading me." He shook his head. "I remember the cave and this stairway and the building—but that's all."

"I've been thinking, Dhal. This place is old and long out of use. But if it once did belong to the Ni and they were chased away by the Sarissa, perhaps they moved to another place and rebuilt their home as they remembered it, naming it Val-hrodhur after their first home?"

Dhal nodded. "It would explain why everything is so familiar to me."

Haradan turned and looked back down the stairway. "You want to go back?"

"Not just yet. Let's see if there are any more steps. If the other Val-hrodhur is a duplicate of this place, there should be more stairs leading up to a cave entrance."

"All right, we can look, but watch your step. It looks as if there've been some recent rock slides."

Following the rock ledge around the side of the cliff, they located another flight of steps leading up to a small plateau. There they found the entrance to the cave. It had been partially obliterated by a rock slide, but after a little work removing stone, there was room enough for a man to crawl over the rubble and enter. But darkness confronted them from that point on, and Haradan would not allow Dhal to go any farther without some form of light.

Haradan led the way back down the cliffside. As they reached the bottom steps, Dhal turned. "We will go back later, won't we, Haradan?"

Haradan dropped an arm across his shoulders. "We'll go back. I know how you feel about this place. It's a link with your people. You know that I would be the very last to deny you that link, but I wasn't going to let you walk into that cave without a torch." Haradan grinned. "Not angry, are you?"

"No," Dhal answered. "Just impatient."

"Your impatience I can handle." He laughed, squeezing Dhal's shoulder. "Come on, let's find Poco and the others and tell them what we've found. After all you've told us about this Val-hrodhur, I don't think anyone will want to miss the expedition into the cave."

They left the cover of the trees and approached the building. But Poco and Efan were gone, their packs lying in a pile near the bushes.

"Poco!" Dhal called, raising his voice. "Efan! We're back!"

There was no answer. "I wonder where they disappeared to?"

Haradan continued on toward the packs. "Probably poking around in the building."

"Haradan, it's too quiet. Listen."

Haradan stopped and looked around, hearing the alarm in Dhal's voice.

Suddenly, Dhal saw movement out of the corner of his eye,

as two men emerged from the shadow of the bushes. Haradan saw the men at the same time. "Sarissa!" he yelled, lunging toward Dhal. "Run! Run!" As Haradan pushed Dhal, urging him back toward the shelter of the trees, four more men appeared from different directions.

Realizing that it was he they were after and not Haradan, Dhal turned back toward the trail he had just left, hoping to draw the men away from his friends. But as he raced to the edge of the clearing, three more men stepped into view, cutting him off. It was a trap—set and waiting—and Haradan and he had walked right into it.

Dodging back to the center of the clearing, Dhal drew his knife. Haradan was fighting with one man while another man lay on the ground clutching his stomach. Just as Dhal ran up, Haradan knocked down the second man. "Keep going," he hollered. "I'm right behind you!"

They ran around a large clump of bushes. Glancing behind, Dhal saw four men on their trail, one fast closing on Haradan. Suddenly he heard something ahead and two more men appeared. There was no way to avoid them. Dhal kept going, lifting his knife. One man ducked away, while the other man threw himself into Dhal's legs. As Dhal rolled over, the first man lunged, throwing himself on top of Dhal—and onto Dhal's knife. His scream shattered the air. Dhal kicked him away and looked for the other man.

But Haradan had already taken care of him. He pulled Dhal up. "Go!" he yelled. "Run!"

One glance downtrail told Dhal that it was hopeless; still, he tried. Turning, he ran upslope toward the first line of trees. He could hear Haradan right behind him.

But they could not outrun their pursuers. Dhal was caught from behind and thrown to the ground. The fingers of his knife hand were pried apart. With five men holding him down, he had no chance to fight back.

After a brief struggle, he gave up. He heard someone order the men to let him up. As he pushed to his hands and knees, he turned to look for Haradan, hoping he might have escaped. But Haradan was there. He lay face down on the ground, four men standing over him. One of the men leaned down and flipped him over.

Dhal's heart froze when he saw Haradan's head flop out of control. Then hands pulled him to his feet. He fought then, fear for Haradan blinding him to the futility of resistance.

Someone ordered the men to let go. Dhal ran to Haradan's side. Gently lifting Haradan's head, he saw the gash over the right temple, blood smeared across the forehead. But it was not the blood that made Dhal's heart drop—it was the emptiness in Haradan's eyes.

"No!" he cried softly. Quickly he felt for a pulse at Haradan's throat. The skin was warm and sweaty, but there was no throb of life there. Summoning his Ni-lach power, Dhal closed his eyes and concentrated, reaching into the body he held, searching for that spark of fire that is in all living things.

Time passed. Seconds? Minutes? Dhal never knew. When he opened his eyes and looked down, he knew Haradan was beyond his reach. Gently he placed trembling fingertips to Haradan's lips, remembering his smile. One moment alive, the next moment dead. It did not seem possible.

Suddenly he felt legs at his back. A hand grabbed his hair, pulling his head up, and something was forced into his mouth. Instinctively he swallowed. For a moment it felt as if liquid fire had been poured down his throat. Coughing and spitting up some of the burning liquid, he knocked the hide flagon away.

He was thrown forward onto his stomach. As his arms were drawn around behind him, someone gave orders. "Take him back to the ruins."

"What about the other one, sir?"

"He's dead. Leave him."

Numbed within and hardly aware of the rough hands that pulled at him, Dhal was jerked to his feet and dragged past Haradan's body. The next thing he knew he was being pushed to his knees. A hand slapped across his face. The sting of pain drove some of the numbness away.

He lifted his head and found a man sitting in front of him on a portable, three-legged stool. The shock of recognition sent tremors coursing through Dhal's body. He shook his head, unwilling to believe.

Then came that familiar voice. "I am no ghost, Green One," Saan Drambe said softly, "nor dead returned to life."

For a moment Dhal could not order his thoughts. Even the shock of Haradan's death was submerged by disbelief. "You—you were reported dead."

Saan Drambe nodded. "As was planned."

"Planned? Planned?" Dhal shook his head. "Why? What of your son? When he learned that you were dead he—"

"Efan is a very good actor," Saan Drambe said calmly, interrupting. "He is not my son."

Dhal's face must have betrayed his bewilderment because Saan Drambe grinned. "It would seem that the boy did better than I had hoped. He had us worried once or twice. I thought he was going to balk at leaving a trail after you healed him. That was beautifully done, by the way. You would never know he had had anything wrong with him."

Efan? While part of his mind said no, that Efan would not betray them, the other part remembered the boy's silences, the eyes that avoided contact. "How?" he asked, sick with the thought of Efan's betrayal.

"What?"

"How did you find us?"

Saan Drambe answered without hesitation. "Efan always had a flare for carving. You would be surprised at the amount of information that can be left on a single, unassuming stick. The boy grew lax the past three or four days though. We didn't find even one of his trail markers, but by that time your trail was pretty well established and we just followed the path of least resistance. That, plus a footprint here and there, was all that was necessary to find this place."

"What has happened to Pocalina-fel-Jamba?"

"We have her. She is quite safe—for the moment."

"Ssaal-lr and Gi?"

"If you're referring to the derkat, it hasn't seen. Nor has your little furred friend, but I assume that both will turn up eventually, if we haven't frightened them off for good.

Animals have an instinct for self-preservation. It wouldn't surprise me to learn that both have left the valley for safer territory. Don't look to them for help."

Dhal knew that Gi-arobi would not leave him voluntarily, nor would Ssaal-lr leave Poco. He looked around but did not see Efan. He turned back to Saan Drambe. "Why all of this? What purpose? What do you want?"

"What other purpose than gain, Green One? You are a part of the legend of the Tamorlee, a treasure that means power and vast riches to anyone wise enough to find it. Down through the years many have tried and failed, but then that only makes the hunt more interesting. As soon as I heard the rumor of a Ni living in the Deep, I spoke with Regent Lasca and convinced him that through you we might have a chance of locating the Tamorlee. He took a lot of convincing, but he's a man forever interested in power, and the thought of controlling even one of the mysterious forces the Ni were able to control was something he couldn't resist. I myself am more interested in the treasure of gemstones and Ni-lach art sure to be found within the Ni-lach sanctuary where the Tamorlee is said to be hidden."

Saan Drambe paused, then continued. "When we realized that we couldn't force you to reveal the location of the Tamorlee, we had to make other arrangements, which included your 'escape' and my 'death.' Once you were free, you behaved much as we had hoped you would. All we had to do was make sure you headed for the mountains."

"Who is Efan, if not your son?" Dhal asked, interrupting.

"Efan is my wife's only brother. My wife, by the way, is very much alive. She has always been more a mother to Efan than a sister. When I told her about the chance for Efan to obtain Ni-lach healing, she didn't question my motives, nor did the boy. They both went along with my plans and didn't think twice about betraying one of your race. I think Efan has found it hard to play the spy, though. He's not the type. I also believe he has some liking for you, but I'm sure that when he understands the riches to be won out of this expedition, his conscience will bother him no longer. But enough of that. Let's talk about the Tamorlee. It is here, isn't it? That's where you and Haradan went?"

At Haradan's name, a flood of anger swept through Dhal. Haradan—dead because of this man's greed! As Dhal knelt there before Saan Drambe, something within him died, an innocence, a trusting that had been nurtured by Haradan down through the years. And in the void that was left, hate was born, cold and hard, and with that hate came a flood of gensvolf cunning and the urge to retaliate, to kill.

"I'm waiting for an answer, Green One," Saan Drambe said. When Dhal failed to reply Saan Drambe took out his knife and with the point of the blade he forced Dhal's head back. "Somewhere it is said that the eyes are the silent messengers of the soul," he said softly. "I would see your eyes, Green One. Look at me!"

Suddenly Saan Drambe's smile faded. Dhal was not sure what the man saw in his eyes at that moment, but he knew what he felt—once his hands were free, Saan Drambe was a dead man.

Saan Drambe withdrew his knife and sat back. "No matter your feelings toward me, Green One," he said, forcing himself to keep eye contact. "It's time to cooperate. One has already died for you. Will you make it two?" He looked at one of his men. "Bring the woman."

Poco was led from the ruins of the building and made to sit at Saan Drambe's knee. Her hands were tied behind her back and she bore the signs of her struggle. "Dhal, are you all right?"

Saan Drambe's hand shot out, fastening in her hair. "Silence," he growled, jerking her head back until Dhal thought her neck would break. "You will not speak to each other!"

Where once Dhal would have lunged to Poco's defense, he now sat still, knowing there was nothing he could do to help her at that moment. Saan Drambe's knife was at her throat a second later. Had Dhal tried anything, Poco would have died.

"Perhaps you don't love her after all," Saan Drambe said softly, pulling his knife back slightly. Dhal watched a trickle of blood roll down Poco's neck. "Talk to me, Green One, or watch the Singer die in front of you."

Dhal looked into Poco's eyes. There was no silent appeal there, only acceptance. Poco trusted him with her life. "Release her," he said. "Then I'll tell you what you want to know."

"You will tell me what I want to know *now*, and I will keep the woman to ensure your continued cooperation. Now, where is the Tamorlee?"

Dhal hesitated a moment. "We didn't find it."

"But you were looking for it," Saan Drambe pressed. "Here, somewhere."

"Yes."

"Tell me what you did find."

"A stone stairway leading to a cave."

"And inside this cave?"

"I don't know. It was too dark to see inside. Haradan and I came back for torches."

"How far to this cave?"

"Twenty minutes."

"Good. It's early yet and we have time to take a look. The girl will stay here. If something happens to me and I don't return, I'm leaving orders that she is to be killed. Is that understood?"

Five minutes later Cerl sar Drambe and Dhal, accompanied by six guards, left the ruins and headed for the cliff stairway. It was almost seven hours before they returned, empty-handed and minus two men. Saan Drambe was not happy.

After entering the cave, they had discovered their way blocked by another wall of loose rock. It looked as if someone had tried to seal the entrance. Saan Drambe put everyone to work removing rubble while he stood and watched from the side, giving directions.

It took them three hours to break through. Once on the other side of the cave-in, Dhal's hands were retied and he was forced to sit with two of the men while Saan Drambe and the rest waded out into the darkness of the cavern, searching for the fabled Tamorlee.

In his mind's eye, Dhal could remember the huge cavern he had seen before. Instead of the darkness, there should have been a glow of green light. Though he could not see, he could sense the emptiness beyond the small circle of light.

Three hours later there came a call to return to the cave entrance. All but two of the searchers returned.

"We'll have to look for the missing men tomorrow," Saan Drambe had growled, tossing the stub of his torch over the cliff. "They're probably lost in those damn tunnels."

Chapter 24

DHAL WOKE TO WHISPERED VOICES. "KNOWING WHAT HE IS, what he represents, how could you betray him?" Dhal recognized Poco's voice. By rolling his head to the side he could see her. She was propped up on her elbows, her body still encased in her blanket. She was talking to Efan. Dhal was surprised to find the boy so close, for the night before Saan Drambe had ordered him to stay away from them.

It was early morning. There was a green mist filtering up through the branches of the trees. The smell of woodsmoke told Dhal that someone was starting breakfast. He could hear several men talking over to his left.

"Answer me, Efan," Poco prodded.

Efan was kneeling, his back to Dhal. For long moments he said nothing, then he spoke, his words barely audible. "I wanted to walk again."

"And now you *do* walk, because of *him*," Poco hissed softly. "How does that excuse your betrayal?"

"Saan Drambe says that the Ni-lach are our enemies. I—I didn't know that—"

"Efan!" Saan Drambe appeared, crossing the tree-shrouded campsite in long, swift strides. The boy stood up quickly, his eyes round in fear. "What did I tell you last night?" Saan Drambe hollered. Grabbing the boy by the arm, he flung him away. "Go on, go help Seen with the fire—and stay away from the prisoners!"

As Efan scurried away, Saan Drambe came over and looked down at Dhal. "What were you saying to him?"

"He wasn't talking to Efan," Poco said. "I was."

"Talking about what?" he snapped, turning on the girl.

"About traitors!"

"Traitor he is, girl, but he is *my* traitor and I won't have you trying to convert him. So keep your mouth closed"—he paused and looked at Dhal—"both of you, or I'll have your tongues out! Is that clear?"

"We understand," Dhal answered.

Saan Drambe looked at him a moment longer, then signaled two of his men. "Untie them and feed them, then detail two of the men to stay in camp to keep an eye on things."

"Only two, Saan?"

"Yes, we're going to need the rest to search the cavern. It's big and there are tunnels all over the place."

The other man looked down at Dhal. "Can't you make him tell you where the treasure is?"

"To be truthful, I don't believe he knows. According to Efan, the Green One has only seen this Tamorlee in his dreams."

"He's never been here before?"

"So he claims."

"How did he find this place then?"

"How do the Ni-lach do anything, Vetch? That may be one of the things we learn when we locate this Tamorlee."

After Saan Drambe left, Poco and Dhal were untied. While Vetch left to get them something to eat, Poco leaned over, ignoring the other guard, and kissed Dhal on the lips. "Something I've been thinking about," she answered, drawing back.

"Thought I might not have another chance." Tears began to well in her eyes.

When he saw the tears spill over, Dhal drew her close and held her, thankful that the guard did not interfere. "You haven't forgotten Ssaal-lr, have you? Or Gi?" he asked softly.

"You think they can help us?"

"They'll try, you know they will."

"But against so many."

"Still they'll try, and we must be ready when they do. Understand?"

Poco nodded. "Dhal—I'm sorry about Haradan. He—he was so good to me. If only—"

"I know. I know. Please, don't talk about it right now."

A few minutes later Poco moved in his arms. "Dhal," she whispered. "You said that you didn't find anything in the cave yesterday. Do you think there is anything to find?"

"I don't know, Poco. It looks so much like the Val-hrodhur I visited, but it couldn't be the same place. The stairway, the cave, the building, none of it has been used for years."

"Or made to look that way."

"Yes," he said thoughtfully. "But if it's only made to look that way, why do I feel such emptiness here?"

"Dhal, about Efan—"

"What about him?" he asked, trying to keep the anger from his voice.

"I think he regrets what he did."

"Regret isn't going to help us, nor will finding the treasure—even if there happens to be one."

"You think Saan Drambe means to kill us, no matter what?"

"Yes, and if Efan isn't careful he may just find himself included on the list. A man like Cerl sar Drambe uses others, then, when they are no longer useful, he gets rid of them. The dead don't talk or demand rewards for their service."

After three days of searching the cavern tunnels, Saan Drambe's men had found nothing, and many were ready to give up. They had been twenty, now they were fourteen. One man Dhal had killed the day of the chase; two men had been lost in the tunnels; two had disappeared from camp; and the sixth man had died in a fall off the cliff when a slab of rock had given way beneath him.

After losing two men from camp, Saan Drambe had ordered all of the packs and equipment brought up into the cavern where they could be guarded more closely. He kept Efan with him at all times, as if he did not trust the boy.

Poco nudged Dhal with the toe of her draak-hide shoe. He caught her eye as she nodded toward the two guards. One had fallen asleep and the other was engrossed in a game of One Man, the soft slap of one card atop another running competition with the crackle of the fire.

Softly Poco spoke to Dhal. "Do you think Screech is responsible for the missing men?"

"The two camp guards, yes," he whispered back.

"Will he be able to find us here?"

"Gi will find me. Screech will follow."

"How soon?"

The card-playing guard looked up for a moment, then returned to his game.

Relieved to have escaped his notice, Dhal turned and saw a strange look cross Poco's face. Her eyes were wide in surprise, then suddenly she smiled. She started to turn her head to the side, then stopped herself. She looked at Dhal and mouthed a few words, but he did not understand.

Suddenly something moved near her shoulder. A small, furred head appeared, two large, golden eyes glinting in the firelight. Gi!

Dhal peered into the darkness beyond the firelight, searching for darker shadows in the gloom, but there was no sign of Ssaal-lr.

Poco was sitting up straight now, giving Gi room to move around behind her. Dhal was not sure Gi's small fingers would be strong enough to untie the cording that the guards had used, but what he could not accomplish with his fingers, he could finish with his teeth.

Five minutes passed. Suddenly Poco's arms moved outward slightly. She nodded. Her hands were free. Now her feet.

Readjusting her position without moving her arms, she brought her legs around to the right. A moment later Dhal saw Gi lying next to her legs, working on the rope at her ankles.

He looked away, afraid of drawing attention to Gi and Poco by staring. He watched the guard play his cards. At the same time he kept his eyes on the cavern darkness beyond. Where are you, Screech? he thought.

Then he noticed the twin flares of light that appeared on the other side of the cavern. Dhal glanced at Poco. Was she free? Her eyes were on the approaching Sarissa.

The man who was playing cards looked up, then quickly turned and hissed at his friend. The second man woke and by the time the others arrived, he was up and adding sticks to the fire. Two of the four who came carried torches. One of them addressed the guards. "Everything all right here?"

"Tomb quiet," the card player replied. "Find anything yet?"

"Yes, that's why we came back. Saan Drambe wants us to bring the Ni to a chamber we've found. There's something carved on the floor. He thinks the Green One can decipher it."

"Can doesn't mean will," the card player said, glancing at Dhal.

"He'll do it if he wants to live," the other replied, moving over to Dhal. "Come on, Green One, you're wanted."

As the man bent to untie the ropes at Dhal's ankles, Dhal cast a quick glance at Poco. He did not see Gi-arobi. Dhal's heartbeat quickened as the card player started toward Poco. "Want the woman too?"

"No, just the Ni." Dhal was hauled to his feet.

"How long will you be gone?"

"Depends on *him*," the man replied, nodding at Dhal.

The guards took Dhal's arms and steered him across the cavern floor. He wanted to look back but did not, fearing any show of concern for Poco might alert the guard and cause him to check her bonds.

As they entered the tunnel beyond the cavern, Dhal consoled himself with the knowledge that Poco would not do anything foolish. She was free, but she was wise enough to play the docile prisoner until Ssaal-lr made his move. The derkat was out there in the cavern somewhere—he had to be. Save her, Screech, Dhal thought silently. She's your responsibility now.

They turned into another tunnel, and Dhal was filled with a heavy foreboding, a feeling that he would never again see his friends. Death thought? If true, he thought, then let it be my death, not theirs.

Dhal recognized the chamber as soon as they entered. There were the large columns, the intricately laid stone floor, and the carved circle. Above he saw the oval opening wherein the Tamorlee should have rested. Knowing that no two places could possibly be so much alike, he felt a chill sweep through him. This *was* Val-hrodhur! There was no mistake. But where was the Tamorlee? Where the Ni-lach? Had his earlier visits somehow warned them of the coming invasion into their home? How long had it taken them to move the Tamorlee, to make everything look so long abandoned?

Suddenly his thoughts turned to Saan Drambe's missing men. Perhaps Ssaal-lr was not responsible for their disappearance. But if the Ni-lach were there somewhere, why were they still hiding? Surely they must outnumber the Sarissa.

"Bring him over here," Saan Drambe ordered, motioning with his hand.

As Dhal was pushed forward, he saw Efan standing behind Saan Drambe. For a moment their eyes met. Traitor, Dhal thought silently, because of you Haradan is dead!

He looked around at the faces of the Sarissa. Not counting Efan or Saan Drambe, they were six. Two were guarding Poco, so five men were unaccounted for. Probably still searching other tunnels, Dhal thought as he was brought to the edge of the stone relief.

"Tell us what this is," Saan Drambe said, pointing down at the stone.

Dhal kept his eyes on Saan Drambe as he answered. "It is what you see—a stone carving."

"You are in no position to play games, Green One. Tell me what the symbols mean!"

The grip on Dhal's arms tightened. "Answer!" the man to his right growled softly.

Dhal shook his head. "I don't know what they mean."

The grip on his arms became painful. Something hit the back of his legs, throwing him forward onto his knees. Dhal felt an arm wrap around his neck. The sudden pressure at his throat made it impossible to breathe. He clawed at the arm but could not break free.

Dhal gasped for air. He was close to losing consciousness when Saan Drambe ordered him released. "The symbols, Green One," Saan Drambe pressed. "Tell me what they mean."

Breathing deeply, Dhal doubled over, his hands coming to rest on the stone circle. Realizing that Saan Drambe would not accept the truth, he lied, interpreting the symbols in his own way. "The circle means life. The suns represent growth and harmony."

"And those lines near your hand?" Saan Drambe demanded.

"Water and flame, symbols of power. The others, those around the inner circle are swords, death omen to any who stand against the Ni-lach."

"And the hand in the center? What does that mean?"

Dhal knew that in the ring world the touching of a real hand to the stone had caused some link with the Tamorlee, but here there was no Tamorlee. Saan Drambe was waiting for an answer. Dhal said the first thing that came to mind. "This is a prayer circle. When one comes here to pray, he sits within the pattern and places his hand so." Reaching out, he started to set his hand in the stone depression.

"Stop him!" Saan Drambe snapped.

Hands grabbed Dhal, pulling him away from the stone circle. "I don't trust you, Green One," Saan Drambe said, moving into the circle. "Efan, come here. Put your hand on the stone. Let's see if anything happens."

"Please, Saan, I don't want to—"

"Get over here! Now!"

The boy slunk to the center of the stone pattern and knelt, his fear of Saan Drambe outweighing his fear of the unknown. Dhal began to understand the power of Saan Drambe's hold over the boy and he wondered what the man had done to Efan to make him so afraid.

Gingerly Efan placed his hand on top of the stone hand. Seconds passed. The chamber was silent but for the sound of breathing. When nothing happened, Saan Drambe snapped at the boy. "Well, do you feel anything?"

"No," Efan answered without looking up.

Saan Drambe looked at Dhal. "Finish what you were going to say."

"Here it is quiet," Dhal said. "The touch of cool stone helps one concentrate."

"Why do I feel that you are lying, Green One?" Saan Drambe nodded to the two men who held Dhal. "Take him back to the cavern. There is no more to be learned here."

The guards' fire should have been visible from the tunnel exit, but the cavern was dark except for the torches carried by Saan Drambe's men. As they crossed the cavern floor, Dhal heard Saan Drambe grumble. "Damn fools, if they're asleep, I'll have their hearts!"

"We haven't been gone that long, Saan," another man said. "It's been no longer than twenty minutes."

"Are you saying you think something is wrong, Dafon?"

"It could be a trap, Saan. We've lost six men already. I would recommend that we approach carefully." At Dafon's words, the pace slowed. Dhal heard the sound of blades being drawn and saw the flicker of light on metal.

"Anyone see the fire?" one of the men asked.

"Should be straight ahead," Dafon answered. "I smell smoke."

The smell became more pungent as they neared the other side of the cavern. It was overlaid by another odor, the stink of burned flesh. Praying it was foe and not friend who had fallen into the fire, Dhal watched as Cerl sar Drambe waved two of the men ahead. Each with a torch in one hand, and a sword in the other, the two Sarissa guards moved forward, stalking the camp.

Saan Drambe turned and looked at the rest of his men. "We'll follow them. Keep your eyes open."

The grip on Dhal's arm tightened as they continued on toward the camp. When they were within a hundred running paces of the camp, the two advance guards raised their torches and beckoned them in. Hurrying, Saan Drambe barked at his men to follow.

The camp was empty, the guards and prisoner gone. The fire had been deliberately doused with water. There were signs of a struggle, packs and blankets thrown about and the extra firewood scattered.

"Something here, Saan," one of the men said, putting his torch down to the cavern floor.

Saan Drambe knelt before a large, dark puddle a step or two away from the still-smoldering fire. He dipped his finger-tips into the wetness, then brought his hand toward the torch-light. The wetness was dark in color. Saan Drambe sniffed at his fingers, then slowly rose. "Blood," he said softly.

For several moments Cerl sar Drambe stood looking down at his hand, then suddenly he whirled around and struck out. Dhal never saw the fist that sent him to the cavern floor. The guard to his right fell with him.

Before Dhal knew what was happening, he felt Saan Drambe land on top of him, crushing Dhal's arms, which were caught behind him.

Saan Drambe's hand closed round his throat. "You!" he roared. "This is your doing! They're out there, aren't they? The Ni-lach! They're hiding—waiting for us! They've taken my men and killed them!" Voice rising to scream pitch, Saan Drambe drew his knife. "Green slime! We were right to slaughter your kind!"

Suddenly Efan was there, grabbing at Saan Drambe's arm and pulling it back. "No!" he yelled. "You promised you wouldn't kill him!"

"Get him away from me!" Saan Drambe bellowed.

"Someone, help me!" Efan cried. "Stop him! No! No, let me go!" The boy struggled.

As several of the guards pulled Efan back, the hand at Dhal's throat loosened. Then he saw the knife. It arced up and out, then Saan Drambe drove it into Dhal's side. A triumphant laugh overtopped his cry.

While part of Dhal's body cringed from the pain, that part

of him that was Healer rose quickly to the surface, muffling the pain and seeking out the wound.

A hand smashed across his mouth. "Feel it, Green One! You can't heal yourself as fast as I can cut you apart! Don't even try!" The hand slapped across his face again and again, breaking his concentration. Then Saan Drambe gripped his knife and turned it in the wound.

The shock of pain was so great that Dhal could not even scream. Saan Drambe laughed aloud and turned the knife again. Gasping for breath, Dhal tried to pull away from the pain but the knife stayed buried in his side.

Pain . . . no. Must concentrate. Breathe . . . shallow . . . pain . . . no . . . concentrate. Cutting the mind from the body was no simple task. Dhal tried—and failed. The pain was too great. The knife was pulled free, then he felt the warm gush of blood wetting his tunic and side.

An open hand smashed across his face again. "Open your eyes, damn you! Death awaits! Look at it!" The knife was held before his eyes, then against his lips. "Taste it! We may not make it out of here alive, but neither shall you! You can keep your damned Tamorlee! I am beginning to doubt it ever existed! I was a fool to even consider it! But I am a fool no longer. You are—"

"Saan!" a guard cried. "Someone's coming. I think it's one of our men!"

Dhal saw the flicker of indecision on Saan Drambe's face. Then, as if coming out of a dream, Saan Drambe lifted his head. "Is it one of ours?"

"Yes, Saan."

The runner arrived a few seconds later, babbling in excitement. They had found the Tamorlee! Everyone started talking at once.

Dhal felt Saan Drambe's weight lift from his body and he knew that he had been forgotten in all the excitement. Ignoring the voices above him, he closed his eyes and turned his thoughts inward, summoning his diminished reserves of energy to heal the still-bleeding wound in his side. He willed the severed blood vessels to touch and reseal themselves, then began work on the torn tissue and muscle. One by one, he repaired the slashed muscles until at last he reached the outer layers of skin. By the time he had sealed the last layer of flesh, he was shuddering with exhaustion.

Carefully he drew in a deep breath. The pain was gone; the healing was complete. He opened his eyes and was surprised to find Saan Drambe still talking with the guard who had announced the finding of the Tamorlee. It seemed as if no time had elapsed since he had gone into his healing trance.

Rolling his head to the side, Dhal saw Efan still in the hands of the guards. The tears on the boy's face glinted gold in the torchlight. For a moment he and Dhal just stared at each other. Efan's shoulders sagged, then fresh tears came. Silently they spilled down his face. For me? Dhal wondered.

Saan Drambe's voice rose slightly, the bark of command returned. "Get everything together, packs, food, weapons. I'll leave no one behind this time."

"Saan," one of the men said. "What about the Ni?"

Saan Drambe turned and looked down at Dhal. After a moment's deliberation, he motioned to two of his men. "Get him up. We'll take him with us. If we run into any more traps, he'll make an excellent shield."

"He won't last very long bleeding like he is," one of the men said, indicating the blood that had saturated Dhal's tunic.

"You worry too much, Dafon," Saan Drambe said. "Lift up his tunic."

Dafon did as ordered, bringing his torch close to better inspect the wound. He wiped the blood away. When he failed to find a gaping wound, his eyes grew round with disbelief. Hastily he withdrew his hand and rose. "There is no wound, Saan, just blood."

"I told you he was a Healer. But it seems no one was listening. You don't kill his kind unless you sever the head from the body." Saan Drambe looked down and added, "Which we can always do later—after we have located the Tamorlee."

Chapter 25

WEAK FROM THE LOSS OF BLOOD, DHAL FELL AGAIN. THIS TIME he almost passed out. Impatient, Saan Drambe ordered that he be carried and the task fell to Dafon, the large, broad-shouldered man who had questioned Dhal's healing powers.

There was no comfort in being carried stomach down, but Dhal could not complain. He still had his life and a chance to keep it, if Ssaal-lr, Poco, and Gi could follow the Sarissa. Though the thought of a Ni-lach treasure stirred Dhal's curiosity, he would have gladly traded the privilege of being in on the find for his freedom and a half-hour's head start out of the valley.

The men were silent as they moved down through the tunnels. The man who led the way counted the offshoot tunnels aloud, his voice echoing eerily down the long-abandoned passages. After passing through a series of winding stone corridors, they reached a stairway leading down. Here the company stopped.

"How much farther, Maur?" Saan Drambe asked the lead man.

"About four minutes, Saan. At the bottom of the stairs there are three tunnels. All of them lead to water, two to the lake south of the ruins and the third to the left and to an underground river that must feed into the lake eventually. It looks like the Ni used the river for transport. We did find part of a rotted boat and some old bones."

"Bones?" Saan Drambe said quickly. "Animal?"

"Man—or Ni. It's impossible to tell."

"What about the Tamorlee?"

"It's on the other side of the cavern, across the river. There are a pair of statues guarding a hollowed-out chamber a couple of steps up from river level."

"Show us the way," Saan Drambe said impatiently.

Dafon readjusted his hold on Dhal's back as they descended the stairway. Dhal was forced to turn his face into Dafon's back else risk having his head knocked against the rock walls as the stairs turned in upon themselves. Suddenly he felt a hand on the back of his head. The hand stayed there until they reached the bottom of the stairs. As Dafon followed the others into the left tunnel, Dhal looked up and found Efan walking behind Dafon. The boy looked as if he wanted to say something, but the darkness of the tunnel fell between them once more and Dhal could no longer see the boy's face.

Traitor? Dhal thought. Or friend still? Or only a youngling lost in the world of adults? As he watched Efan's shadowy form march along behind Dafon, he came to understand a truth about men, about their vulnerability and their fears. Like the many facets of a fire stone, each man had many faces, both dark sides and light, and from moment to moment the spirit force could change. Efan had been a stranger, then a friend, then a traitor. What was he now?

The air became cool and damp, the footing treacherous with slime. Twice Dafon slipped but caught himself. Dhal heard the squishing sound of water beneath the men's boots and realized that at certain times the tunnel they walked was probably under water.

The tunnel ended abruptly, opening out into the river cavern described by Maur. Saan Drambe and some of his men went straight to the river's edge.

"Varga!" Saan Drambe yelled across the river to the man who had gone ahead. "Varga, what have you found?"

As the last of the echoes died away, Varga appeared on a ledge overhanging the river. "Come see for yourself, Saan," Varga cried gleefully. "You won't believe it! There are thirteen wooden chests back here, all of them filled with Ni-lach jewelry and carvings the likes of which you've never seen! It looks as if they might have been trying to take it out with them when they left!"

"Don't touch anything, Varga," Saan Drambe yelled back. "We're coming over."

Leaving Dafon, Efan, Dhal, and two others on the near side of the river, Saan Drambe and the other men stripped to their breeches and waded into the water, three of the men carrying torches. Several of the men swore at the ice-cold water.

Dafon let Dhal down from his shoulder and ordered him to sit quietly. Efan stayed close, his face turned to the river. Silently they watched Saan Drambe and his men reach the other side and pull themselves up onto the rock shelf below the inner cavern.

Dafon ordered the two guards with him to scout along the water's edge. "The river runs in that direction," he said, pointing to the right. "Follow it and see if there's anything we could use to build some kind of a bridge. I think we're going to need it."

The two men quickly disappeared around a bend of rock. For a minute or so Dhal could see the reflection of their torches on the water, then that too disappeared. Across the river he could hear voices and see the shadowy figures of Saan Drambe and his men.

Minutes passed. Sitting there on the wet dirt, Dhal felt coldness creep into his body, followed by a strange lulling of the senses. The cavern took on a dreamlike quality. He was a watcher, seeing but not feeling, aware yet half asleep. The loss of blood had weakened him more than he realized.

"Wish they'd hurry," Efan said, taking a step or two toward the water's edge.

Suddenly they heard a terrified scream. As the echo bounced off the cavern walls, a cry for help came from downstream where Dafon's two men had disappeared. Dafon grabbed the torch from Efan and started running down along the riverbank, leaving Efan and Dhal alone in the darkness.

"Dhalvad?" Efan's voice quavered.

"I'm here." Dhal could just make out Efan's form against the faint glow from the torches on the other side of the river. He reached up to meet the boy's questing hand. "Help me up," he said.

Cerl sar Drambe's voice came from across the river. "What's going on over there? Dafon, where are your lights?"

Dhal felt the boy draw breath to answer and squeezed down hard on his shoulder. "No," he said softly.

"Answer me!" Saan Drambe hollered, raising his torch high overhead, as if to throw light over on their side. Other torches appeared along the river shelf.

The cavern was silent. The only sound Dhal could hear was the soft gurgle of water as it rose from some underground source. He listened for voices downstream but it was as quiet as it was dark. He did not know what had happened to Dafon and the other two men, but he was not going to wait around to find out. Already Saan Drambe had ordered two of the men into the water to see what was wrong.

Dhal's legs were shaky and the wet moss was slippery beneath his feet. Slowly he began to back away from the water's edge, pulling on Efan's shoulder, silently inviting him to come along. The boy came.

But they had gone no more than ten steps when Efan stopped. "Dhalvad, look!"

They both stared at the river. The swimmers' torchlight reflected across the water and showed a strange roiling movement behind the men, who seemed unaware of the change. Dhal thought it looked like some kind of a whirlpool, then suddenly a great shadowy form rose out of the water.

"Look out!" Efan cried, running forward. "Behind you!"

It was a water draak, not as large as the one they had seen in Sar-ruel, but still dangerous. As they watched, the draak's head dipped down toward one of the men in the water.

Lunging forward, Dhal grabbed Efan's arm. "There's nothing you can do, Efan. Come on, let's get out of here!"

A second later one of the men in the water was gone when a single snap of the draak's jaws severed head from body. The other man was swimming madly for the riverbank, his torch gone. Dhal and Efan could hear his sobbing gasps.

At the call for help, Efan shook free of Dhal's hand and ran toward the water's edge. A wedge of darkness overshadowed them both, then there was a great splash. Dhal heard a single scream, then a wave of water washed up over the riverbank, knocking him from his feet.

Dhal rolled over in the darkness, then somehow he was on his hands and knees, water swirling around him. Someone got a hold on his tunic and pulled him up. He felt the bite of sharp claws. He slipped again, then strong furred arms caught him up and carried him away from the water's edge.

"Screech," he cried. "Efan! Find Efan!"

A few more steps brought them to the safety of the tunnel, then the arms relaxed and lowered Dhal to the ground. Ssaal-lr turned and went back to the underground river as other hands reached for Dhal.

"It's Poco, Dhal. Are you all right?" She patted him anxiously, looking for injuries.

"Gi here too, Dhal," the olvaar whistled.

The roaring hiss of an aroused draak echoed through the cavern. The water creature had turned its anger on the flickering lights and shadow forms on the other side of the river. The battle lasted only a few minutes.

All torchlight was gone. Poco, Gi, and Dhal sat quietly in the darkness listening to the water draak make a meal of its victims. Dhal felt Poco shiver against him and pulled her close. Minutes passed. Dhal grew worried about Ssaal-lr and Efan. Had the derkat found the boy?

At last, with a snuffle of air the draak slipped below the

surface of the water. They waited in silence. "Think it's gone?" Poco asked softly.

"I think so."

"What called it?" she asked, keeping her voice whisper soft.

Called? Had the Ni-lach left a guardian for their treasure? Or was it only the voices and the lights that had roused it from the depths of the river?

A soft coughing sound broke into his thoughts. "We're here, Screech," Poco replied.

"Efan? Did you find the boy, Screech?" Dhal asked.

He felt Ssaal-lr's warm breath on his face, then furred hands touched his head, gently moving it back and forth. Efan was gone. Dhal's last feelings of anger toward the boy dissolved as he realized that Efan had died trying to warn others of their danger. No matter that they were Dhal's enemies.

"Efan's gone," he told Poco.

"I had a feeling," she said. "Come, let's go. We left several torches back on the stairs. They should be enough to light our way out of here. If not, Ssaal-lr can lead us. His eyes are better in the dark than ours."

Chapter 26

*S*ITTING ON A KNOLL TO THE EAST OF THE RUINS, DHAL LOOKED downvalley, his thoughts on the treasure Saan Drambe and the others had died finding. It had taken Ssaal-lr five days to find another tunnel leading to the other side of the underground river, days that Dhal had spent sleeping and eating, trying to regain his strength.

Poco, Gi, Dhal, and Ssaal-lr had slipped quietly into the cavern one night, to sort through the wooden chests. Just as Varga had said, the treasure consisted of Ni-lach jewelry and intricate wooden carvings. Poco chose for herself a pendant carved in the form of a seven-pointed star. While the others picked and chose things they would like, Dhal searched through the jewelry. None of the gemstones inset in the rings and headbands were shards of the Tamorlee, and of the Tamorlee itself there was no sign.

Where is it? he wondered. What had happened to the great crystalline lifeform and the people who had guarded it? Questions, always questions, but never any answers.

Dhal watched Poco emerge from the trees and cross the open ground in front of the abandoned training center. Stopping at the main doors, she poked her head inside. He knew she was looking for him and called to her.

She saw him and started up the rise, her movements sure and graceful. Dhal nudged the furry bundle in his lap. "Wake up, Gi. Company coming." The olvaar rolled over and looked up at him, golden eyes heavy with sleep. Around his neck Gi wore a golden chain with a small pendant dangling free, the only thing he had taken from the wooden chests. Dhal had a feeling that the olvaar's interest in the chain was only momentary; the olvaar were not collectors of anything but stories.

Breathing easily, Poco dropped down in front of him. "I wondered where you two went. I came to tell you that Ssaal-lr saw two of Drambe's men leaving the valley headed south toward the pass."

"When?"

"Just a little while ago."

"What did they look like?"

"One was a big man with heavy shoulders."

"Dafon," he said softly.

"What?"

"I think his name is Dafon. He must have found another way out of the cavern with one of his men."

"Screech didn't get a good look at the other one, but the man was hurt. Screech wanted to go after them but I told him no. I don't think they'll make it back alone."

Dhal thought about the men and the path that lay ahead of them. Though it would be a long and lonely trek back to Port Bhalvar, the Sarissa had proved to be resourceful in escaping the cavern alive. "They might make it," he said. "I don't think I would bet against them."

"You want me to send Screech to stop them?"

"No."

"But what if they live to return to Port Bhalvar? Won't they bring others back here?"

"If the Sarissa come, they come, Poco. It doesn't matter any longer. The Ni-lach might have ruled here once, but no more. All this"—he waved his hand toward the valley—"belongs to draak and gensvolf now. Let them keep it."

"What about the rest of the treasure?"

"We have all we can carry. Let the draak guard the rest. It will be as safe with him as it would be if we tried to hide it."

Poco nodded in agreement. "Well then, I've got everything packed so we're about ready to leave. Do you want to start this afternoon or wait until tomorrow morning?"

Dhal looked down at the ring on his finger. When Ssaal-lr and Gi had buried Haradan, Gi had salvaged the leather pouch at Haradan's belt. Inside the pouch Dhal had found the fire stone that had introduced him to the Tamorlee and the ring world. Not one other fire stone had they found in the treasure chests.

Poco reached out and placed her hand over his. "Dhal, is something wrong?"

He shook his head. "No, I've just been thinking." Though none of them had been overly talkative in the days following their escape from Saan Drambe, they had made plans for their departure. Their destination was to be Janchee and then Port Sulta. But now Dhal was not so sure that that was where he wanted to go.

"Thinking about what?" Poco prompted after a long silence.

"About Val-hrodhur." Dhal took a deep breath and looked Poco straight in the eyes. "I have to go back."

"Why?"

"I have to know where it is and what happened here. I have to know if Val-hrodhur has been created more than once. It might give me a clue as to where the Ni-lach have gone and how we can find them."

"What if you meet Danner or l'Tamorlee again and they won't let you go this time?"

"I have to go, Poco, even if I risk capture. I must know what has happened to the Ni-lach. I must learn the truth for both of us."

"Dhal strong enough to use ring now?" Gi whistled.

"I'm strong enough, Gi, and I thank you for your concern."

"I wish one of us could go with you," Poco said softly.

"No, it's something I must do alone. Will you wait for me to return?"

"You know we will. How long will you be gone?"

"I don't know. An hour, a day, perhaps longer." Dhal picked Gi up and handed him over to Poco. "But if anything should go wrong, wait no longer than a week, then start for Janchee. If and when I can, I'll follow."

Holding Gi in her arms, Poco shook her head. "We won't leave without you, Dhal. We'll wait, won't we, Gi?"

"Gi waits, yes."

Dhal knew where he wanted to go this time. Gazing into the fire stone, he willed the swirling colors to form a picture of the Tamorlee, the glowing crystal that rested in the cavern. He was not aware of the movement or shift from world to world—all he noticed was a sudden stillness in the air, warmth replacing cold.

One moment he was sitting with Gi and Poco on a hill overlooking the abandoned training center, the next moment he was sitting within five or six paces of the Tamorlee. For long moments he just sat and stared, then he stood up and approached the crystal. Reaching out, he laid his ring hand against the surface of the stone. It was cool to the touch, smooth and hard.

He heard footsteps and turned. Two Ni-lach stood there, one female, one male. Both looked a little nervous. The female spoke. "Seeker, we were told to watch for you. You are Dhalvad sar Haradan?"

He hesitated, then nodded.

"L'Tamorlee waits for you. He hoped you would return. Will you come with us, please?" When he did not respond, she held out her hand. "Don't be afraid. Come, take my hand. I promise, you shall not be harmed this time."

Slowly Dhal proffered his hand. As they moved away from the crystal, the male came up on his free side and startled him by taking his other hand.

Instantly Dhal pulled it away, reading entrapment in the male's action. The female stepped forward. "Meer, let me take our guest to the sun chamber," she suggested softly. "You go and tell l'Tamorlee that the Seeker has arrived."

Meer looked at Dhal, then nodded. Turning, he trotted off toward the cave exit and the stairway leading down and outside. Following the gentle pull on his hand, Dhal allowed himself to be led from the cavern down to the sun chamber, the same place where he had laid hand to the stone relief and had locked into the crystalline lifeform called Tamorlee.

He stared down at the carved lines in the stone, remembering the strange warmth that had reached out and touched him, the pressure within his mind, as if something was trying to get inside his thoughts, and the pain as he fought against that intrusion. Here is the place for answers, he thought silently, and this time I won't run away before I know the truth.

He turned to the Ni standing beside him. Her green hair, caught into a single braid over her right shoulder, was streaked with glints of silver. She was older than he had first thought. Her gray eyes regarded him calmly. If she had been afraid of him, she was no longer. "What is your name?" he asked her.

"Ceera."

"Ceera, how did you know I would be there in the cavern?"

"We didn't know. We were only told to watch for you, as were many others. L'Tamorlee was sure you would return."

"When you were given the order to watch, did l'Tamorlee say *why* he thought I'd return?"

"No. He only said that there had been a misunderstanding between him and you and that because you were a Seeker, you would return. He said it was imperative that you not be frightened away again. Dhalvad sar Haradan, it is rumored that you are a Healer as well as a Seeker. Is this true?"

"Yes." He started to explain about his healing power when the sound of hurried footsteps interrupted. Danner, Thura, Meer, l'Tamorlee, and two others entered the sun chamber. Ceera stepped back a pace, bowing to l'Tamorlee.

L'Tamorlee acknowledged her presence with a nod, then his eyes went to Dhal. Hoping Ceera hadn't spoken falsely, Dhal inclined his head to l'Tamorlee. "Greetings, sir."

L'Tamorlee bowed. "Greetings, Dhalvad sar Haradan. We are pleased that you have returned to us."

"I'm sorry to have to intrude upon you once again, but I had to come. I have questions that *must* be answered."

"As do all Seekers," l'Tamorlee responded carefully, stepping forward a pace. The other Ni stayed where they were. "I wish to apologize for the violence of our last meeting," he continued. "It was uncalled for. It had been a long time since we guested a Seeker and we made demands that were not in keeping with our customs."

"Apology accepted," Dhal said, matching the Ni's tone. "I think perhaps the fault was not yours alone. As I told you before, I'm new to the ways of the Ni-lach and in my ignorance may have seen enemies where I should have seen friends." *I hope,* he added silently.

"Perhaps," l'Tamorlee said softly. "Now that that is settled, will you tell us how we can help you?"

Dhal looked at the Ni Speaker and decided to trust. His own world could not supply him with the answers he needed. He hoped the Ni of this ring world could. "I'm lost," he began. "Your world and mine seem much the same. I have found a place in my world that is a duplicate of all you have here, minus the people and the Tamorlee. I'm confused and would ask if the Tamorlee has ever known another home site identical to this one? The Learning Arc, the tunnels, the cavern, has it all been built before, in another land perhaps far from here?"

The Ni Speaker frowned. "No, not to my knowledge. The Tamorlee has been here as long as any can remember."

"Is it possible that there is more than one Tamorlee? Another crystal? Another group of Ni who have patterned their home after this place? Perhaps a group of Seekers or long-ago visitors to your land?"

L'Tamorlee nodded. "I suppose that could be possible, but I think it highly unlikely. If there was more than one Tamorlee, I believe we would know about it. Seekers have traveled far in our world and never once has any reported finding another crystal like the Tamorlee. It's our belief that the Tamorlee is unique, its origin and life force as mysterious as the gifting among some of the People. Some say that the Tamorlee was created by the Ni thousands of years ago. Others claim that the Tamorlee was here before the Ni and that our contact with the crystal is alone responsible for our special talents."

"And the truth?" Dhal asked.

"The truth is that we don't know. Not even the Tamorlee knows. The Tamorlee's conscious memory goes back hundreds of generations of Ni, but it doesn't go back to its own beginnings. Its first memories are of the original Seekers, those Ni who carried shards of the crystal for good luck in their wanderings. When these shards, or fire stones as they came to be called, were carried back to Val-hrodhur, there was a rejoining with the Tamorlee. The crystal wakened and began to learn, absorbing all that the fire stones had recorded while with the Seekers.

"It took many years for the Tamorlee and the People to form a working relationship. The first step was more spiritual than physical, a joining with the Seekers which instilled the feeling of reverence for the fire stones and the large crystal from which they came. Then came the revelation that the crystal was another lifeform rather than a spiritual force."

"Lifeform—not god," Dhal said.

"The term god is rooted in the sun travelers' language, Dhalvad. The Ni knew nothing of gods when first they met the Tamorlee. If they worshiped at all they worshiped life and the right of all lifeforms to exist. The crystal was not a god to them, but only another lifeform, one to be studied. The original Seekers were a curious and wandering people and the crystal's thirst for knowledge was just as great as their own. Once they understood that and discovered that the Tamorlee remembered all it was ever taught, they learned that they could use the crystal to help teach the following generations of Ni. It seems a fair trade to us. We help the Tamorlee learn and it in turn teaches us and remembers for us, so that no knowledge is ever lost."

Dhal felt a great tiredness wash over him. He must have looked unsteady on his feet, for suddenly Ceera was there, her hand under his arm. "You're very pale, Seeker. Would you sit down?"

L'Tamorlee moved forward and helped Ceera lower Dhal to the floor. When he asked if Dhal were ill, he told them about Saan Drambe and what had happened in the caverns in his world. His small audience sat quietly through the telling. L'Tamorlee interrupted only once, to ask a question concerning the Ni-lach healing power that Dhal had used to close the wound in his side. "How long ago did this healing take place?"

"Seven days ago."

"Like most Ni gifts, the use of such power is draining. It was unwise for you to use the fire stone so soon."

"After all that's happened to me these past few weeks, it seemed important that I return here, sir. I'm alone, the last of the Ni in my homeland. I and my friends have nowhere to go. If you or the crystal could only tell me where you are in relation to the place I found in the Mountains of the Lost, we would know which direction our path lay. I would like to bring my friends here, where they'll be safe from the Sarissa and others like them. I would like to learn more about my people. Please, can you help?"

"We can try," l'Tamorlee said softly.

"The crystal?"

L'Tamorlee nodded. "Once before I asked you for your ring and you refused me. Do you still feel the same way?"

When Dhal did not respond, l'Tamorlee reached out and tapped the ring with his finger. "It is a part of the Tamorlee, Dhalvad. It records all that the Seeker experiences. When each Seeker returns to Val-hrodhur, he brings the fire stone to this chamber and places the stone there, in the small hollow above the palm print. Then the Tamorlee is activated and all that the fire stone has absorbed is transferred to the crystal. From what you told us before, the ring you wear was worn by your father and perhaps his father before him. Should you activate the Tamorlee, all the information that your fire stone holds will be freed and we could well learn about your father and where your homeland is. The Tamorlee has evidenced a great interest in you. I know it would like a joining. The ring is the way."

"You've already told the crystal about me?"

"Not my doing, your own, the day you laid your hand on

the stone and failed to remove your ring. Had the joining been complete you might already know the answers to your questions."

Dhal glanced beyond Ceera to the stone pattern, then to the green crystal that hung over the stone relief. Did the Tamorlee hold the answers he wanted? Dhal looked to l'Tamorlee. There seemed to be only one way of learning the truth. Slipping the Seeker ring from his finger, he offered it to l'Tamorlee.

As the Ni Speaker took the ring, he looked deep into Dhal's eyes. "Do you ask a joining, Dhalvad?"

"Yes."

The eyes softened. "The ways of the Tamorlee are unknown to you. Your choice shows courage. Because it is your first joining, I think it wise that someone attend you. Agreed?"

L'Tamorlee indicated a slender, middle-aged Ni who wore his hair cut short. "Breen is qualified to assist in a joining, as are Danner, Thura, and myself. The choice is yours."

Dhal glanced at the others, then turned back to l'Tamorlee. "I would have you."

"I am honored. Shall we begin?"

While the others moved back to the wall of the chamber, l'Tamorlee led Dhal to the star pattern and positioned him facing the palm print on the floor. Then, walking the outside circle, he touched the fire stone to the points of the star.

Dhal was aware of a subtle change in the green light overhead. Crossing over, l'Tamorlee told him to match his hand to the handprint on the floor. As Dhal's fingers slid into place he held his breath, ready for the strange, pulling sensation he had felt before. Nothing happened.

Dhal looked up. L'Tamorlee was watching him and read the question in Dhal's eyes. "The crystal is only activated by a fire stone. When you touched hand to the stone before, you were wearing your ring and were captured and held by an energy we call polu. It will happen again when I place the ring in its proper place. Ready?"

Dhal nodded. L'Tamorlee covered Dhal's hand with his own, then carefully placed the stone in a small circular opening a hand's span in front of Dhal's fingertips.

The flush of warmth came so quickly that Dhal nearly pulled away, but he could feel l'Tamorlee's arm around him, and in his mind there was the whisper of the Speaker's voice.

Dhal felt himself moving forward down a long corridor of green light. L'Tamorlee was there, speaking softly and calming his fears. Dhal could not see him but he could feel his presence. It was like a cloud of morning mist, which one can feel yet never capture and hold.

The warmth increased. Cloaked in l'Tamorlee's embrace, Dhal was nudged forward. When he reached the end of the corridor, the green light began to change to gold, then deep red. There were shadows within the colored mist, all of them pulsating with life. As questions formed in his mind, the shadows melted into pictures and he was drawn into those pictures as he had once been drawn into the ring world. Worlds within worlds within worlds—was there no ending?

Confused by all that he was experiencing, Dhal felt panic rise once more. But l'Tamorlee's voice came to him. *I'm here with you. Don't be afraid. You are but seeing our world as recorded in the fire stone. Watch and learn. It's what you came to do.*

So Dhal watched and saw those who had carried the Seeker ring before him. The Tamorlee revealed brief glimpses of his brother and his father, then other faces, most of them Ni. He saw places that he recognized, the Enzaar Sea and Annaroth, then he came upon scenes that were unfamiliar. He saw small riverside communities where Ni lived high above the ground in sheltered platform homes; he watched Ni-lach diving from cliffside ledges, plunging deep into the sea where they swam and raced one another; he saw a gathering of Ni-lach dancers who sang and guided draak for fun and challenge.

Then there was a shifting in the scenes and the fire stone showed the great Ni city of Jjaan-bi hidden high in the branches of a forest of centuries-old aban trees. The Ni who carried the Seeker ring to Jjaan-bi stayed there many years, and scene upon scene folded one over the other: names, places, information, everything was recorded from the most important to the least important.

A sense of peace grew within Dhal. The fire stone had absorbed life as seen through the eyes of those who had carried it, recording thoughts, actions, and all else that came within its sphere of perception. Peace came from knowing that nothing would be lost, that no single Ni would pass beyond remembering once held by the Tamorlee.

Time passed. Once again Dhal felt l'Tamorlee's voice within his mind. *The crystal isn't satisfied, Dhalvad. There is something wrong in the joining, a variant which seems to have something to do with you and the fire stone you carry. We must search further.*

We?

We are one now and must remain so until the variant is understood.

Dhal became aware of an undulating movement around him. He lost all sense of up and down, then there was a strange softness wrapping around him. He could not see any bonds but he could feel them as they wove themselves around his body.

L'Tamorlee, what is it? What's happening?

Suddenly there was another presence within his mind. *You are Ni-lach child, but not one of mine. Seeker you are, and Healer, and mystery guest within my realm. You would learn where you come from. I too would know the answer to that question. Stay. We will learn together.* It was the crystal speaking to him. Awed by the impossible, Dhalvad forgot to be afraid.

Dhal was sitting on the cool stone floor of the sun chamber, the voice of l'Tamorlee speaking softly in his ear. "All is well, Dhalvad. Wake now."

Breathing deeply, Dhal lifted his head and straightened up. "Are you all right?" l'Tamorlee asked, as he and Danner helped him to his feet.

Dhal looked at them, the shock of the knowledge gained making him tremble. "Alternate worlds!"

L'Tamorlee smiled. "The fire stones don't lie, Dhalvad. In your time the theory of alternate worlds has become a reality."

Dhal shook his head, hardly daring to believe. For months

he had lived with the thought of a separate world entrapped within the ring stone, a world which he could visit once he had learned to unlock the door. To discover that there *were* other worlds, not one within another, but rather standing side by side, was enough to make one feel lightheaded.

"What's all this about alternate worlds?" Danner demanded. "*Is* there another Val-hrodhur?"

Dhal turned to the Ni and shook his head. "No, Danner there is—was—only one Val-hrodhur."

"Was?"

Dhal looked at l'Tamorlee and saw him nod. L'Tamorlee answered Danner's question. "In Dhalvad's time Val-hrodhur is dead."

"His time?" Danner echoed.

"I realize that this may be difficult to accept, but what we are going to tell you is the truth, as the Tamorlee interprets it. You see, Dhalvad is a Seeker, but he doesn't come from *our* time. He is the son of our future. The Val-hrodhur he has found in his time is this same place, but long abandoned. The fire stone he carries is a shard broken from our present-day Tamorlee—that's why he returned here and not to some other time. We can't be sure of the number of years separating us, but I should think they might number in the thousands, because the crystal didn't recognize any of the names Dhalvad uses to describe his world."

"You're telling us then," Thura said, "that at some time in the future—our future—the Tamorlee will be moved from this place."

"Yes," l'Tamorlee said.

"Why?"

"According to all that Dhalvad has told us about the Sarissa war against the People, I would guess that the Tamorlee was moved for safety's sake."

Leaning down, l'Tamorlee plucked the fire stone from its place on the stone floor. "This stone is new in our time but old in Dhalvad's. It had recorded hundreds of years of Ni-lach history before it ever came to Dhalvad. In him, it found a very special Seeker, one able to transport it back to its origin where it could disgorge all of its information to the Tamorlee."

"But why didn't it go to the Tamorlee of his time?" Danner wanted to know.

"Because it isn't in *our* world any longer, friend. You all know how long it had been since we guested a Seeker. Is it because they are so few now, or is it because they've gone *elsewhere*?"

L'Tamorlee's emphasis on the last word roused Thura. "Elsewhere—as in an alternate world?"

"Yes, Thura. The fire stone Dhalvad carried back to us speaks of doors to alternate worlds, of the energy patterns which create those doors, and of the Ni-lach Sensitives who guard them. It will be years before we're able to assimilate all the information Dhalvad brought back with him, but when it is accomplished I believe we will find that his coming to us at this time will direct us to new paths of learning. Now that we know that there are other worlds which touch ours, we can send our new Seekers to look for them. For if the future is to be as Dhalvad describes it, we may have need for one of those doors, not only for the safety of the Tamorlee, but for the continued existence of the Ni-lach."

Thura turned and looked at Dhal. "And you, Seeker, will your search for the Tamorlee in your own time continue?"

"Yes," he said, looking down at the fire stone. "I'll keep looking. Something inside of me tells me that I hold the key to unlock the doors to those alternate worlds. Once I understand the key, I believe those doors will open."

"Perhaps, child," Thura said softly. "But do not go too boldly, for doors that open can also close."

L'Tamorlee touched Dhal's shoulder. "I think it is time you were leaving us, Dhalvad, lest you become locked within our time forever." Leaning forward, he touched his lips to Dhal's forehead. "May your search be successful, Seeker Dhalvad."

Dhal stood on the rise overlooking the ruins of the Learning Arc. The shadows of night were fast closing in. He could see a campfire down in the field. Poco, Screech, and Gi were waiting for him, just as they had promised.

As he started downslope, he began to make plans for the future. First they would go to Janchee, then on to Port Sulta in Letsia, and from there perhaps to Jjaan-bi which, he had learned from the Tamorlee, lay to the northeast of the Enzaar Sea.

Somewhere there had to be other Ni, either those who, like himself, had been accidentally left behind as the Tamorlee was taken into another world, or those who had chosen to stay and resist the Sarissa. Surely he could not be the last Ni on Lach.

About the Author

Marcia Joanne Bennett was born on June 9, 1945. Raised in a rural community, she has spent all but a few of her working years in central New York State.

After graduating from Albany Business College in 1965, she spent the next seven years in banking.

Several years ago, she established a small craft shop in her hometown. While running the shop she began writing, a hobby that quickly became an addiction. Her other interests range from reading, painting, and basketry to astrology and parapsychology.